ELLEN FLOOD

ELLEN FLOOD

Sad Songs and Happy Dances

ELLEN DEMERS

Ellen Demers

For Ellen Flood, the Irish grandmother

For William Bennett, my grandfather

For Ellen and William's children; Alice, Billy, Jenny, George, and Mary.

For Ellen's sisters here in America; Mary Anne, Bridget and Kate and brothers and sisters in Ireland: John, Jim, and Rose. And their parents, John Flood and Anne McCormick.

For my parents, William Bennett and Phyllis Tenney

For my brothers and sisters and their children and grandchildren

For my husband, Stephen Demers, for his encouragement and support

For my son, Nathan, who served both as support and as my editor. His hard work got us here.

For my cousins Charlie and Anne Naff, who found Ellen and Mary Anne Flood in Westmeath, Ireland

For my Irish cousins, Tom and Sheila Nally and Family, who introduced me to Ireland and the family

For my friends who followed and encouraged me on this book journey; Florence who set me up for a literary consult, Mary who enjoyed reading some chapters, and Janine for her continuing interest in my book. And others along the way who listened to me talk about it.

INTRODUCTION

This is a re-imagining of my immigrant grandmother, Ellen Flood's life and that of her family. I used genealogical and historical sources for the period in which she lived. I visited and researched her part of Ireland in County Westmeath, as well as Dorchester, Lincoln, and Dover. My book is fiction, a novel, not a memoir. I created dialogue and some events in the story, while others certainly happened. My father's recollections of his boyhood on the farm in Dover helped bring their story to life.

I hope you will enjoy her story. I liked telling it.

~Ellen Demers

CHAPTER 1

America

IRELAND TO AMERICA

John Flood was against it entirely, our going to America. He could not bear to lose any of his girls. I thought I had never heard anything so sad as my father weeping in the night and my mother murmuring comfort. Mary Anne and I wept too that night.

It was in October when I left Ireland. I woke on the morning of our departure and stepped into the kitchen. I turned to face my mother, whose eyes were full of tears, as were my own. I quickly went out to the forge to see my father. He stood there in his big apron. He was hammering iron to shape it like he had thought he might change the shape of our thoughts when we talked about going to America.

The bright glowing coals smelling of hot iron and the banging of the hammer were a part of him. He was short; a small man with black but graying hair, strongly built and muscular from his work. He looked at me but did not speak. His eyes were bleak.

I sat there while he began to busy himself. Then, I got up, went over, and put my hand on his shoulder. His own calloused one went up and covered mine. I left it there. It was like a caress. Ma was resigned to it, our leaving. She was making breakfast. I think she told herself stories of how successful her daughters would be in America.

We each had one small bag packed, my sister Mary Anne and myself. The thought of the ship waiting for us in Queenstown filled me with both fear and wonder that we would be on it. Imagine, the Flood sisters going to Boston. I tried not to think about it all at once because if I did, I would never get myself off the front step. I'd driven myself daft the day before, walking all around and telling myself it would be the last time. The roses were still in bloom and the thick, green hedges came right up to the lanes. The leaves were beginning to bronze. That day, it had been mostly fine on my long walk, but the temperature was going down. The wind blew clouds across the sky. I had on my shawl, but got caught in rain, making me damp on this soft day. It did not become a wetting rain though as I continued my walk over the fields to Empor School where my best friend, Sean, was waiting for me.

We took the path together along the Royal Canal to the village of Ballynacargy and past a bridge and back again, holding hands, watching the boats. Then for a last visit to the churchyard at Saint Matthew's where he left me after shaking my hand. "Best of luck, Ellen," he told me. I'd wanted a kiss, though. I gave him a piece of paper with my address. He promised to write. I thought he would come to Boston.

I had myself in a state by the time I returned and had to run to the bedroom to gain back my composure before anyone noticed. I wanted to bawl. After I put my shawl to dry by the kitchen fire, I helped Ma with supper, another last thing. My brothers and sisters stared at me. I grabbed baby Rose and cuddled her. Eight-year-old Bridget broke the silence by telling us about school. She had no sense of what was to happen the next day. Jim is the tender one. He looked sad. Kate was probably imagining joining us some day in America. My brother, John, looked stoic, like he could not be bothered by his sisters leaving. I didn't think my brothers would ever want to leave home. They had their place in our small town land.

There had been plenty of arguments during these last few months after Mary Anne and I announced our decision to emigrate. My father would go get a drink and walk out to sit alone in the forge some evenings. We told him we loved them both, but we wanted more, to be independent, to make money, and to marry and have children.

"You girls romanticize everything," he told us. "You don't deal in the facts. What do you really know? No one ever comes back to tell us."

"We will write," we say, "And you will be proud of us."

"I want to be proud of you right here in Ireland," he countered, "where I can see you and my grandchildren."

"Who will protect you," he protested. "You've never been out in the world, I cannot bear to think of you on that ship alone, and what if no one meets you?"

At that we agreed later, he was finally facing the reality of our leaving because now he was worried about the ship and our arrival in Boston.

Sometimes I have the idea that this is my destiny, a fanciful notion not supported by my sister who thinks herself more sensible than me. She had spent the last few days packing and checking our tickets. "We are going to find work and husbands," she declared.

That last morning we found we had a ride to Mullingar if we left soon. There were hearts breaking all around. Small Bridget did not understand, saying we would be back in two weeks. We stood in the main room of our small house, which smelled of turf fire and home. They gave us their blessings. First, our father and it came out hard because he was full of sadness. His voice shook a little and then steadied. We bowed our heads.

"May your days be many and troubles few.
May all God's blessings descend upon you.
May peace be within you.
May your hearts be strong.
May you find what you are seeking wherever you roam."

Then our mother in her quiet tone.

"Until we meet again
May God hold you in the palm of His hand."

We all made the sign of the cross. I knew in that moment and our parents did, too, that we would never see each other again, except in heaven. So many had done this and survived, and I supposed we would, too. Ma was crying. Kate was crying. "I will write," I told them, "as soon as we arrive." But my words were thrown against a storm of grief.

We went outside, all the family. It was a damp day in Rathcaled. It did no good to prolong the leaving, so we departed, our faces wet with tears. On the way, people waved at us and we waved back, although our eyes were almost blinded with those tears. I could not help thinking during our day's travel of what they would be doing at home while we rode the train away from them.

We were traveling with our friend and neighbor, Bridget Raftery. She had relatives in Dorchester, Massachusetts. We had never traveled so far and in one day. The train ride from Mullingar to Ballymahon was our first and then we took another train to Queenstown and the city was a marvel, all shops and the sea, and at the docks, a massive ship, the Aurania, to take us over.

"Your tickets are in order, but you are much too early," the agent told us, eyeing our small bags. "But I can take your luggage for you."

We knew that we did not want to let go of our belongings, so, I said, "No, thank you."

"Come back in four hours," he said briskly.

I turned to the others and said, "We must get a cup of tea."

"We are not to spend money," said my sister, stiffly.

We were all tired and nervous, our crying at the leave-taking having been followed by giddiness and now replaced with a real fear of getting on that ship and sailing away from home.

"Well, then," I said, "We can just stand here or we can go explore the town." And we did and even had a cup of tea and something with it. We had a few coins in our pockets.

There were massive crowds on the dock when we went back and the ship still stood there waiting for us. We marched right up to the ticket master and presented our tickets again, this time getting them stamped. Then we joined a long line of people to board. Nerves cannot adequately describe our feeling at that time.

The voyage was long, but we were not sick and made new friends. We had our first view of New York from Ellis Island, rode a ferryboat, and soon boarded a train for South Station in Boston and then had our first ride on a streetcar to Dorchester.

We stayed with the Raftery cousins on Grange Street. Sometimes I could not breathe naturally when I thought of what we'd done in leaving Ireland and coming here. The Rafterys were good to us, but we needed to find jobs. I was seventeen years of age in the year of 1904. Bridget Raftery's cousin knew of an opening and walked my sister Mary Anne right to the house. She had been hired as a maid immediately. That was a week ago. She had gone forward with the first part of our plan and left me behind.

One morning I stood outside the door of the Intelligence Office. It was where they told me to go for a job. With a very short prayer to the Blessed Mother and pulling myself up to my almost five foot height, I let myself in the door.

"Good morning," I said to the imposing woman seated behind the desk. "I am here about getting a job as a domestic."

She looked me over. After inquiring about experience of which I had none, she told me there was a lady coming in the next day who was seeking a girl. I would be the only servant, and it was here in Dorchester. She said I should come in the next day promptly at ten o'clock. I agreed immediately and thanked her politely.

"You should consider yourself lucky to have walked in at a good time, in view of you having no experience," she told me sharply. I made sure to ring the doorbell on the way out.

I met Mrs. Bernstein the next morning at the Intelligence Office. She wore a smart, dark green suit and her hair pinned up under a small felt hat and held her gloves in her lap. She sat up straight in the chair facing mine with her feet flat on the floor. She was pretty with dark hair, medium height and very well-spoken. Young though, I thought, and maybe not accustomed to interviewing likely maids. We made our introductions.

She began. "My husband and I have no children," and then she continued, "But he thinks I should have someone to help. I've not been in the best of health recently." at that point a little shadow seemed to come over her face, not exactly a frown but a look as though she did not want to think about something. "I need a maid for the housework while I involve myself in other matters. It will give me more rest to have someone take over the chores."

I told her I had journeyed here from Ireland with my sister, who already had a position. She asked me if I had experience working as a maid and I told her, "No, but I helped my mother run the household and I know how to do chores." I added. "I have a lot of energy and like to do things right." She was silent for a minute and then nodded her head.

"If you can do simple cooking and are willing to work, Ellen Flood, I would like you to come work for us." And she allowed herself a smile.

"I can cook," I replied, "and do housework. I can learn whatever you need me to do."

"I think you could be satisfactory," she said in her low voice. Then she looked very directly at me and said, "I would like you to come on Sunday evening at five o'clock. My husband and I will both be home and it will give you time to settle in before starting your duties on Monday." She reached into her small purse and pulled out a paper. "This is the address and how much we will pay you." Then she looked at me again and seemed to prepare herself for the next communication. "We are a Jewish family and you are probably Catholic. Does that present a problem?"

I looked at her and said, "No, but I will need time off on Sundays to go to church."

She nodded and said, "Then I will see you on Sunday evening." She gracefully rose, turned slightly to shake Mrs. O'Brien's hand, thanked her for setting up the interview and walked out the door.

CHAPTER 2

The Maid

So, on Sunday next, Mary Anne and I stood outside twenty-three Shafter Street, on a rainy, dreary November night. We had one shared umbrella. The house had a neat door, curtains in the windows, and stood in a quiet neighborhood. We rang the bell, and the door opened. Mrs. Bernstein beckoned us inside and showed us where to put the wet umbrella in the stand. Mr. Bernstein stood briefly. We did introductions. Then it was time for Mary Anne to go. I walked her to the door where she gave me a quick hug. And she was gone into the rainy night. The tears rose to my eyes, but I quickly blinked them away, shut the door behind her and turned to face my new employers.

"I'll show you to your room," Mrs. Bernstein said, getting up from her chair. I followed her up the stairs, bag in hand. Their house had a third floor and my room was up a last steep flight of stairs. I saw the small bed first, neatly made, and then a lamp, the bare floor, one window, and a wooden chest. I'd never had a room of my own. There was also a pitcher and basin. I would put up the small crucifix my mother had given each of us, only weeks ago. I had to remind myself this was to be my new home. I banished sad thoughts before they overcame me. I had a job to do and grand plans for my future, and this was where it all started.

"After you get settled," she said, "come downstairs and I will show you the other rooms. In the kitchen, you can warm up some soup and have some bread for your supper."

"We have already eaten." She looked at me and smiled. "It was nice of your sister to come tonight." I shook my head, and smiled back, and she left, shutting the door behind her. I turned and put my belongings away neatly.

I went downstairs just a short time later. I'd not had much to unpack. The house had bedrooms on the second floor and a water closet; a toilet, a marvel to me. The parlor I'd seen. Downstairs, there was also a small dining room, a little room she called her sewing room and then the kitchen with sink, stove and icebox, a large table and a wooden floor. In the back was a washing tub. The small pantry had shelves with dishes, and underneath, pots and pans as well as bins of potatoes and onions. The kitchen door led out to a side yard and walk. The only window did not let in much light. There was a small lamp attached to the wall. When Mrs. Bernstein left me, I had my soup and bread, cleaned the sauce pan and dishes, turned off the lamp, and headed upstairs. I'd been informed how many chores there would be for a single maid, and I expected that tomorrow would be a long day.

Up in my room, getting ready for bed, I told myself that I had been well-received, and it had been very thoughtful for her to provide me supper this night. If only it wasn't raining. I could hear it clearly, hitting the roof just above my head. It was not making me feel cozy. Instead, this was the loneliest Sunday night I had ever experienced in my life. I knelt to say my prayers, and then climbed into bed, I told myself my new life would begin tomorrow, but still I cried that night. The next morning, I awoke at six, poured water from the pitcher into the bowl to wash, and then shrugged into my work clothes, stockings and shoes. I brushed and pulled my hair up onto my head. I visited the toilet in a closet on the second floor, briefly, before going downstairs to the kitchen. I quickly applied the match to the gas lamp and turned it on. The coal was in the stove and I lit it, filled the kettle from the sink and put it on to boil. Another marvel was not going to the pump for water.

They did not seem to be up yet. I checked the icebox for milk and eggs, and the pantry for bread, and made myself a cup of tea.

A short time later, I turned and greeted Mrs. Bernstein as she came quietly into the kitchen. "Good morning, Ellen. I am glad you are up early. It will give me a chance to show you how to prepare breakfast. Mr. Bernstein likes to eat at half-past seven. Here is an apron. You have two; one for mornings and one for afternoon company." There followed instructions on the boiling of eggs and toasting of bread and where to find plates, silverware and napkins and how to set the table which she supervised. Then she looked at the watch pinned to her blouse and went through the door to the dining room. A few minutes later, I came in with the tray. Mr. Bernstein, in suit and tie, was seated at the table, just opening his newspaper. He looked at me and then seemed to allow himself a smile as I placed the food in front of him. As I stood there and poured his coffee, I thought that what this house needed was the sound and excitement of children.

Every morning, now, I get up at six o'clock to light the kitchen fire, checking that that there is adequate coal. I grind the coffee. The stove, it has gas burners, so I've had to learn that. I have to scrub the stove top every day. Once a week, I apply stove blacking. Always the same for their morning meal; eggs and toasted bread with butter. After breakfast, I run in and open the parlor windows just a bit, on these cold days and while the room is airing, I run the carpet sweeper, another marvel. Later, I do the bedroom and upstairs hall. The kitchen floors, I scrub with soap and water on my knees, at least once a week. My duties are fine, but I am at them from morning to night. The evening meal is meat, usually, and potatoes and vegetables. They eat a lot of chicken which comes plucked for which I am glad. Supper all has to come out ready at the same time, and that has taken some practice. And then there are the dishes in the sink and the pots and pans. And then scrubbing the sink and taking the garbage out.

On laundry day, the clothes go into the big wash tub twice; once to wash and then to rinse in clear water, then through the wringer. So far, I have hung them outside on lines to dry. When it gets cold, I've been told, I will hang them on a wooden rack for that purpose in the warm kitchen. Oh, yes, I do like baking day. It makes the kitchen warm. There is plenty of flour and sugar and tea, too. I make oatmeal bread and a currant cake which they like very much. I enjoy being in the warm kitchen. The ironing, too, keeps me warm. I do sing while go about my duties. It makes the time pass. I don't think Mrs. Bernstein minds it. One day she smiled at me as she passed the kitchen. She plays the piano in the parlor. I love to listen to her. I also daydream, even as I go about my work. I make up stories in my head and imagine myself in another place or think about the dance that my sister and I go to on Thursday nights. I'm sometimes still lonely and anxious for letters from home. I worry when there is not a letter that there might be something wrong. It is very quiet upstairs when I go to bed. I only cried myself to sleep the first night. Now, I say my rosary and turn off the lamp and fall right to sleep.

The kitchen, to me, is dark and full of chores and yet I cannot deny some rest there because often when I am sitting so weary, I am comforted by the neat space and the clean tablecloth I put on at the end of the day. My bedroom is pale and full of my thoughts and dreams. It is where I think and write and pray and sleep.

"My mother was a kitchen canary."

~Bill Bennett, age 90

CHAPTER 3

Dorchester Musings

I am aware of my appearance. When I lift up the edge of my skirt to climb the stairs with the basket of laundry, I try to carry it gracefully, with one hand holding my skirt and the basket balanced against my hip. I think my ankles look nice when I do that. My mother would not approve of my vanity. I can see myself in the big mirror hanging over the bureau in their bedroom when I am cleaning. I check my appearance every day when I am dusting and straightening, looking to see if I am tidy, but my mother would call me again, vain, because I spend too much time examining myself in the mirror. I am proud of my small waist, which I see when I turn to observe if my apron is tied properly. I look straight into the mirror to see green eyes and clear skin; no freckles, and brown hair, not red. I have fine hair, always falling out when I pile it on top of my head, even with the pins and combs I put in, despite a natural wave. I've tried to put it into a fashionable pompadour when I go dancing, but it just falls out, making me a mess. Mary Anne and I used to do each others' hair.

I don't think I'm outstanding pretty but am said to have a nice smile, which I practice in front of the mirror, thinking of the lads I will meet at the dance. I like the pretty afternoon apron with the lace on it for company. For the dances I have my best skirt and the blouse with the tucks in it which I believe shows off my figure. I would like to have silk stockings, but they are too dear.

There is a cousin of Mrs. Bernstein, a lady who sometimes comes to the house. She holds a prejudice, I've found, against the Irish, particularly Irish maids. She does know I can hear her when she speaks to the other ladies being entertained in the parlor.

She dresses in nice clothes and has formal parlor manners but does not have class, like Mrs. Bernstein, who treats everyone with kindness. Cousin Beatrice, as she is called, tries to embarrass or insult me by the way she addresses me and that demanding way she shows. I cannot change the expression on my face or show any temper. When I am serving, I have to stay agreeable and keep my tone very even. I think every time she comes it's a test. My mother would say, "Offer it up."

I'm doing fine, working for the Bernsteins. She is precise about her requirements, but always pleasant. One afternoon she would be having the ladies over again for tea and I thought about how I would be on display. I did hope when Cousin Beatrice came, I would be able to hold my tongue.

The ladies were making polite talk to each other. It all seemed to be going well, but of course I had overheard Cousin Beatrice, who was watching me very closely, refer to "those disorganized Irish maids" to the lady seated beside her. Then she suddenly demanded hot tea. Now, I had only a short time in which to brew hot fresh tea for her and bring out the tray of pretty sandwiches and thinly sliced pound cake for everyone. Two trips or one, I thought. Which would be satisfactory? All eyes were on me. I'll do it right, I decided, for Mrs. Bernstein because it mattered to her.

In the kitchen, I grabbed the kettle, turned on the hot water, placed tea leaves in the pot, took the plate and went immediately back into the parlor to serve.

"Where is my tea?" demanded Cousin Beatrice with a scowl. "Oh, Ma'am," I said in a sweet tone, " I did want it to be perfect for you and have set the kettle on to boil again. I will bring it presently. Would there be something else you would like also while I'm at it?"

Two of the ladies tittered and Cousin Beatrice glowered at me. Mrs. Bernstein smiled quietly and referred to the weather and coming holiday. I went back into the kitchen to fetch the tea, holding myself straight and head high. Well, I thought, that went well.

I thought of Sean all the time. Sean had been my best friend in Rathcaled, and next to me, the smartest scholar in our country school. I had supposed we could be more to each other. He is the second son of a farmer and had plans to emigrate, like me, when he could earn the passage. I thought that was our plan, for him to join me in Boston. We were that close already. I even supposed I was in love with him. I told myself this story while I did my work and we did write letters back and forth, although mine were more frequent than his. But I didn't think boys wrote as often anyways. "Feelings change," Mary Anne said, "especially when you are far away from each other. After all, your Sean never promised he would come to Boston, and you never had an agreement between you."

Then I got word from Sean. He had decided to emigrate to Australia with friends from Mullingar. I was crushed. I told Mary Anne that maybe now I would never marry, which she said was nonsense.

"You're in America," she said. "Things are different here. You do not have to marry Irish. There are plenty of young men to fall in love with and have a proper marriage. Don't be silly." But my dream was my dream and Sean was always in it and I'm not at all good letting go of an original plan. I raged at Sean for a while and wrote him a very strong letter, but I knew it was all over and sent him another one wishing him well. I suppose he survived the first one. I did not really care when I wrote it.

CHAPTER 4

Mrs. Bernstein and Me
(1907)

BIRTH

I knew that Mrs. Bernstein was expecting again. It was because I'd seen my own mother's waist expand that way and the small belly form. Also, she'd not left for me the rinsed out cotton rags from her monthly periods to launder for more than three months. I knew what that meant. I had been there for a loss she'd had months earlier. And I knew now she'd lost another pregnancy before my time here. She seemed well this time. I was very pleased about a baby. She said nothing. I'd begun sewing up in my room at night, a small gown with careful stitches. I lit a candle at church each Sunday for special intentions.

She still went out, but started her days a bit later, remaining in bed and quickly dressing before joining Mr. Bernstein at breakfast, just sliding into her seat at the last minute. He would glance at her when she wasn't looking, with a serious expression on his face. He had started telling her to nap in the afternoon and not do the stairs so much. She would hush him.

I didn't understand how Mrs. Bernstein would think I did not know she was expecting a baby, and further still why she would not want me to know. I thought it ridiculous. But she seemed to need to have this secret. I had also learned that well-brought up ladies did not talk about such things. I suppose she was afraid to lose another baby, too, but I could see she was further along this time. One day, I found her sitting on a step, out of breath to go the rest of the way upstairs. We looked at each other. I spoke first. "Mrs. Bernstein, I think it would be better for you to rest on your bed. It is quite common, I understand, to get fatigued more easily during this time."

She looked up at me. "I should have been aware you would know. I have not felt comfortable talking about it."

I took her hand and eased her up. "You are getting larger, ma'am and you will have to change your ways for now. I am aware of that much. I know you are praying and so am I. Maybe we are alike that way."

She smiled a little. "It is the same God," she said. "So in that way we are the same. This time seems different. I've been sick a little in the mornings and oh, so tired."

We walked down the hall to the bedroom. "I will wake you when you want," I offered.

"Yes," she said. "Wake me an hour before supper. I will want to freshen up. Mr. Bernstein, too, is worried, but he doesn't think I know that. He tells me it will be all right. We would both like to believe it."

"Rest," I said.

As I went back downstairs, I thought about how lovely it would be to have a baby in the house.

(Five months later)

Mrs. Bernstein had gone into labor early. It was not yet her time, and that was a concern. I stayed with her. Mr. Bernstein soon sent me next door to get her friend Mrs. Pearson and to call the doctor. When the doctor arrived a short time later, he looked worried and went in to attend her, closing the door behind him. Mr. Bernstein had chosen his place in the hall and was not leaving it. I was called back in and we stood ready to help. I did hope for the best. I was willing it so and praying as fast as I could to myself.

Someone had placed a small basket with a blanket inside, on a table near the bed, as well as a basin of water and washcloth. As Mrs.

Bernstein's cries grew louder and more frequent, the doctor got busy with the bedclothes and Mrs. Pearson moved in next to them.

One loud groan and the baby came out and the doctor, after looking at it briefly, cut the cord and placed it in the basket and turned back to Mrs. Bernstein who had gone deathly pale. So, she was not well. I looked into the basket at the tiny thing that had come out and thought I saw a flicker of movement around the nostrils. I do not know how I did what came next.

It was a little boy, and he felt cold. He seemed to take another little breath. I grabbed the basket and went quietly out of the room while they were attending to Mrs. Bernstein. Mr. Bernstein did not even see me go by because he'd gone into the bedroom and Cousin Beatrice now stood in the hall. I moved quickly down the stairs and into the kitchen where the oven was still warm and put the baby in the basket inside. I kept my hand on him. I kept rubbing him gently. And then I heard a little mewling sound and the hands and feet moved a bit. I had never heard a weaker or more welcome sound than that baby crying. I began to breathe myself.

Mr. Bernstein came into the kitchen, red-eyed and miserable-looking. "She'll be all right," he said. He blinked at me. I had my hand over the baby in the basket. He'd been followed by Cousin Beatrice. "Oh my God," he said. That's all, and I reached in and carefully placed the tiny boy wrapped in his blanket into his father's arms.

Cousin Beatrice could only stand there, for once, quiet and out of words for me. She'd have looked comical if not so sad, her cheeks still wet with tears. She did love her Cousin Anna, but I'd known that.

We stood, the three of us. Mr. Bernstein looked ready to collapse, so I took the little one from him and nodded toward the stairs and up we went, up to his mother. I was really worried because he was so delicate. I knew truly he might not live, but kept that to myself.

Mrs. Bernstein was facing the wall. The doctor was packing his bag with a solemn look on his face, which quickly changed to one of astonishment when he saw me carrying my small bundle. I let him look. He saw the baby's tiny breaths. He nodded quietly. I went over to her.

"Mrs. Bernstein," I said, "You need to look at me."

I'd never spoken to her that way, and she turned at my voice.

"Here is your little miracle," I said, and handed him over to her trembling arms. Doctor went right over then and touched the infant briefly and then looked over at me. We both had the same fear. Our eyes looked alike. But I believed she should see and hold her child.

I left the new mother and father together and headed over to the door where I was met by Cousin Beatrice. She looked at me in bewilderment. I won't say all her prejudice faded away, after all, I was still the maid and Irish. She put her hand out, not knowing what to do with it. I decided to shake it. I suppose she would regret that later.

She whispered, "Thank you." and floated out the door and down the hall.

Doctor Devlin, that was his name, followed me down the stairs. He seemed to be looking at me for the first time.

"What did you do? He wasn't breathing."

I told him. "He was cold, but I thought I saw him breathe a little, so I took him in his basket and put him into the warmed oven and then just rubbed him and prayed until he began to cry a little."

"How on earth did you think of that?" he said.

"My mother had a tiny one, still and cold like this one, and the aunts put my little sister in the warmed oven and she survived," I told him. He could only look at me.

Then, he said, "I am making you the guardian of this infant. He is weak and undersized. You know he still might not survive? He is underdeveloped." I took a big breath at that. "If he doesn't feed properly, he'll need a bottle with a special nipple or maybe an eyedropper if that doesn't work, until he gains some weight. I will send the supplies and help you. He won't sleep much and will need to be fed frequently. Keep him warm with a water bottle and blanket. The mother is still recovering, so it will be up to you. You will be in charge day and night. I don't know about your other duties, but the baby must come first. And there will be no company, not even family." He was firm on that. "He is too delicate. We want no germs." I felt frightened that our baby might not live despite what I had done. But there was hope.

The doctor then said, "I'll be going back up again to check on mother and baby now." And off he went. "I want you to come up in a few minutes." I nodded and busied myself in the kitchen. I thought a cup of tea for all involved would be a good thing. I had a lot of nursing ahead of me. I'd helped Ma after her births and cared for new babies. I knew what to do. This would be the healthiest baby in Dorchester if Ellen Flood had her way.

I hummed to myself. This had been a remarkable day. I said a quick Hail Mary to the Blessed Mother in thanksgiving and thought of all the candles I had lit. I did feel very full of myself. I wondered what they would name the little boy. Mrs. Bernstein and I could do this. I was sure of it. Our baby would be fine, I told myself.

CHAPTER 5

Our Baby

The days and nights after Benjamin was born were not mine. They belonged to the baby. His mother and I spent all our time on this precious child, because, you see, the life that had been given was not at all certain. Although the Doctor was pleased with each tiny weight gain and we were impressed with open eyes and wiggling hands and feet, he seemed to be looking for other signs, medical ones that we could not fathom.

I knew most babies were bigger. I'd had to cut his diapers in half and hem them all in one evening with Mrs. Pearson, who had a sewing machine. His clothes looked like dolly clothes. The little gown I'd made him was still much too big. Doctor would come and weigh him on a small scale he pulled out of his black bag, nod, and put it away. I remembered my sister being tiny, too, and keeping all of us up at all hours with her cries.

Mrs. Bernstein's milk had come in after a few days, so we did not need to use the little bottles much, although he would take a bit if you held him just right and his mother was sleeping. But it was better for such a little one to be breast-fed. Such had been the experience of the Doctor.

Mrs. Bernstein or I slept in the baby's room next to theirs each night. We shared the night, taking him into the rocker to soothe or feed him, letting him sleep in our laps. He was never left alone. His little eyebrows were coming in and some black and downy hair, after a few weeks. His father, too, when he was home, would hold him in his lap in the rocking chair, sometimes feeding him a little from one of the bottles.

Mrs. Pearson was proving herself our friend by coming over each day, so I could get some rest or get a few chores done.

Our baby was turning the corner, I was sure. Each night he slept a little bit longer, sending both of us to his crib one night, me from the rocking chair where I'd been dozing after putting him in. We checked to see if he was breathing. We couldn't help it. He was fine, lying peacefully, his little chest going up and down and the breaths coming softly in and out, as I put my finger under his nostrils to check. We could see a flickering of his eyes under his eyelids, as though he was dreaming.

"He's playing with the angels," I said.

"He's certainly happy," was her response, and we both smiled down on our darling.

A little while later, we both heard him cry, and she rushed to get him, taking him to their bed and so I slept upstairs in my room for the first time in many weeks, waking at five in the morning and wondering where I was.

That morning, Mrs. Bernstein kept the baby with her while I went down to the kitchen to make Mr. Bernstein his breakfast. Not a regular occurrence these days. He looked very happy getting his coffee and paper and was delighted with the eggs and toast. I guess breakfast downtown is not so satisfactory, maybe lacking in the service he was used to at home.

He said, "I don't know how to thank you for all your hard work taking care of Benjamin all these weeks." It was nice to hear him call our baby by his name. Then, he continued, "I really think you deserve some time off and I will make sure you get it."

"Thank you, sir," was my reply and "We've all been working hard. I am so glad young Benjamin is getting to be so healthy. I think he smiled this morning." That was the most conversation we'd ever had. It pleased us both.

The next morning, after Mr. Bernstein went to work, we decided to take the baby downstairs. Mrs. Bernstein felt she needed a change and decided to sit in the sewing room. We brought Benjamin down in his basket. It was cunning, the way he seemed to look around before falling back asleep. It was as though he knew he was some place new.

I walked to the butcher for lamb chops. I thought I would serve them with potatoes and peas. I sent Mrs. Bernstein upstairs for a nap in the afternoon because she looked tired after another long night we'd had. I took Benjamin in his little basket into the kitchen and we had our tea together, very cozy.

Again he seemed to be looking around as though to say, "Where am I now?" When he cried, I fed him with one of his little bottles and he quieted and fell asleep.

Later, towards supper time, I heard Mrs. Bernstein come down the stairs in a great rush, calling out that she'd not slept so long since our baby arrived. I think I saw Benjamin turn a little in his basket at her voice. She reached in and lifted him out, asking him if he'd been good. "He's been a little angel," I told her. And that's how Mr. Bernstein found us, in the kitchen with supper still not ready to go on the table. But they didn't seem to mind and wandered off to the parlor with the baby after I laughed and told them to get out of my kitchen.

Ellen Bars the Door

The following afternoon. Cousin Beatrice rang the doorbell. I was quite pleasant to her and asked her how she did. She was polite back to me. She held a beautifully wrapped package which she announced was for was the baby. I held out my hands to take it, but she wouldn't let go.

"I'm here to see the baby," she declared

"I will go right up and have Mrs. Bernstein come down to see you," I said, just as forcefully but keeping a pleasant tone. I thought it would be wise for her, not me, to tell this lady that the baby could not have visitors yet.

I invited her to sit.

"I am family. Send Anna right down and we will settle this." She remained standing.

I guessed that we were not friends anymore. I knew she would regret that handshake. Soon enough I would be hearing about Irish maids who took too much on themselves.

"Yes, Ma'am." I left her scowling in the front hall and went quickly upstairs.

I told Mrs. Bernstein that Cousin Beatrice had arrived, and I'd barred the door.

"Oh, dear," was her weary reply. "I suppose she's not happy."

"Not at all," I told her.

"Well, we can blame it on the Doctor," She sighed.

I heard them talking downstairs, Mrs. Bernstein's quiet tones and Cousin Beatrice's louder one. Then I heard the front door close. Mrs. Bernstein was a little pink in the face when she came back upstairs.

"I told her that Benjamin's grandfather had not even been allowed to see him yet, but still, she was not pleased. But you did the right thing."

One morning when I was unwrapping the baby for his bath, I noticed that his little limbs were plumping out. His eyes danced as I gently tickled behind an ear. Mrs. Bernstein stood behind me and said, "He's not exactly fat, but surely he's rounder."

"He's lost his rag doll look," I said. "He's very handsome too." She smiled her agreement. We stood together in admiration of our baby.

"The doctor comes today. Maybe we'll be allowed company soon." She looked as though she was pretty sure she wanted this. "I want his grandfather to see him."

"And Cousin Beatrice," I added. And we both laughed a little at that.

The Doctor examined Benjamin and weighed him. Benjamin reached for his finger, making him smile, a rare occurrence. He was very serious, our doctor.

"Well, he's thriving," he announced. "There's really some significant weight gain. I think we've turned the corner. Our baby is doing very well."

He turned to Mrs. Bernstein. "Another week and maybe this young man can meet his relatives."

We all smiled at that and as the Doctor packed his bag, he declared that he hoped all of his families would follow directions like we had and with that; he was off, not even waiting for me to see him to the door. We had lost some of the formality in these weeks of caring for Benjamin. Sometimes the Doctor even joined me in the kitchen for his cup of tea.

Tea Party

Mrs. Bernstein was to give her first tea party since Benjamin was born. Cousin Beatrice was first on the list, followed by old friends, some of them from her temple. The synagogue, they called it, was several streets over and they attended almost every week. Those ladies would be coming too.

The plan was for me to prepare a nice repast, as Mrs. Bernstein called it, and serve it up, in my best apron, of course. And when she gave me the signal, I was to bring Baby Benjamin, all dressed up, for their admiration. I did hope Benjamin would be aware of the importance of the occasion and behave like a little gentleman. He would hopefully wake up happy from his nap in the sewing room.

At four months old, he was not yet what my mother would call, "strange" with other people. That would come later, being shy with faces he didn't know. He did tend to gurgle and smile a lot, I would excuse myself after serving, and get him from his nap. He did usually wake up happy and I'd explained it all to him the night before, as he gazed up at me as I changed his diaper and put him in his little night-clothes. I did think we had an agreement. It would be a while, though, before I could promise him a sweet for good behavior.

I heard the first sound from him as I finished clearing up from the serving and the last round of tea. No one was getting ready to leave yet. They'd been promised the baby. Cousin Beatrice, though, had already had her private showing and was busy telling the other ladies all about him.

Benjamin smiled at me from his crib. I lifted him up and talked to him while I changed him into his little dress and bonnet. He cooed at me, moving his arms and legs all around, and seemed to be talking as he stretched.

"Remember," I said, "Be charming. This is important." I liked the way he looked, his dark hair grown in, bright eyes and nice healthy color to his skin. Oh, yes, our baby was more than presentable. He was superior.

We came in from the sewing room. Well, I never heard such cries of admiration. I handed Benjamin to his mother, and they all gathered around, their figures in lovely afternoon frocks, all moving around like something from a play. Benjamin played perfect baby and charmed them all. He laughed and allowed hands to hover over him. He seemed to like the attention. I stood ready to take him if he cried. This went on for about fifteen minutes before Mrs. Bernstein handed me the baby, so she could say goodbye to her guests. As the ladies moved out the door, I took him upstairs

"Well," I said to Benjamin, "You've been a success, my little lad, and your mama is proud of you." We talked it over, he and I, until I heard the front door close and Mrs. Bernstein came up the stairs. She looked delighted and reached out for her little son.

"Our baby enjoyed his first outing," I said.

"Oh, yes, Ellen," she replied. "I've been judged as a good mother. "

"There was never any doubt," I said back.

And with that, I took myself downstairs to start supper.

CHAPTER 6

Mary Anne's Wedding
(1909)

WILLIAM

Mary Anne was married to Frederick at Saint Paul's, our parish church on Saturday. It had been a year since she and Frederick were betrothed. My sister had wanted to work longer and earn more money before they married. Frederick worked for a farmer out in Lincoln. I like him. He is tall and quiet; Swiss, with light-colored hair. Mary Anne is small, brown-haired and not at all quiet. She looked beautiful in her dove gray suit. She wore flowers in her hair and carried a small bouquet. We'd dressed her at our friends' the Raftery's house before the church. She is only a bit taller than I am, but looked quite majestic walking down the aisle. We'd found her some shoes to match the suit, surely an extravagance, but so pretty, and silk stockings. Those were from me. I'd saved up. We were a happy group walking to the church with all our friends.

Frederick waited there. Next to him stood a young man I'd never met. Mary Anne smiled at her Frederick as they said their vows. Frederick looked very handsome in his suit and tie. He stood tall and smiled back at her. Father Kelly proclaimed them man and wife.

We walked back to the Raftery's house after the ceremony, a very lively group. Mary Anne was laughing as she tripped along. There was a lovely party. Tea was served and a bit of something stronger to celebrate the occasion. There were sandwiches and little cakes. Then, we pushed the furniture away and piled up the rugs and commenced to dance. Someone had a fiddle, so it was lots of fun. It was hard not to have the family with us, but we would both write to them at length. Mary Anne was the first Flood sister to marry. They would begin their family out in Lincoln.

Now, here is my news. I met William Bennett, Frederick's friend who stood up for him while I stood up for Mary Anne. So we spent all day together, but not alone. He is very handsome and I believe I looked nice in my new skirt and blouse. I had a pretty dark red jacket to go with it, so I looked my best. He has black, curly hair and eyes that sparkle and he smiles a lot. He comes from a large French-Canadian family and lives with them in Lincoln. He also works on a farm. He did make sure to not take up all my attention, but to be jolly with everyone. He made us laugh, trying to dance the Irish dances. He asked to see me again, and I said, "Yes." It's all I could think about the rest of the day.

After the party, we all got on the streetcar with the newly married couple and rode with them to North Union Station, where we waited until their train arrived. "You must come and see me soon, Ellen," my sister whispered to me. Then the sign came up on the board for their train, stopping at South Lincoln Center. We all followed them down the platform to put the bridal couple on the train and waved our good-byes; some of the lads shouting.

Just before William jumped on the train, he reminded me in front of everyone. "I'll see you on Thursday, Ellen." They all turned and looked at me. Of course, he'd already asked for directions, so I knew he meant it. My friends teased me all the way back until Annie made them stop. I was happy, though.

When Mrs. Bernstein welcomed me home from the wedding, I did tell her that a young man had asked me out on Thursday. She said to be sure to introduce him to her. I also described the wedding and how beautiful Mary Anne looked. She did remark how I would be missing my sister, and I agreed. But part of my mind was now taken up with William Bennett. I thought I would always remember my sister's wedding, as the day I met him. Oh, well, I had a lot to think about as I busied myself in the kitchen preparing the evening meal. Small Benjamin was already in bed. I was not hungry, so I just served and cleaned up and went upstairs to my bedroom. It had been a good day. I prepared to write a letter to our parents, giving the details of the wedding, but decided not to tell them about meeting a young man, not yet. William would seem forward to my mother, who might not approve of me seeing him alone so soon after meeting him.

A few days later, I sat in the clean and orderly kitchen and watched the door. William said he would be there at three in the afternoon. My cup of tea had cooled. I had dressed in my best skirt and blouse and had my hat and jacket on a chair. I'd taken time with my hair, hoping it would stay up and polished my boots. I wanted to look nice. I'd never had a young man call before. I'd never encouraged it. William had insisted he would pick me up, "properly," he called it, where I lived. Mrs. Bernstein would meet him, too. So, I faced that chore.

When the knock came on the door, his smiling face greeted me and right away his hand came up with flowers, early daffodils. I love them. "Country flowers for a country girl," he announced. He looked good in nice shirt, neat pants and cleaned boots. I put the flowers in a clear glass.

Then I led him through to the sewing room and knocked on the door. Mrs. Bernstein responded with a soft "Come in, Ellen."

William addressed her as "Ma'am", and said clearly, "Pleased to meet you." And then, charmingly, "Thank you for letting me spend time with Ellen." This produced a smile from Mrs. Bernstein.

"Enjoy the spring weather," This from her as a way of gentle dismissal, and off we went through the kitchen and quickly out the back door. William reached for my hand and pulled me along.

"Now," he said cheerfully, "What shall we do first?"

He quickly determined we should take the streetcar into town. He was still holding my hand. I did think of what Mrs. Bernstein would think of that and my mother and our relations and neighbors, were I still in Ireland; Ellen Flood and a young man holding hands in public. But I liked it and he held it easily, without fuss, and he just kept talking.

We rushed to get the streetcar as it came down Washington Street. After dropping money in for both of us, he asked if I would like to get some ice cream.

"Your sister says you have a sweet tooth. We can go to Baileys and have ice cream." I wondered what else Mary Anne had told him about me.

"Yes," I told him. "I would like that." But then I wondered if I was dressed right. We had looked in the windows at Baileys, my friends and me, at the glory of marble counters, mirrors and fancy little tables and chairs and stylishly dressed people sitting nicely at those tables having their treats.

Once off the streetcar, he guided me down to Temple Place and in the door by Tremont Street. A few minutes later, we were enjoying our ice cream, with chocolate sauce and whipped cream, all in silver goblets placed in saucers to catch some of the delectable stuff. I was in heaven. I glanced once at our reflection in a mirror and we looked fine. I finished it all, even scraping the last of it, unwilling to have it all gone. "That was excellent," I told him, and "Thank you very much." He looked pleased.

It seemed that William had our afternoon all planned. Next, we went "window shopping" back at the big stores on Washington Street, because, he said, "I know girls like to do that."

We looked at all the lovely things in the windows; Easter hats and shoes and beautiful dresses. I thought to myself that I should buy some feathers and flowers and pin them on my plain hat. I told him I was enjoying myself very much.

"We are having a grand time today," I said. Then, hoping I was not being too forward. "I like you, too, William."

Well, that just made his face light up. We walked over to the park, the one they call Boston Common. like a real couple. We strolled down the paths and across Charles Street, and on the other side was the Public Garden. And over a very pretty bridge where we stood for a while looking down on a small pond. He pointed out the swan boats and said we would take a ride some day. We gazed at flowers all set up in beds; daffodils and red and white tulips. I observed society ladies in their big hats and some with parasols open on this sunny afternoon. We did look nice, though, William and me in our best clothes.

After a while, we sat down on a bench where we could watch the ducks and swans. It did remind me a bit of the Royal Canal near our home in Rathcaled on a quiet day. William teased me because my feet did not touch the ground if I sat back. We perched for a while. "I love the city," I told him. "But how do you know your way around, being a country boy?"

"I met Fred when we both worked on the same farm. He had lived in Dorchester when he came over and still had friends here in Boston. He brought me in with him and we went around. I noticed Fred started, in his quiet way, to talk about a girl who was part of a group he knew and your sister attracted him. Soon, he was in Dorchester every Sunday and I did not go in so often. So, when he asked me to stand up for him, I was surprised, then very pleased. And the rest of the story is that I met you."

"I like working on a farm," he continued. "I would like to manage a farm some day."

That did give me some thought because I had become convinced I wanted to marry and live in the city. But it was way too early to think of that, I told myself, and pushed it far back in my mind.

We chatted some more. He was really easy to talk to. He told me about his family in Lincoln. He has several brothers and sisters. He is the oldest, and he doesn't seem very old. I thought I must be older than him. Was that important when we seemed to get along so well? Then he turned to me and said we should go to a little tea shop he knew of on the back of Beacon Hill he called it. "The Irish are always wanting their tea." I laughed at him. I seemed to do that a lot. We had tea and muffins. I felt very special. I told him about life in Rathcaled, how the place is called a town land and was a lane with families on it, all knowing each other very well and how many brothers and sisters I had back in Ireland.

"You should come out and visit your sister at Easter." he offered. I just smiled at him.

And then it was time to go back because he had to catch his train from North Union Station and insisted on taking me all the way back on the streetcar first. "It is proper to escort a lady back to her home." he informed me. I laughed at that.

"A lady," I said. "Me?"

"Yes", he said quietly and a bit seriously, I thought, "a lady."

It was getting chilly out on this March afternoon, gorgeous, though, with the sun just coming through at the end of the day. I could smell the outdoors as we walked back through the park. I pushed the collar up on my coat. William reached over and touched my hair briefly where it was slipping out of my hat. The crowds, flowing around us, were just beginning to push toward the streetcars to go home.

We were quieter walking back from my stop. He escorted me right to the back door and waited while I unlocked it, then held my hand in his larger one and asked if he might come in to take me to Mass on Sunday. "I cannot often get in on a Thursday," he said. "And would like to see you again soon."

I said, simply, "Yes," and gave him the time.

And then he touched my cheek and said, "Good bye, Ellen. I'll give Mary Anne and Fred your regards and tell them you'll be out to see them soon." Then he took off rapidly down the sidewalk before I could say anything about that. Boyish, he was, but he had a determination in him that matched mine. I'd seen that right away.

What an afternoon it had been! I spent the evening reading and writing letters and thinking about William and me. Later on, Mrs. Bernstein came into the kitchen and asked me if I had a good time. I replied. "A lovely time, Ma'am." and she smiled.

"He did seem a nice young man," she said.

And that was that. He had the spark I'd been looking for. William did begin to come to church with me almost every Sunday and we would go walking together and with our friends, too. I liked spending time with him, although I am several years older than him. It doesn't bother William who, I'm sure, has figured it out based on the age I was when I came over. It bothers me a little. He was beginning to mean a lot to me and that both pleased and worried me. I did not think I was ready yet, but at home I'd have been married by now, probably to a farmer, and here I was walking out with a farmer. He is more than that, though. He really has an inquisitive mind and we can talk together. He comes from a big Catholic family like I do. I had noted he didn't drink at the wedding party. I'd not have minded if he did. He was still after me to go out to Lincoln to see my sister. I was not ready to meet his family, though, so Easter went by.

CHAPTER 7

A Disagreement

LOVE AND COURTSHIP

William and I had been walking out together for several months. After church one Sunday, he said he could not come on Thursday to see me because it was a very busy time on the farm. He would be in on Sunday next. William stood there holding his hat and looking sad, not with his usual smile. The thought did enter my mind that I could go to the dance that evening. I'd not been for a long time; ever since meeting William. My friends wrote, telling me they missed me. So, later, I made a plan to meet them in town Thursday afternoon.

Sure, I was very fond of William and he was special to me. But I'd have no amusement all week long. I did think it would be all right to have some fun. I had no thought of the lads at all. I just loved to dance.

Thursday afternoon, I dressed up and met with our flock of girls in town. Maybe I should have known better than to go to the dance, but I didn't think it wrong of me to go either. The girls took my mind off it for the afternoon, all of us laughing and talking together. Few of them were walking out with anyone yet, and maybe that's why they encouraged me to come out with them and have fun.

So, at the dance that evening, when the music began, I stepped out and danced, Well, I paid no mind to the boys who wanted to dance with me and after a short time, got ready to leave. My heart just wasn't in it. I said goodbye to my friends and left early. The image of William just kept coming into my mind, even as I had tapped my shoes to the music. So, I caught the streetcar home to a cup of tea and my book and looking forward to Sunday when I would see William again.

On Sunday, after Mass, William was outside. He'd been talking with the people we knew. We'd not sat together because sometimes he was a little late because of taking the train in, so I waited for him to come over. He was all in his best clothes and me wearing my new hat, which I hoped he would notice. Sundays were nice. I thought it would be our usual Sunday until Annie came by with a warning look for me. Well, I didn't know what that could be about until I looked more closely at William's face and saw thunderclouds. "You went to the dance," he said, and did not smile at me, not at all. Well, I'd already been feeling bad about that dance. I do not know if I'd actually planned on telling him I'd gone.

I informed him I'd gone and left early and hadn't really danced with any boys anyway and missed him, but he did not seem to be prepared to accept that.

"Maybe you would rather not have me take up your time, this Sunday?" That was said with the look of a boy on him. I guessed he was hurt, but I was not going to back down. He was beginning to make me mad.

"You are daft to think I don't want to spend time with you. I wanted only to see my friends and have some fun. I missed you."

All the joy of spending our Sunday afternoon together was leaving me then. I wanted to cry.

"I don't understand you, Ellen. I would never go anywhere without you. You must know how I feel."

Well, I didn't like the way he'd turned this into something it wasn't. So, I turned to him and said, "William, I'm sorry you feel bad, but I've done nothing wrong. I left the dance early and went home. If you don't want to spend the afternoon with me, then go." I was feeling that sorry for myself because I didn't think I'd done anything wrong.

He didn't say anything at all, just looked away. So then I lost my temper. I stamped my foot and walked away as fast as I could. I'd have no more of this. That surprised him. William had never seen this side of me before. I didn't care either at that particular moment. Well, I sped down the sidewalk and wasn't looking back so didn't see but felt his hand on my shoulder as I continued my race down the sidewalk and with everyone watching us. He must have had to run to catch up with me. I pushed away and kept going, but then stopped when we were well away from the crowd at the church.

"Ellen, I spend all my time with you because you are more special to me than any girl has ever been in my life." Well, we'd had short lives, so that didn't impress me. But he went on. "I don't want any of those Irish boys to take you away. I don't know what I'd do without you. Please don't be mad."

I wasn't quite ready to let it go, this treatment of me, but I listened to him and did hear what he was saying. And. I truly did not want him to see other girls out there in Lincoln, and he was a good looking boy. I did not think I was jealous, like he was showing me. I'd never thought he'd carry on this way or I'd not have gone to the dance. I hadn't had a good time, anyway.

Well, that afternoon we were careful with each other in a way we'd never done before. I would still do what I wanted to do because no man would tell me what to do but I would try not to hurt his feelings again, although I did think he had hurt mine by not showing he trusted me. I would not be dictated to either.

When William brought me back later that Sunday, something had changed. He was quieter than usual and so was I. We had a lot to think about. And I thought it all came about because of a foolish dance. I told him I probably would not be going to any more dances. I said "probably" to him, although I really had no intention of going again. He seemed to take it well. I guess it was a truce we were making between us.

I wondered, though, if I should be worried that William had acted so jealous. It felt like I broke something by going to the dance. But he needed to think, too. Although we had made our peace on Sunday, things had changed and I thought I needed to make a new plan about me and William, and I needed my best friend Annie to talk to me about it.

I had Annie for tea. I started. "Thank you, Annie, for warning me about William on Sunday. I had not any idea he would find out or if he did, be upset like that."

I asked her what she thought of me going to the dance.

"Well," and here she hesitated. "I know you didn't mean anything by it, just looking for some fun, but I know how boys can be."

"What about our independence?" I said. And we looked at each other then. We'd had long talks about that Even though we worked as maids, we did whatever we wanted on our time off. But perhaps I had not been entirely fair to William?

"You were a sight running down the walk and William after you. We were all a bit worried when we saw that." And then she paused. "We never saw you like that before, losing your temper, and with William!" And then her eyes twinkled a little bit. "You can move really fast!" I laughed at that. Then she took on a more serious expression, "Are you and William all right now? I wondered when you wanted to talk to me."

"We are all right, but now I think we will need to make an understanding between us, not because of the foolish dance but because it's the right thing to do."

"Do you love William and do you want to marry him some day?"

"Yes, but I'm not ready to marry yet."

"Then make that agreement between you. You promise not to see any other boys and he promises not to see any other girls and you tell him you are not yet ready to marry and be done with it, as my mother would say."

"Annie, you're brilliant." She laughed at that, and we quietly sipped our tea some more. She chose the next moment to tell me she had just started walking out with someone herself. "Annie!" I said, "And we've been just talking about me all the time!"

"You know him, Ellen. It's Tom from the dance. A few weeks ago. He asked to take me walking on my Thursday off."

Well, our group was beginning to change if Annie was making plans and I expected the other girls in our group would also be choosing young men. This place we found ourselves in, all working as maids and being by ourselves, was about to change. I thought of us all with families of our own. It was a lot to think about.

After I saw Annie out, I went upstairs to my bedroom, prepared for bed, and then went to sleep, peacefully, after I'd said my prayers, more comfortable now I'd made up my mind to accept the next changes in my life.

We did welcome another baby in late fall, another little boy they named Raymond. William and I had just arrived back from a day together and I was summoned upstairs to help. I gave Benjamin to William to mind in the kitchen for several hours while I assisted with the birth. This time, everything went very well and after William left to stay overnight with our friends, the Raftery's because it had gotten quite late, I sat in the rocker with a sleeping Benjamin, thinking what a good father William would make. And that night, my last thoughts as I went to sleep were of William.

CHAPTER 8

Winter (1910)

I spent Christmas with our friends, the Rafterys. William and I had exchanged gifts and kisses under the mistletoe. He came religiously every week. I'd not yet managed a time to go out to see my sister in Lincoln. Mary Anne and I wrote letters all the time. I promised to go out in the spring. January was cold. I could not get warm at all except when I was in the kitchen cooking. At night, I knew enough to get my clothes off down to my shift and quickly climb into bed and under the sheet and two blankets where I would warm one spot and try to stay in it all night long. I could scrape my name in the frost on the window with my fingernails.

And so, when William said we should go ice skating on a small pond he knew of on our Thursday afternoon, I was not enthused. "Why would I want to spend my time off out in the cold, William?" I asked him. Then he promised me a hot chocolate drink afterward.

"I can borrow my sister's skates," he said. "They are mad about skating." He did not tell me how well he could skate. I knew myself to have good balance and plotted out what to wear, not my best woolen skirt, but extra stockings and the shawl over my coat and a woolen hat and those big mittens and the large, red scarf I'd knitted that I could wind around and around me.

William arrived at the kitchen door that Thursday, after I had served lunch, bearing two pair of skates he had in a cloth bag. He looked very pleased with himself. He showed me the skates, wooden things with leather straps and metal blades. They didn't look like they would hold me up. We left for the pond. William helped me attach the skates to my boots and then walked me onto the ice where I stood there afraid to move but not wanting him or anyone else to know. He said he'd be right back and skated quickly to the center of the pond, making me feel quite abandoned. I was cross for him, skating away and leaving me there. My face was cold and felt flushed with both the cold and the aggravation I was feeling.

Then I watched him. He was graceful and fast. He had on a knitted hat over his black curls and his face was all pink and it being William he was smiling at the day and everyone in it. His hands were in his pockets and he made it look so easy. I think I was scowling when he came back to me though I had been admiring him. He took my hands and began to pull me across the ice, skating backwards himself. At first I felt scared, although I didn't show it. But then it began to feel good, like I was blowing across the ice and I felt so light. Nor did my ankles buckle under me from being up on the blades.

He let go, then, and I went away across the ice by myself. He shouted, "Put your hands out, Ellen, and just push your feet back and forth. Let yourself go. You're doing fine." And I did! It felt like dancing. I felt so full of myself and graceful, too, until I fell down. William didn't look as concerned as I thought he should, maybe he was even laughing a little, but I got right back up again and did not let him enjoy it too much, the sight of me on my backside.

So, we stayed out there a long time. I had not learned to stop yet, but instead of asking William to show me, I watched him and the others and soon learned to do it myself. I practiced that a few times and then William took me by the hand and we flew across the ice together. I began to hum, but eventually as the afternoon got older, it did seem a good idea to stop and warm ourselves. There was also the promise of hot chocolate. So off we went, and I burnt my tongue on it, and had to get my warmth from my hands around the hot cup for a while. It felt so cozy being there with William, and I'd had a wonderful afternoon for all my doubts. I drank the chocolate left at the bottom of the cup like a greedy child. It was funny how he could both make me feel like a child having fun and at the same time, a woman having feelings about her young man.

Back at Shafter Street, as he got ready to leave me just inside at the kitchen door, we made our plans as we always did. I thought that the Rafterys might have mentioned having a sled, I told him, and we could borrow it and I knew of a hill where I had seen people sledding and would he like that? He looked delighted and supposed I did know how to use a sled. "Of course," I told him rather sharply." What could there be to riding a sled on snow down a hill?" He gave me a glance from his eyes all full of glee and I did wonder about that.

"Remember," he said, "You promised you would come by train on a Sunday out to Lincoln to see your sister and visit with me, too." "And," he added, "to also meet my family?"

"When it gets warmer," I said quickly, with a smile. "And no prospect of a snowstorm."

"It's not such a long way," he responded and then, "Would it be such a bad thing if you were to be left in Lincoln due to some bad weather and not able to get back for a few days?" He was grinning at me like a boy.

The next week, we borrowed the sled. "The hill is much too high," I declared, "and I'm not going down it," William laughed at me. "Look at the small children going down the hill," he said. "You can do it. I'll go down with you."

"Two on a sled!"

That really made him laugh.

"Is that so bad, Ellen?"

He sat on the sled first, and then I arranged myself in front of him. I prepared for the worst but thought that all the over clothes I had on would save me when we overturned. I sat stiffly while his arms went around and his hands gripped the rope and he planted his two feet on the turning part at the front.

He teetered just for a moment at the very top of the hill and down we started down before I could change my mind. There was a whoosh of air and the metal runners took us over the snow and off we went. A few bumps later, we arrived at the bottom of the hill. It was exhilarating. I tumbled off the sled, gathered the rope and began to pull it up the hill.

"I'm going down alone this time, William," I called out. He looked surprised. I liked that. I went down alone and felt like I was flying and landed safely. He showed me how to go down on my belly. We did take turns, and I consented to ride together again. We never crashed and I had been fearful of that, although I never let him know. I have my pride. My sister would say, enough for several people.

Being outside in all the snow on a sunny, cold winter afternoon and going down again and again made me giddy, and we laughed and teased each other a lot.

It's times like these I feel so full of energy and freedom, too. And there is always an excitement being with William. He is my match for energy. I am not always thinking of other things like when I am doing my chores. He takes up all the room I have and I think I do that for him too.

The afternoon was not long enough. We headed back after several hours on the hill. We left the sled leaning on the porch rail and walked fast all the way back. William made me laugh when he teased me about my small size and being so brave on the sled. As we reached the kitchen door and I opened it, we were laughing together and as we stomped our feet on the step, Mrs. Bernstein came into the kitchen smiling.

"Well, you must have had a good time," she said, smiling.

William pulled off his hat and smiled back. "Ellen learned all about sledding this afternoon, Ma'am," he said, grinning at her.

"He's a terror," I told her, "making me do things and liking it."

"It will be another year before both Benjamin and Randall will be ready for a sled, but I think my father has and old push-sled for babies and I'll see if I can get it. The fresh cold air will be good for them as long as we bundle them up." Mrs. Bernstein looked very pleased with her idea. I could picture little Randall with only his tiny face peeking out from all the clothes and covers.

"You should offer William a cup of tea, Ellen, before he has to get his train back."

And with that, she turned and went back to the parlor. My mother would not have given us such privacy.

William drank his tea slowly at the table and ate his piece of pound cake and preserves. We talked quietly about his family's doings and those of Mary Anne and Frederick. I felt pleasantly warm after the cold outside, not exactly sleepy but contented with both time and place. I wished he could stay longer.

So, he put his cup down into the saucer, picked up the last of the cake crumbs, and put it in his mouth. It was always the same, stretching out the time before he had to leave.

He got his coat and hat on and stood there holding his mittens, and then I walked him to the door. He stood there looking a bit serious, I thought, after our happy afternoon. Well, he pulled me in for a hug and I went too and there was a kiss. I did not push him out the door. We remained a minute that way and then he was off with a "Goodbye, Ellen." I watched him down the street. The kiss stayed with me.

End of Winter

The branches of the big blue spruce tree outside my window were finally free of snow but bending backward to a March wind, swinging back and forth and bouncing. But there was a blue sky that day and even with the still cold temperatures, I could feel spring coming. The air smelled fresher in the early morning. The birds were singing now, sitting on branches where you could see them and hear their songs.

We danced, William and I, one Sunday afternoon in the Bernstein's kitchen. I sang a tune loudly and got up and danced myself, after pushing the chairs out of the way. I put my hands up over my head and got my feet going, clicked my boots and whirled around and then, facing him where he sat on a chair, pulled him up and had him face me and put my hands behind by back and did a few steps which he copied. But he was minding his feet, and I told him he was doing fine, to look up and dance. I sang slowly and then faster, and we moved to my beat. And then we were both going up and down and turning and I took his hands and we danced together. It was fine. I stopped just for a moment and he pulled me over. I rested there for a moment and then stepped out again. William joined me and we were laughing when Mrs. Bernstein appeared at the door, holding Randall by the hand. They clapped their hands. We took a bow.

"How wonderful," she said.

I began to explain, but she stopped me.

"You were just having fun" she laughed. "And now I'll leave you alone to finish William's lesson." And she quickly left.

"Tea," I said, after showing him a few more steps.

"I'd rather we danced," he responded

"We'll dance at our wedding," I said quickly, astonished at myself for saying it. "Some day," I added.

But he gave me such a look of pure happiness, I felt myself melting, Just a little.

"It's the dancing and the music I love," I told him.

We were both a bit breathless and sat down and had that tea. Then he left for home, as always.

We walked all over on those spring afternoons. I talked to William about my home and family in Ireland and even shared some letters from my mother. I tried to explain the small place I came from, the town-land of Rathcaled and village of Ballynacargy nearby and a few miles away the market town of Mullingar, and further, by train, Dublin, all strange to him. I told him the largest place I'd seen before Boston was Queenstown, where we boarded the ship.

On those afternoons, we both knew when to head back to Dorchester for me to return to my duties, and then he would take the train back to Lincoln. One day I told I was ready to go out there for a visit to see my sister. He immediately added "and to meet my family."

"Easter is late in April and this still March, I'll be ready to go out then.

"Well, he was surprised. I don't think he expected it so soon. William and I agreed I should come out early on Easter for the day. He would pick me up at the train station. First, I would have to ask for the whole day off into the evening.

So, I went to Mrs. Bernstein to ask for the Sunday off. She nodded her head quietly and then surprised me by saying perhaps two days would be better. She did not see why I should not leave on Friday afternoon and return on Sunday night. I thought that generous and thanked her. I would let William know on Sunday and send a note off to my sister.

I felt like skipping back to the kitchen but controlled myself and walked. I sang the rest of the morning while I did my chores. I could not wait to tell William.

CHAPTER 9

Lincoln (1910)

PROMISES

By Good Friday afternoon, I had made the kitchen clean, ironed the boys' little clothes for the Sabbath and hung them up. I'd cooked a chicken, and it sat in its pot in the icebox, all ready for the evening meal. It was only left to throw off my work clothes and change into the skirt, blouse and jacket I'd prepared for the trip to Lincoln. I had until Sunday evening to be back. I felt like one of the Irish Travelers, myself. Adjusting the hat on my head, I moved quickly downstairs, bag in hand, to say goodbye to Mrs. Bernstein. The boys were in for their naps. She gave me a look and appeared satisfied with my appearance.

"Well, Ellen, you are to see your sister again. You must be excited."

"Oh, yes," I replied. "It will be lovely to see her and Frederick."

"And William," she said, smiling.

"Well, be very careful. Remember that you are on a train and in charge of yourself. I would suppose someone will be there to meet you?"

"William promised." I answered.

Then she nodded. "We will miss you and look forward to seeing you again on Sunday evening."

"I'll be back before Benjamin goes to bed." I answered.

That was all. I was out the door and down the walk, swinging my small bag. At Park Street Station, I changed to the elevated and that brought me to North Union. I soon had my ticket and sat on one of the big wooden benches, holding onto my bag and waiting for my train to Lincoln. At last, they posted the gate number. I headed over there. One high step up and I was in the car and then in a window seat. I did not want to miss anything.

First, we stopped in Charlestown, where I believe they have a lot of Irish. Next was Cambridge, where it was beginning to look leafy. Then we were speeding through fields and by trees and houses. I got a little anxious, then, not wanting to miss my stop. I was to get off at South Lincoln Station. And then we were there and William standing on the platform. I tried to catch his eye, but it was not until I'd grabbed my bag and moved to the open door that he saw me. He just had this big smile on his face. He gave me his hand to step down and led me to a horse and buggy.

He pointed out things as we trotted along. It seemed to be mostly farms we were passing. As we pulled up at the house, they must have heard us coming because both my sister Mary Anne and Frederick were standing on their porch. She must have just finished some dishes because she still had a towel in her hands. I ran quickly up the steps and into my sister's arms. I had missed her so much! Frederick quietly shook my hand and then my sister pulled me into the house.

"We'll have tea," she said. She was as excited as I was.

"I can't believe you are to be here for two whole days."

I noticed William still stood at the door, hat in hand, grinning away.

"You'll be back for supper," she ordered. "At half-past six." He nodded, gave me a happy look, and off he went. Frederick had also departed for somewhere. So, there we were in her kitchen, alone. Mary Anne flew around, getting cups and saucers. Soon, we had our tea, and then she pulled her apron off.

I looked at her closely, and she flushed. "I wanted to tell you in person," she said.

I said it for her, "You're expecting!"

She wasted no time on her triumph, but sat herself down and looked straight at me.

"What about you and William? Frederick says you are all he talks about."

"I am very fond of William," I said.

"Don't be so prim," she said back to me. "You make a lovely couple."

"In my own time, I will decide." That was my answer. My sister always made me feel stubborn. She just looked at me. There would be much more about this before the two days were over.

"Anyway, we'll have a nice supper later. You'll meet Joseph, our boarder, too. He'll sleep in the storage room for these two nights and you'll get the bedroom. He thought that the right thing to do for the young lady, he calls you. He's shy but also walking out with a local girl which has saved your William from much worry." Mary Anne had a sharp tongue, but she was almost always smiling and that did take the edge off.

"The Bennetts," I said, to take us off the subject of William. "What are they like?"

"Well," she said, "William has brought his three younger brothers by. One is big already and the others are still little boys, all of them very friendly like your William, and he has three younger sisters, one just a baby, also another brother, not so much younger than him. William is, you know, the oldest boy in the family. I think his parents dote on him. He says they are, all of them, looking forward to meeting you."

Mary Anne must have seen something in my face because she changed the subject by telling me how pretty I looked and how she liked the feathers in my hat and the smart jacket which I reminded her I had worn at her wedding. "Don't you look like city," she said. "I miss the city myself, but I also like it out here in Lincoln because it reminds me of at home in Ireland. Don't you agree with me?"

"Yes," I said, "The air is is different and oh, how good to be in all this green again of trees and shrubs and how the roads go through the fields like at home," I told her.

I decided to ask her when her baby was due and she said in about five months.

"We've saved up and will have the doctor to the house," she said. "I'll write the parents soon, too, when a little more time has gone by."

There was potato chowder for supper and fresh peas, too, and asparagus, which I'd never had, drenched in yellow butter, and extra potatoes, too.

William returned for supper. I walked him out when it was time for him to leave. Quite late it was, and he touched my hands and then my face a little, having turned quiet. We had a kiss then; a chaste one by priest standards and then another one, a bit more exciting than the first. He stopped and stepped away. I don't think anyone had noticed us from inside. They were well away from the door.

"See you, tomorrow, Ellen. I will be here before noon to take you home to meet the family. They've planned a big noon day meal. I'll have you back here by evening and then we'll all go to church on Easter Sunday."

He looked like he could have said more, but climbed into the buggy, the horse already hitched up and off he went, down the now dark road.

Mary Anne showed me a small bed and a table with an oil lamp. The outhouse was in the back and she said she'd show me the way.

She stopped and gave me one of her looks but instead of going on about me and William, she asked me if I would be the godmother. "I'll be honored," I said happily. I was already planning a little baby wardrobe, and I knew small things would arrive from Ireland. I also had a thought of them not seeing their first grandchild and felt sad about that. I suppose I was getting tired to be turning my mind that way. Why, I thought, a little later as I climbed into bed after saying my prayers, did there always have to be sadness next to happiness? Well, I suppose I could pray about it, but I did tend to fall asleep quickly at night before I got much serious praying done.

I woke at dawn, not knowing at first where I was but soon remembered. I smelled coffee, put on my clothes quickly and went out to the kitchen. Mary Anne had made porridge and there were slices of brown bread on a plate. I quickly ran to the outhouse and then back in to ask her if she needed any help.

"The men have work today," she said. "It will be a shorter day on Saturday, but they still start early. When everything's done. We'll all eat together and then you can help me with the cleaning up."

"What time is William coming by?" she asked.

I told her he had told me he'd be here to get me before noon.

"You'll be fine," she said, smiling at me. "Do you have a neat skirt and blouse, not too fancy?"

"I do." Now we were coming to the sisterly things I missed so much, like getting ready to go out.

After we ate and the men had gone out the door, I went to my room and pulled out the blouse I planned to wear. I had three acquired after some scrimping and had made them nice with new collars and buttons. I brushed my skirt. It would have to do. I thought I looked nice but not too dressed up. When I came out, Mary Anne looked me over.

"All right," she said. "You look sweet and not too city and your hair is up nice, too. We'll have a tub tonight, so we can both bathe and wash our hair for Easter Sunday. You'll have time for that when he brings you back later, and you and I will have another visit."

I could tell she thought we'd have much to talk about after my visit to William's family.

"We'll send the men out to play cards down the road and have the house to ourselves for a few hours. I'll have Frederick arrange it." I liked how my dear sister ran things.

"I wish William and Frederick could meet our family in Ireland. Do you think of them all the time like I do?"

"Yes," she nodded. "But things change. Already now, the parents are older and the children have grown up without their sisters. It is not the same home now we're missing, and that is sad in its own way."

Mary Anne loaned me a pretty shawl and when William came by, I was ready, but already counting the hours when I could be back here, God forgive me. I'd never have shared that with him. He looked so pleased with himself and with me.

William let me be quiet on the ride out to the house. We went a distance down a long road to get there. I could see an old house and a porch as we got closer. And someone let out a shout, and I heard running. Three boys raced down the road toward us.

"My brothers," he said, laughing. "I told them to be quiet and not scare you away, not that I've ever seen you timid."

They stopped by the buggy and seemed to have nothing at all to say, no plans at all beyond running to meet us. They just stared. "How are you keeping?" I said, smiling. "We are well," said the oldest one, and the others nodded. "Ma is waiting, Willow." I turned to look at William.

"My other name," he said, smiling at me.

The boys, still full of energy, now galloped back down the road where I could see clearly a couple standing on the porch with some other children. The woman was holding a baby.

We pulled up in the buggy and the oldest of the boys helped me down. I straightened my skirt and walked toward them. I could see William's mother was a bit taller than me and his father the same as William and looking like him.

I greeted Mrs. Bennett and held out the spring flowers that Mary Anne had picked that morning. She reached out for them with the arm not holding the baby, a little girl who was clinging to her mother tight and examining this stranger very closely.

"My mother," said William and "my father." He added, "This is Ellen."

"This is my sister, Martha." I nodded, but she looked at me, though, not totally unfriendly, not as happy to see me, I thought. She was a year older than William, and I thought she would not be welcoming a girl who might take her brother away. That thought astonished me because it meant I'd come to a decision about William and it was sudden. She had reason, I admitted to myself, to fear losing him. The younger girl looked at me shyly. She told me she was twelve.

"So, Ellen, we finally meet you. Welcome to our home," said Mr. Bennett and his wife smiled her welcome and we went in. There was one big room that seemed to take up all of the first floor. The table was set for dinner and I could smell roast meat.

Then I asked if I could help. Young Florence reached out her arms to me and I took her. "You keep the baby," Mrs. Bennett said.

"What's your name?" I asked the baby as she let me hug her. She just looked at me.

"Florence," replied the youngest of the brothers. "Her name is Florence." I asked him how old he was.

"I'm Stephen and I am six years old and Robert is nine, and big Walter is eleven."

"So," I said, "Robert, Walter and Stephen," and looking at the girls now busy in the kitchen, "Martha and Alice.", "And Francis," they added, and I looked over and saw a boy who seemed closer in age to William.

I was feeling very comfortable.

William had gone outside with his father to talk when he saw I was occupied. Walter headed out there with them. Francis came over and introduced himself to me before going out to join them. He had his brother William's smile, but maybe not so outgoing. He seemed quiet, and still a boy.

In a very short time, Mrs. Bennett called us for dinner. William and his father and all the brothers came in the door. The girls set bowls of potatoes and vegetables, and gravy on the long table as well as a plate of sliced bread and another of butter. I realized I was hungry. Martha took Florence from me and took her to her chair. Stephen and Robert pushed to sit by me but their mother said William should sit on one side of me and Alice on the other side because she was a girl and older. Martha sat by the baby. The boys looked disappointed and then she said they could change seats for dessert and they were happy again.

We bowed our heads and said grace, except for Florence, who waved her spoon and called out, "Eat." We all laughed at her.

A large roast chicken was set out on a platter, and Mr. Bennett carved it. My William had his father's curly black hair. They were both built solid. You could tell they worked outside. Their skin turned brown from the sun.

Dinner was not quiet. I managed to eat while at the same time, telling them about my family in Ireland and, to the children, who wanted to know why I talked the way I did. I told them about working in Dorchester and going in town to the city. Six-year-old Stephen told me I was pretty and then turned red as his brothers laughed at him. William reached out and patted his head kindly.

William and his father worked out at farms. The other children, except Martha, were still in school, or scholars as we would say in Ireland. William had some chance at getting a job at the grain store when there was an opening, but that could take some time. They discussed that around the table.

We cleaned up before dessert and I did get my apron. The boys ran about outside.

William and his father stood on the porch while Mr. Bennett smoked his pipe. We cleared the table and I dried dishes while the girls put them away.

There was pie for dessert, made from apples they'd kept in a cold cellar from the previous fall. It was good. I had tea and the other grown-ups had coffee and we sat and relaxed on kitchen chairs on the porch all that Saturday afternoon, while Baby Florence ran around from one lap to another.

I had caught William looking across the table at me during dinner and his mother looking at him. He would be a good husband, I thought, and I would have a family again in his. They did not seem to have noticed I was older than their son, and that had been one of my worries. If they did, his parents showed no signs of caring. I did not trouble myself with the details of that future I'd just mapped out for us. Nor did it trouble me to be making plans before I'd accepted William's proposal. I had rarely been so sure of anything. Mary Anne would be so smug when I told her.

Finally, at about five o'clock, William said that he should be getting me back and went off to hitch up the buggy. Mrs. Bennett removed the now sleeping little girl from her lap. Martha carried her off after giving me a half-smile.

Mrs. Bennett stood up to take my hands in hers. "I have the feeling you are very important to my son, and I like you very much. You young people must do what you desire, but I know after meeting you what I want. Remember that, Ellen."

"I think I know what I want, too," I said to her in a low voice. She nodded as Mr. Bennett came over and then he also took my hands in his. "We will see you all at Mass tomorrow and then you will all come back for Easter dinner."

"I will see you tomorrow," I told them. "Thank you for the wonderful visit."

William helped me into the buggy.

"God bless," Mr. Bennett called out.

The boys chased us down the road until we left them behind and then William put his arm around me and that's how we stayed until we were almost back at my sister's house. And then we sat properly again.

Mary Anne was at the door before the buggy came to a complete stop. Our mood was broken, but I think we were both philosophical about it because we would spend time together tomorrow after all.

"Do you want to come in, William?" She said nicely as he helped me down from the buggy.

William smiled and said he would see us at church the next morning.

"So," she said, "How was it?" I'd not even taken the shawl off and we could still hear the clopping of the horse's hooves going down the road. The water was boiling for tea. I supposed I could drink some more.

Frederick and I talked about the early spring weather while Mary Anne set the table. Frederick let us do most of the talking. I congratulated him on the coming baby and he smiled at that and said he was pleased. He seemed, like Mary Anne, to think it important that they would be having the doctor come.

"I am working very hard," he declared. "I will have my own farm some day and a house for all the family we will have together."

Mary Anne spoke up then. I'd never known her to be quiet for anyone. "Ellen will have a family, too, with William, and won't it be grand when our children come together." I just looked at her. Frederick cleared his throat and just pushed his chair back and said he had some chores to do before he headed down the road to the Smiths. He pointed to some pots of water he'd set on the stove to heat for our intended baths. I immediately said I could handle the pots. He nodded and then headed to the door.

She soon had towels warming by the stove and blankets over the chairs. We both got down to our shifts, shivering a little, because it was cold in the kitchen on this late April afternoon. Then I poured hot water into the tub and filled the pots again. Ma had taught us how to do our Saturday night baths. I told her she should be first. I held the towel up while my sister got out of her shift and slid into the hot water I handed her the big bar of soap and while she was soaping all over, I ran to my room to get her surprise, a bottle of shampoo from Jordan Marsh. I poured out a little into my hand and lathered up her wet hair, and then I poured warm water from a pitcher to rinse. I told her she should relax for a bit in the tub and then I'd be taking my bath.

I held out the towel to her while she got out of the tub and she was soon sitting in her shift, wrapped in a blanket, in a chair by the warm stove while I poured more hot water in for me. I just pulled the towel off as I sunk into the tub. After a while, she came over and we shampooed and rinsed my hair and then I relaxed until the water began to cool. Out I came, wrapping up, first, in a towel, then my shift, and then a blanket. We both sat there a while, quiet and comfortable in the warmth and with the lamp, now lighting the kitchen on this spring night, making it cozy. I knew we were both thinking of bath nights at home, so long ago now that we could measure it in years, not weeks or months like when we first came over. So, we sat there a while in our shifts but all warm wrapped in our blankets and our thoughts.

We prepared to dry our hair by the stove. I knew it was time to talk. I started first. "William's family is very nice and welcomed me fine," I said. "Seeing him with them made me understand how he is. They are lively and friendly and his parents are very kind."

She nodded. "But what about you and William?" The girl always went right to her subject.

"Now, don't be smug, Mary Anne, but I do think I want to marry him sooner than later." She looked very satisfied at that. "Of course, You're meant to be together. I've known that since our wedding." And then, "When will you marry?"

"He has to ask me again."

"Again?" Her voice went up.

Now, that made me feel foolish, but I couldn't lie about it. I'd been holding all this to myself, how it was with William and me. I saw how it would seem to her.

"I think we have an understanding, William and me, and I will tell you when we have decided."

"There you go, prim, again," she said, putting her hands in the air.

"I want to do things my way," I responded in a sharper tone than I meant to use.

My sister surprised me, then.

"You need time," she said. "I do understand that, sister. We came here together from Ireland, found work, told each other everything until I moved away and now you need to do it your way."

We spent the rest of the evening talking about our future. I did ask her if she thought it wrong of me to make plans in my mind before we were betrothed, and she said she'd done the same with Frederick, who had not been as forward as William. But she thought we should make it proper very soon.

We got the rest of our clothes on then. God forbid they find us in our underclothes sitting by the stove, even with coverings over us. A while later, a knock came at the door and we told the men to come in. Frederick dumped the water outside from the tub and then we all headed to bed, knowing we had an early start to church in the morning.

CHAPTER 10

Easter Sunday

Easter morning, I slept a little longer than I usually do. Mary Anne was just getting up then, too. Frederick was coming in from the garden where he'd been doing the watering of early spinach and sweet peas. Joseph was nowhere to be seen, having set off to walk to his girl's house. After a trip outside, I finished dressing. More formal today, I wore my red jacket and my hat with the feathers, too. I also had on my best stockings and had shined my shoes. It only took a few minutes to wash my face and put my hair up. Mary Anne looked very pretty in her outfit of skirt and white, starched blouse and gray jacket. We'd be fasting to go to communion, so no breakfast. It was a bit chilly out, but I thought the sun would warm us as the day went on.

By half-past eight, Frederick was helping us into the buggy for the ride to Concord for the nine o'clock mass. In Concord center, near a pretty green, there were wagons and buggies everywhere. I guess that most had come in from the farms. We did not see any Bennetts and thought they must be already inside. We could hear the organ music as we headed over to the white, wooden church and up the stairs.

We walked almost to the front of the church, only four pews back, where I saw William poking his head out, looking for us. He stood up and positioned himself in the aisle to let us into the pew, a very full one. The children were trying to quiet their excitement at seeing us. Their parents smiled at us in greeting. Mr. Bennett had his missal and she, her rosary beads.

A rush of more organ music started up, and we all stood as the priest entered in his beautiful white vestments and began the prayers after bowing to the altar. It was neither a large church, nor grand, but did have stained glass windows and polished wooden pews. All of us made the sign of the cross. We spoke the Latin responses and sang the songs.

We went outside. The Bennetts knew everyone. Things quieted down after a while, and families began to return to their buggies and wagons. Everyone was in their Sunday best. Florence had on a little dress and bonnet. Martha looked like a young lady and Alice very sweet like her name. Both girls wore hats today. I think there had been Saturday night baths all around because the boys looked very shiny and clean.

William climbed up beside his father to drive the wagon and big Walter, too. The rest of them sat on benches. Mr. Bennett then called out that there was room for me too if I cared to join them. I got a look of approval from my sister, and so climbed on. Mary Anne and Frederick would follow us.

Several country roads later, not far at all, we arrived. This time I knew where the aprons were and wrapped one around me right away. Mary Anne came into the kitchen, too, while the men remained outside on the porch. The boys were chased out and Mary Anne was allowed to help set the table. Mrs. Bennett did not remark on my sister's condition, but I knew she'd noticed.

It was a merry group that sat down to dinner, but we did quiet down long enough to say grace. Little Florence, though, was fast asleep and had been put into her crib to nap. We had ham and potatoes, carrots and early spinach and butter, lots of butter and bread. Each adult had a glass of wine, home-made, they told me. It was potent. All the food was luscious, all grown in the garden, and ham from a pig killed the previous fall. We cleaned up before dessert, this time a fruit cake and coffee and tea, again served on the porch where we sat wrapped up warm against the April chill.

The afternoon went much too quickly. I did not want it to end. William had been attentive all day, and it had been so pleasant being with them all. But by almost four o'clock, it was time for me to say my goodbyes. William went off to hitch up the buggy. My sister looked sad. The boys made a slow trot alongside but seemed tired, maybe stuffed with all that food. They waved as we drove off. William put his arm around me as soon as we turned the corner. He was quiet again, but I didn't suppose that would last. I decided to take the initiative.

"Yes, William, I will," I said from where I was tucked under his arm.

Well, the man was a marvel. He just pulled me closer and replied, "Of course, you will marry me, Ellen." I would have liked to surprise him a little. It seemed everyone had known this was to happen, except me.

"But, William, you have to ask me, again, formally, and then I get to say 'yes' and then we will be betrothed. My sister did tell me we should do it properly."

And we did, stopping the buggy so he could say the words to me and me back to him, and that was that. There was a kiss involved. Then, I told him he had to write to my father in Ireland. He didn't groan at that but told me to give him the address and he would do it during the coming week.

I felt so sad when the train pulled in at the station. So much had happened in two days. We stood up from our bench and he walked me over to the train. I already had my ticket out and William carried my bag, which he handed up to me as I climbed up the tall step. There wasn't anyone else getting on, just me. I got a window seat on the side of the platform. The train pulled out and the last thing I saw of the station was William standing on the platform waving. In my bag was a thick ham sandwich Mrs. Bennett had given me, all wrapped up in paper, and a large slice of cake. I supposed I would have it later, before I went to bed. I sighed at taking on my duties again.

It was getting dark. I could hardly see anything as the train sped through fields, then, darkening streets with shadowy, leafy trees, then the city lights, as we sped through Charlestown and then right into Boston and North Union Station. The station was nearly empty. The streets were quiet, walking back to Shafter Street from the trolley. It was only six in the evening. I'd arrived back when I said I would, to see little Benjamin to his bed. I thought he must have missed me the previous two nights.

I let myself in the kitchen door and set my bag down on the floor. Someone had lit the lamp. Mrs. Bernstein called to me. As I walked toward the parlor, I thought that I would not share the news about William and me, not yet.

Mrs. Bernstein looked at me. I felt so different from when I had left that I wondered if I looked different, too.

"How is your sister?" she said in her low voice.

I thought that I could share her news and told her about the baby, and Mrs. Bernstein was delighted to hear it. I then went on to tell her how pretty and green it was out there in Lincoln and how it reminded me of Ireland. I was chattering, I could tell, so she wouldn't ask too much about William.

Then she smiled at me and asked how William was saying what a nice young man he was. I had to tell her about the Bennetts and the meals I had and how we dressed up for church and how nice they were, too. And yes, William had met me at the train. I think she had more to say but instead said I must be tired and Mr. Bernstein was upstairs, playing with Benjamin who had missed me and would I like to go up and say "hello" before he went to bed?

I used that as an excuse to leave the conversation and run upstairs to see my boys.

She did smile and look closely at me, though, before I left the room and hoped I'd had a very nice time with "your William." I fled.

Benjamin squealed when he saw me, and Mr. Bernstein laughed as he flew to me. I suppose he had not known when he would see me again. Such little ones do not understand time. I got hugged again and again and finally shushed him because his baby brother was already asleep.

After putting Benjamin into his nightclothes, and into bed in the room he shared with his sleeping brother, and assuring him he would see me again in the morning, I went back downstairs to the kitchen and began to clean to my standards which meant I had to scrub the sink and put a new cloth on the table. I checked the ice box for butter and the larder for eggs and bread. When I'd arranged everything the way I like it, I sat down with a cup of tea and my sandwich from Mrs. Bennett and ate it, saving my cake for the next day. I put out the lamps and called a "goodnight" to the Bernsteins seated in their parlor where they were reading.

"We're glad you're back," called Mrs. Bernstein as I passed through..

I thought of William. I suppose I shouldn't have thought of him in bed beside me, but I did and I felt his kisses again and heard his voice, teasing me and laughing. I told myself I was betrothed now to him and how I should also send a letter to the parents, after his or before, I wasn't sure. Oh, I thought then, first a letter to my dear sister or I would never hear the end of it. I didn't feel sleepy anymore, now that my mind was filling up with feelings and plans. So, I contented myself with a picture in my mind of me and William on our wedding day, me in my best clothes and he in a suit, and my sister there and the Bennetts and with that realized there would be no other Floods at my wedding, making me sad and awake again. Finally, I calmed down and went to sleep after the sensible part told me to do my work and the week would go by before I saw William again. When did I start talking to myself the way my mother had talked to me back in Ireland?

CHAPTER 11

The Interview (1912)

It was spring. I reminded Mrs. Bernstein I would be leaving soon, in only a few weeks. My wedding would be on the twenty-ninth of May, the day before Decoration Day. William had rented a house he knew of in Lincoln and we would move right in after the wedding. The Bennetts would have tea and sandwiches and cake at their home after the church ceremony. We would go home to our house afterwards. It delighted me to think of it.

Mrs. Bernstein first looked like she did not want to hear that I planned to leave. I could tell she did not want it to be so close. But she recovered quickly and said that of course she was not surprised, having known I would stay with my sister before the wedding. She did allow herself a sigh and then smiled at me.

"I will take you to the agency to hire a new maid," she said cheerfully. "You can help me choose. I will hopefully hire another Irish maid." Then we both laughed as both of us said, "Cousin Beatrice" at the same time who had become much nicer to me as time went on but had never entirely changed her mind about Irish maids. She was never one to back down from an opinion or a belief. We smiled together at what her reaction would be to the employment of another Irish girl.

At five and three and a half years of age, Benjamin and Randall must be told. And I could make them no promises either. Lincoln was far away for me to travel, and I'd have new responsibilities. I needed to make them understand how important they were to me and that I'd never forget them. I did not look forward to that conversation.

So, one morning when Mr. Bernstein was home, Mrs. Bernstein and I went off to the agency. The same one I'd gone to. Mrs. O'Brien had arranged for a girl just over from Ireland to meet with us. I knew she thought it quite irregular to have the current maid come, but neither Mrs. Bernstein nor myself were bothered by that. I thought the new girl should be strong enough to handle the work, but more important that she love children. I'd been loyal to this family, too, and she should be capable of that.

So, we got there before the appointed time and she was there already, dressed nicely and sitting with her hands folded in her lap. She looked to be about eighteen years of age. I could tell Mrs. Bernstein was impressed she'd arrived early. We were introduced, and the girl stood up and sat down again when we did. Her name was Kathleen, and she came from Westmeath, so she and I talked about that briefly. I did not know her family, but she came from a town land not far from Rathcaled, so we noted that.

Mrs. Bernstein went right to the point. The position was for a single maid for the household and there were two young children. She would live in. The work was hard and the hours long. Did she think she could handle it?

And then Kathleen gave nearly the same answer I'd given years before.

"I can work hard and learn what I need to know."

I just loved hearing her say that and in her Irish brogue and looked over to see Mrs. Bernstein nodding, but not smiling yet. She could be very reserved, although always fair and kind.

"And," Kathleen added, "I love children and am used to them because I come from a big family."

At that, Mrs. Bernstein allowed herself to smile. "They are lively little boys," she said.

Then Mrs. Bernstein glanced over at me before saying exactly what she'd said to me at my interview, "I think you could be satisfactory." Well, that was just so nice to hear again and to know how satisfactory I had proven to be. It was like history repeating itself.

Kathleen smiled and seemed to relax a little in her chair.

Mrs. Bernstein went on. "My Ellen leaves us to marry in weeks." She gave the date and continued. "This is when I would like you to start." She handed Kathleen a piece of paper with the date, address, and what she would pay her. Then Kathleen, smart girl, handed her a paper on which she had written the address where she was staying with friends.

We all stood up, then and Kathleen, who was taller than me with black curly hair worn up, just smiled all over and thanked Mrs. Bernstein for the job. I knew she would be running back to whatever house she was staying at with the good news.

Mrs. Bernstein shook hands with Mrs. O'Brien who, after a moment's time, reached out to shake my hand too. I felt quite like the matron and it came to me I would be respectably married soon.

So, we walked into the late, cool, spring morning and Mrs. Bernstein suggested we go for tea and sandwiches in town. We hopped on the streetcar and got out at Park Street Station, and she took me to a small restaurant. We ordered chicken sandwiches and tea. I sat there with my employer like two ordinary women having lunch. It was grand. We talked about the boys and she commented that David should have time alone with them to experience the work that went into taking care of them. We both smiled at that. It was such a lovely lunch we were having that I actually forgot the time. I was not used to sitting so long over a meal. Then Mrs. Bernstein paid the bill, and I thanked her for my lunch. We went to Jordan Marsh, then, and she bought me a pretty blue hat to go with my wedding suit. She did have me try on several before concluding this was the best one. I thanked her, again.

When we arrived home to Shafter Street, it was to find no one home. Mr. Bernstein had left a note that he'd taken the boys to the park. We both observed at once that there would be no naps this day. Mrs. Bernstein thought she would enjoy her book, and I went upstairs with my hatbox to try on my hat again. The hat did make me look different, stylish maybe. I was pleased with it and there was still plenty of time before I had to start supper, so I could write a letter to my mother about this exciting day. Only a few weeks, I thought, and then out to Lincoln to stay with Mary Anne before the wedding. My heart jumped in me. Then I looked around this room that had been my home for so long and pictured someone else in it, and that gave me a strange feeling. Always, I thought, happiness and sadness together. I'd learned that about life. And then I heard the boys' voices as they came in the door and prepared to go downstairs to greet them, but then thought maybe I would just stay up here as planned and write this letter. I was, after all, almost a married woman.

CHAPTER 12

Leaving Dorchester

ELLEN AND WILLIAM 1912

The time went by very quickly from the hiring of the new maid to the week before I was to leave the Bernsteins. Kathleen was due that very week to spend a day training. She'd written a very proper note back to Mrs. Bernstein, stating she would arrive in the morning ready to work. I had written to Kathleen and explained exactly how to get there by streetcar and telling her to come right to the kitchen door.

I'd had the talk with Benjamin and Randall. I could tell it had never occurred to them that I could leave the family. They'd thought it would go on forever as it was now, and William would just keep coming to the house to take me out. They were astonished to hear we would marry. Randall, the younger, wondered if I'd be back in two weeks after the getting married was done. Then, I suggested we go to the park, thinking they'd heard enough for one time. They ran upstairs to get their coats then. I knew there would be more questions.

I heard the knock on the door at nine in the morning, right on time. Kathleen and I smiled at each other as I let her into my kitchen. Mrs. Bernstein had said she'd see her in the sewing room for a short talk and after I'd take her around the house, upstairs and down. We'd planned for Kathleen to spend the morning and leave after lunch. When Mr.

Bernstein returned with the boys from their walk, we would have introductions and I would take the boys into the kitchen with me for an early Saturday lunch and let them spend some time with me and Kathleen together.

After Mrs. Bernstein's talk with Kathleen, Mr. Bernstein came in with the boys. He shook Kathleen's hand and welcomed her to the house. He had some difficulty knowing what else to say, so went and sat down in the parlor. The boys just stared at her. She smiled at them but said little. For once, they had nothing to say.

As we walked into the kitchen, Randall took my hand and then, after a moment, so did Benjamin. We were a quiet group until Randall saw the cake which he loved and called out to his brother, "Ellen made cake!" Then, getting down to business, asked Kathleen if she knew how to make cakes. It seemed she did know how to make cakes and pies, too. That seemed to satisfy Randall and also Benjamin, who was quietly listening. We had sandwiches. The boys showed off their manners both by sitting up straight and using their napkins but soon their curiosity overcame them and they both started asking Kathleen questions like why did she talk like Ellen and could she sing and was she getting a husband soon like Ellen, this from Randall.

The rest of the morning went well. The plan was for that early lunch for the boys and then serving the Bernsteins their meal in the dining room while the boys rested upstairs. Kathleen helped me with both the preparation and the serving. I'd loaned her an apron. She did very well. After we'd done the dishes, it was time for her to go.

"I will love your boys," she said, "And the Bernsteins are lovely people, too. I feel so lucky to have this position. I never thought I would be welcomed in this way, but instead, just set to work. That's what I'd heard it was like."

I watch Kathleen walk away quickly down the street, looking so pleased with herself and the day as she should be. I wished I felt so lively, but knew I'd feel better soon. I'd still be a week here and so much to look forward to. So, I closed the door quietly and put my mind to supper and how many treats I could give my boys in a week and that took over my mind but not entirely.

I woke on the morning of my departure to Lincoln feeling a little like I had when I left Ireland all those years ago. This would not be an easy day. William planned to arrive mid-morning. I'd written Mrs. Bernstein a letter of appreciation to be opened after I left. In it, I'd also written simple letters to the boys, telling them to be good and how I'd always think of them. Well, I was getting bothered just thinking about that, so I stopped and got practical again.

I stripped the bed of sheets and put clean ones on for Kathleen, who would be arriving this afternoon. I'd written her a little note of welcome, so I put that on the freshly made bed. I realized I was all prepared with my bags packed and yet really not ready at all.

I kept to my routine this morning. The boys came downstairs with their parents for breakfast, which I served. They chattered away as usual. I thought this was the last time I'd do this. I knew William would be there soon, so I hurried through the dishes and cleaning so I could spend some time with the boys. I'd wrapped two small books for them and had the letter ready for Mrs. Bernstein. Mr. Bernstein had said goodbye before he left for work, shaking my hand and telling me how much he appreciated all I'd done during my time with the family. He also wished me happiness on my coming marriage. Then he handed me an envelope.

I had the boys at the kitchen table drawing me pictures when William knocked at the door. I'd brought my bags and hatbox down earlier, so that was done. I'd thought I was ready until I saw William with the bouquet of flowers. Benjamin ran to the door and opened it. William, as always, had smiles for them. It seemed like a regular visit, but this time when I left with William, I would not be coming back. Randall still told everyone that Ellen would be back in two weeks. Even his brother had given up correcting him. William praised their drawings.

It was time to go, but for all my planning, I did not really know how I was going to do this. Mrs. Bernstein saved me by coming into the kitchen. She was all smiles.

"So, today is the day you begin your new life, Ellen. I am so pleased for you and William." So, I thought, she was determined to make this easier for me.

And then she looked at her two sons and they said together, "We will miss you, Ellen. Thank you for all you've done for us." I thought they must have rehearsed that a number of times. But they'd not practiced the next part. They ran to me and hugged me-hard. I felt my eyes beginning to tear. These had been my first children.

"We need to let Ellen go, now," Mrs. Bernstein said as she gently pulled them to her. She, too, had a tear in her eyes. I could only nod and hand her the letter. "For you to read later," I told her. Then I reached over for the two packages I'd put aside for Benjamin and Randall and handed them over. "Books for you and think of me when you look at them." They solemnly took the books from my hand and thanked me.

William had placed himself by the door, looking a little sad himself. And then he picked up my two bags and, addressing Mrs. Bernstein, told her how lucky his Ellen had been to be with them and how he would take good care of me. Neither words nor charm ever failed him. With that, I gave my boys a final, quick hug and shook hands with Mrs. Bernstein, who took both my hands in hers, just for a few seconds and with a "Stay in touch, Ellen," she let me go.

I knew there was no prolonging it, so, as William held the door open for me, I walked out ahead of him, moving forward, but not without giving one last look back at them, and just in time to hear little Randall turn to his brother and say, "Two weeks, Benjamin. She'll be back in two weeks."

We walked down Shafter Street for probably the last time together as we left this house where I'd been happy. The tears came then. So, I used my handkerchief, and we caught the next streetcar, the first part of our journey to Lincoln.

I began to feel better and asked William who would be meeting us at the station. "My brother Walter will be coming to get us in the buggy. I expect you will be fussed over by my mother and my sisters are so excited, too. They have a surprise for you." And at that, I turned to him, but he'd closed his mouth and there was no getting it out of him. My spirits began to rise. I could not wait to see my nephew, who would be almost two years of age now. I turned to William and remarked that this would probably be the last peace we would have until we went home together after the wedding.

He liked hearing me say, "home," and grinned. "We should look out for my brothers. They seemed inspired by the prospect of a wedding and might be up to some mischief."

Our sister, Kate, would be my bridesmaid and his brother Francis, the other witness. Oh, Kate. She'd taken a position in New York City, one she had heard of from a friend and had not stayed at all long in Boston where I'd have kept an eye on her. She worked for a family in a big house with many servants and was very happy in her position. Mary Anne and I plotted to get her back closer to us.

The train pulled in and thirteen-year-old Walter was there, sitting in the buggy with a big smile on his face. "Big Walter" as they called him, was even taller than I remembered. He very importantly greeted us, climbed down and took the bags and then got back up again, waiting while William put me on.

As we pulled up in front of the house, Mary Anne opened the door and standing right beside her was a tiny boy, clinging to his mother. He eyed me as I climbed down from the buggy. Mary Anne was smiling away for both of them. From the little one, we got a wave and a stare. Looking more closely at my sister, I thought she might be expecting again.

She greeted William and Walter, while her own little Walter stared from behind her, and she pulled me in. They turned around to head home after William told me their mother expected to see me on the morrow, which was Sunday, for dinner, after church. She had something to show me, he said. But he would leave us now to visit.

Once inside the door which we carefully latched against the baby, I hugged Mary Anne and then crouched down to say hello to my nephew who gave me a small smile and began to trot around the kitchen on his little legs.

"He is so handsome," I said, then with a look at my sister, I asked, "Are you expecting again?"

"In the fall and you will be here to help me," this said with a smile as her hand went to her back. "I am more tired this time."

I asked when our Kate would arrive and was told she would come two days before the wedding and leave the day after. We agreed we wanted her closer.

"But she loves her position," I said, "being in a big house with other girls for company. She has more excitement than we did, being the only servant in the house."

"We should really be thinking of you," my sister said then, "Let me see what's in the box."

I pulled out my smart hat with the feathers to go with the blue suit.

"It makes you look taller," she laughed after admiring it, although she was only an inch taller than me. I let her try it on and said it made her look taller, too. And we both giggled at our nonsense. Our Kate was just a bit taller than either of us. We hoped she wouldn't be putting on airs, coming from New York City now.

The next day, after Sunday Mass, I rode back with William and his family to their house. The good smells were coming out the open kitchen window. They'd left the meat to roast slowly in the oven. They turned up the heat under the vegetables and potatoes. A little while later, we emptied them into big bowls and Mr. Bennett was called to lift the roast pork from the oven onto a platter where he sliced it with a big knife, at the same time, giving little pieces of meat to anyone who came near. We sat down in no time at all and said grace, this time with little Florence joining in from her chair by her mother. We all smiled at her.

When dinner was over, the men and boys headed outside and the rest of us cleaned up, me drying the dishes. Then, instead of going right to dessert, Mrs. Bennett and the girls drew me into the bedroom and there on the bed was a quilt, unlike anything I had ever seen. It was big and had all kinds of colors and designs on it; blues and yellows and even purples, diamonds, circles, and squares and each square sewed together. It was large enough to cover the whole bed. I ran my hands over it, telling them how awed I was. I think I showed it, too, because they were all smiles. I thought I might cry it was so beautiful.

"We made it together," said shy Alice.

"It took a long time," offered Martha, smiling at me. Even little Florence, it seemed, had had a part in it, sorting out the pieces for the quilt. There followed a description of how they had made it. At that point William came in and told me how he'd kept the secret of the quilt, although many times, he had wanted to tell me. I told them how I would cherish it and could picture it on our bed and then blushed a little talking about our bed, but no one minded and I kept asking about colors and patterns because I was truly fascinated. And then, it was time for dessert, so we went back to the kitchen, but not before I ran my hands over it again. It seemed to me that it was like life, this quilt, with all its designs and love in it. I could not say exactly what I meant, but it did make sense to me in that way. I thought I might explain it to William later.

After a long time sitting on the porch, William and I went off to hitch up the buggy to take me back. It was a lot of work, I thought, hauling me around and it would be good to be in one place. I knew he got paid pretty well working for a farmer which was good because I would no longer be working and that would be new to me. I'd left yesterday with my last pay and that something extra from Mr. Bernstein. It bothered me I would no longer be sending money home, but it was understood that when a girl got married, she was done with that.

Back at Mary Anne's, William carried the quilt into the house and we lay it on the clean table. Mary Anne was beside herself with both the beauty of the quilt and the work that had gone into it. "Truly an heirloom," she declared, "something to have forever." There was a wooden chest in her bedroom, not a full one, and we agreed to put it in there. I knew, in the next days, I would visit it often. There was some talk of the house William had rented, all cleaned, furnished and waiting for us. Mary Anne described the curtains and other things, but we could tell when William had had enough of that and he was asked to supper. He told us tomorrow was an early day for him, so he would go along home.

He did want to know what we would be doing all week. Mary Anne thought I should have a rest first and get to know my nephew, and she had some things for me, too, and our mother had sent a package. And at that, my eyes lit up, but she said we should wait until tomorrow for all that.

Looking right at William, then, my big sister said, "Ellen and I have much to do before the wedding and you will leave us to it."

William grinned and said he would, but she should expect to see him every day after work because he would not have me so close and not come over.

The next day, when the little one went in for his nap, Mary Anne ran into her bedroom and began to rustle around and then came out with a parcel marked from Ireland and presented it to me. I opened it very carefully. First was a letter on top, which I did decide to open later. I thought it might make me cry. My mother had sent lace for the table, so lovely. I put that aside and found a pair of rosary beads, pretty ones, then a Saint Brigid's cross for our door and a beautiful shawl she'd knitted in white. I wrapped it around me and thought how I would wear it on my wedding day with the blue suit, how perfect. And then I looked at my sister through my tears. I'd been so busy with the package, I had almost forgotten she was there. She understood my tears and had some of her own, too. We were our mother's daughters for all she was so far away.

After a few minutes, she went back into the bedroom and came out with another box. I opened it to see a lovely embroidered nightgown, just beautiful, white with red roses. It was exquisite. I wondered aloud how she had found time to sew it and with all those tiny stitches. I loved it. Also, in the box were kitchen towels, all hemmed and perfect. And then she made me laugh by saying she expected to be sewing little garments before too long because Walter needed cousins. So, we sat in the kitchen until the baby woke up, just chatting and looking over my treasures.

We put the bread out to cool, and the currant cake went in. Mary Anne kept a clean house, so we only had some straightening out to do before starting supper, a stew which could sit on the stove until we were ready to eat. I'd already moved my things to the bedroom. I asked my sister if she would mind if I read my letter and she thought that would be fine. She was going to sit until it was time to put supper on the table.

My mother had written to me.

Dear Ellen, You will soon be married, my second daughter in America, to have a wedding. I miss you both very much. I do have faith, as does your father, that you have chosen a good husband in William. The rosaries are for you to pray together. Do not ever hesitate to call on the Blessed Mother for help. Think of me when you hang the Saint Brigid's cross on your door. God will protect you. I felt sad at the end, when I finished your shawl because I could not, myself, place it over your shoulders on your wedding day. We will go to Mass to pray for God's blessings on you. I know you will make a good home together with William. Give little Walter a hug from us. You are in our hearts every day and we pray for you, too. Keep an eye on your sister, Kate. I worry about her. She's a good girl but still very young to be away from all her family. I do not like her in New York. Your father sends his love. God Bless.

Love, Mother and Father

And so, I cried a bit out of love for my parents and missing them. I sat on the bed for a while, the shawl around me until I felt better. I thought I would show the rosaries to William. It would be a nice practice to say the rosary together each night, on our knees, as we'd done in Ireland. But I did think he might be too tired some nights. Well, we could make the attempt. Prayer had helped me down on my knees each night in my little room at the Bernsteins. We would be a good Catholic family.

CHAPTER 13

Our Sister Kate

The days went by fast and one morning William came to pick me up to go meet our sister Kate at the station. When the train pulled in, there she was, waving to us from the window, all smiles. She was so pretty, and I knew William noticed it too. She ran across the platform with her bag and gave me a hug. She was dressed fashionably in a slim gray skirt and jacket and nice felt hat, and she was not a bit strange with us. He bundled us both into the buggy then, and we rode all the way to Mary Anne's house without stopping once with the talking. It seemed she was very happy in her position. I'd asked that right away. Mary Anne and the baby were waiting on the front step, and our Kate jumped down before William could help and ran over to hug her other sister while Walter looked on, amazed at the arrival of another aunt. His life had been so quiet before. He let Kate give him a hug but then looked to his mother for support and got picked up where he watched the proceedings quietly.

I encouraged William to come back later for an early supper. We both looked at each other, knowing that in two days, we would be married. Kate took a while to settle down while we set the table for tea. She kept saying how nice the house looked and what a happy time this was, and how nice it was to be a bridesmaid. Then we had a few minutes with our tea before she was off again, this time to get her bag from which she pulled a pretty package and handed it to me. Inside was a lovely pair of gloves. "You will wear these at your wedding," she said. "You will look so elegant." I smiled and thanked her. I was really happy with the gloves.

"It is good to have nice things," I said to Kate and ran to show her my hat, which she admired. It did not take long for us to start acting like sisters again. We wanted to know all about the house where she worked in New York and what was it like. She enjoyed telling us. I did feel that by letting her do this, it would make it harder to tell her how grand it would be for her to work nearby, but we let her go on. Frederick was very nice when he came home and welcomed Kate to his house. He also looked like he wanted to go right back out again.

She had her two days before the wedding and one day after, but was leaving that day and I might not see her at all until her next visit. So, when Walter went in for his nap, we got her to the table and brought up the idea of finding a position closer to us, her family. Well, she looked a bit surprised at that after all our listening to her talk about how much she loved New York and said so.

"Kate," I said to her, "I know how you work hard and have fun, too. I had a long time before I met William. We girls went to the dances and had lots of friends, but," and with that I pointed to Walter now sitting in his mother's lap. "Wouldn't you like us to be all together?"

"I would like to see you more often," she declared. "But I like my position and my life even though the work is hard, but I have such freedom like I would never have at home and I know you like your independence, too, for all you are married and almost married."

And then she gave us such a sweet but mischievous smile. We forgave her, but at the same time I know both Mary Anne and I felt disappointed. Then Mary Anne said that maybe our little sister would feel differently when she met someone to marry and have a family with, and she looked at us with such a look of disbelief that would ever happen to her. We laughed together.

Our Kate shared the bed with me that night, and we did talk until we both fell asleep from exhaustion. It seemed she did not yet have a

beau, but several lads she liked, but was not ready to walk out with anyone. She had gone on that afternoon to describe her life in a big house,
and it was fascinating. Always, there were girls to talk to, and they slept
together in one big room and one had to be careful of the cook who was
very strict but could be motherly, too. The family she worked for was
prominent in New York, and the children were cared for by nursemaids.
Kate did housework all day long. She was excited that they would go to
a summer house later, and she'd been told it was on a lake and quite
nice. Kate was drawn up by her life right now, I could tell, with the
excitement of a girl.

One more day, I kept telling them, and after that, I would no
longer be a single girl. I would be a married lady and William's wife.
Well, Mary Anne had no patience for my imaginings, just like on the
last day before we left Ireland, and she had checked tickets and ship
times while I walked all around, telling myself it would be the last time
I would see our home. Instead of agreeing that going to Boston was
some kind of destiny, she had reminded me we were going there to find
jobs and eventually husbands and to have families. And with the same
determination, now, she suggested all the items on our list of things we
had to do to be ready for tomorrow. So, I pressed my skirt and blouse
and hung my jacket to lose the wrinkles, found my best undergarments
and new stockings, but took some pleasure in modeling my hat again.
Mary Anne just shook her head at us as she sliced bread to bring to the
Bennetts next day. She had made a cake, too.

"Imagine," I told our Kate, "I will depart here as Ellen Flood and
leave the church as Ellen Bennett." At that, Mary Anne grabbed a dish
towel and chased us out of her kitchen, telling us if we could not be
useful, to at least get out of her way. Kate grabbed Walter and asked if
he wouldn't like to to come play with his aunties in the bedroom and
we carried him off where we amused him singing songs and dancing
around until we heard his mother's call from the kitchen asking if we
thought we might like some tea.

Mary Anne, at the table with us, said she had never drunk so much
tea in her life than she had, first with one sister and then with the other.

We began to talk of home. Kate said that Pa had become old before our mother, but he still worked the forge every day. Jim was our talkative brother and had got himself a job in the village working at the grocery where he was a great favorite. Bridget was lively, but Rose was quiet, like her name. Our brother, John, was also quiet. Kate expected things were about the same as when she left because time moves so slowly in Ireland and we agreed with that. She said nothing was as green as our part of Ireland, she missed the smell of peat smoke and sometimes would dream of home and did we too? We both said we did, even sensible Mary Anne. So, we sat and talked most of the afternoon until it was almost time for Frederick to return for supper.

Kate and I offered to help our sister then with anything that needed to be done. I ended up pressing her skirt. Kate entertained the baby. I'd not be seeing William this night because it was not felt to be proper before the wedding. I don't think he had that opinion but was overruled by the women.

CHAPTER 14

Together

Kate and I did not stay awake so long that night because we knew we would be up early the next morning. Church was at ten o'clock and then time at the Bennetts and then home with William. I'd be thinking of my parents back in Ireland at their prayers and I said mine, too. And before I knew it, I was waking up in the morning and remembering why this was a different and important day.

Mary Anne had bathed Walter, who was fussing at the little shirt and petticoat she'd dressed him in and was trying to squirm out of it. She instructed Kate to keep him clean while she dressed. He did look darling. Frederick had appeared in his suit looking very handsome and also being the calmest of us all, took Walter. Kate dressed next, looking very stylish in a light beige ensemble. Then both my sisters took me into the bedroom and put me together. A few minutes later, I was dressed and ready to put my hat on. There was a mirror in the hall and I stood there thinking I did look nice. Kate had done my hair, and I tucked it under my new hat. I felt pretty. My sisters joined me in the mirror and we saw three smiling young women, eager at the day and the occasion, all with the same brown hair and the same smile. And then, Frederick came in, handed Walter to Mary Anne and offered me his arm and walked me to the buggy followed by Mary Anne, holding the baby, and Kate. Mrs. Bennett had sent flowers from her garden the afternoon before and we each had a bouquet. He got us all on. Then off we went down the green country road.

When we arrived in Concord Center, it was an ordinary day for people going about their business, some glancing over to see the bride and her family go into church. Our guests were already inside. The organ started up as we entered, and Frederick walked his wife and son to a front pew. We'd rehearsed this, so he knew what to do. He came to the back of the church and the wedding march started and everyone stood up. I wasn't shaking at all, but maybe was a little nervous with being the center of attention, and then I saw a solemn William, standing at the front of the church with his brother Francis at his side. When he saw me, he got his big smile on and I was all calm again. Kate walked up the aisle first, looking very nice, and then it was time for Frederick to escort me to William.

We faced the altar. Then we knelt. Everything we would now do together. And we said our vows and there was more music and then Father Lynch blessed us and we turned and went back down the aisle, while people all stood up, smiling at us. They would be coming to the Bennetts now. When William and I came out the front door, I think we made a fine-looking couple, all smiling and happy.

So, William helped me into the buggy and we waited while everyone else climbed into wagons and buggies. I did notice our Kate had a ride in the Bennett wagon. The Bennett boys had managed to tie empty tin cans to the back of our buggy and they made a big noise and everyone laughed at us as we led the way to the house. Some of the townspeople looked over and smiled. It was our day, and we prepared to enjoy all of it.

Once at the Bennett house, we all climbed down and up on the porch and we went inside where the table was just covered with food. Everybody was all dressed up and made a nice picture, all gathered around to eat and drink. We had some of Mr. Bennett's potent wine. There were many toasts and then the singing started, mostly in English, but some in French, too. All the songs were lively, no sad ones at all.

Then, someone pulled out a fiddle, and the rug was pulled back and the table was moved and the dancing began. Well, that was lots of fun and the dances were fast and we girls got up and did the jigs and the boys joined us and it was such a joyous afternoon and over so soon.

It was time to say goodbye. I came over to William's mother and father first. They looked happy for us. I saved the last hug for our Kate because I did not know when I would see her again. As William and I climbed onto the buggy, I heard Mr. Bennett call out, "Goodbye, Mrs. Bennett." I did notice the noise makers had been removed, I thought, at Mr. Bennett's direction, so we would not arrive at our new dwelling with clacking and banging. Everyone shouted good wishes to us as we left. I thought they would be celebrating for some time longer, but we were headed for home, now. I was so tired and excited, it was hard to know how to feel, exactly, so I just settled into William's shoulder and he drove, a little fast, I thought, to our destination.

There was a stillness to the evening as we drove out and a cool breeze starting up for all it being late May. No one was watching as we passed several houses on our road. Lights were on, but all was quiet. William stopped the cart, and I saw a small white house with black shutters and a little porch. We both got out and William opened the door, making it squeak. He quickly lit a lamp, and I saw the small, neat kitchen and pretty white curtains with Mary Anne's tiny stitches, bare kitchen table, and to the side through an open door I could see our bed with the quilt on it. I could see how everything had been put in order for our home-coming. I kept hearing the quiet, so different from the festivities we had just left. I did not feel lonely though because William was there. It did occur to me that we had never been entirely alone like this before. It was a strange feeling. I looked over at William who seemed to be expecting some response from me, so I told him truthfully how nice everything was and he looked a bit relieved.

"I know it is a small space for us, but it won't be forever. Some day we will have a house of our own, but this one is clean and you will make it pretty." He looked at me then.

"I love it, William," I said softly and moved over to give him an embrace. We both stood there for a few minutes, holding onto each other.

"Remember, Ellen," he said with a very straight face, "Father Lynch said he expected great things of us." I pushed him then and sent him out to get my bags while I changed into something simpler than my bridal clothes. I hung my hat carefully on a hook in the bedroom and decided to take my shoes off too. When William came back in with my bags, I insisted on emptying my clothes into the small chest of drawers which I discovered already had my new husband's clothes folded inside. It was not all the way all dark yet, so we sat together at the kitchen window and went over the day. We were not hungry for the sandwiches, so I put them in the icebox.

As it did really begin to get dark, we lit the rest of the lamps, both in kitchen and bedroom, and then he went back out again to tend to the horse which he'd stabled in the small barn. I took the opportunity to undress and put on my new nightgown. William came back a few minutes later and looking at me, proposed we go to bed. He quickly put out the kitchen lamp, and I climbed into bed and waited for him while he removed his suit, which I directed him to hang carefully because I would not have the ironing of it, and his shirt, too. He laughed at me, then. And he climbed in beside me. I'd not thought much about men sleeping in their under drawers but William did, I observed and then he turned to me, and turned again to put out the lamp and then it happened, as my sister said. We were both young and knew what to do. And then we went to sleep, and it seemed, in the morning, he wanted to do it again and maybe, I thought, I would be carrying a baby sooner than later. So we slept some more, and that was nice because neither of us was used to sleeping past dawn.

It was Decoration Day and in Lincoln, that meant a small parade of veterans to the monument in the center, so we dressed after breakfast and drove into town because William was eager to see the parade and hear the music and I did not like to miss anything either, so off we went. Some of his friends were there, and he proudly introduced me as his wife. The men removed their hats and their wives took my hand and said how pleased they were to meet me. They were mostly farmers and knew William and his family very well. So we followed the parade to the cemetery where people went around putting flowers on graves and then some settled down for picnics.

We returned home. William looked at me and proposed another ride. He said we could take a country ride since he had the whole day off and he knew some pretty places to go. But then he surprised me by informing me he had the time of Kate's train and would I like to say goodbye to her?

I immediately said, "Yes." I promised the rest of the day would be ours. I quickly packed our sandwiches of the day before and some cake and a glass bottle of water, too. Then I ran out to where he was waiting for me in the cart and pulled myself right up with no help at all, and off we went.

Kate was standing there alone at the station, waiting for the train, a small bright figure in her traveling clothes and red hat. She looked bored. I supposed she and Mary Anne had said their goodbye adequately. I could imagine small Walter's confusion at not one, but two aunts disappearing. Kate glanced over when she heard the cart and put on a huge smile and ran over to us. I climbed down and gave her a hug. I'd been doing a lot of that the last few days. We sat on a bench together, the three of us, until William went off to walk the horse and then I turned to her and asked again if she wouldn't like to work nearer to us, and she gave the same answer, then laughed and said that Mary Anne had asked the same question that very morning. She was never solemn for very long, my little sister, and she was smart too. I knew she'd go far. Kate had said our younger sister, Bridget, was also lively. Well, we would have to see what happened with her.

Kate and I sat close there on the bench until we hear the train coming and William came back and we stood up. He grabbed her bag and moved toward the train. I was not the one leaving this time. We watched her climb the big step and as William handed up her bag. She did have a quick look of regret on her face, but then the big smile came and the last sight of her was at the window, waving. And that was that.

We headed away from the train station and toward Lake Walden in Concord. It is a very large lake, he told me. A long time ago a writer lived there called Henry Thoreau. A few farms could be seen but mostly woods and in some places, only room for one vehicle if any ever came our way. It was peaceful, as so were we after all the excitement of the last few weeks.

We arrived at the lake. After tying up the horse with water and feed bag, we climbed down a slope to the water. We found a place under a tree. I opened the bag of food and we began to eat. I wrapped my skirt around me to get comfortable. William sat down and stretched out his legs and we ate our sandwiches and drank some water. Then he put his head in my lap and we both fell asleep. Shortly after we woke up, some people passed by, hiking around the lake, and I was determined we would do that, too. So William sighed, and we got up. Much of it was hilly, but we completed the circle and I did enjoy being in such a lovely place and told him we should do this every Sunday, and he did remind me that Sunday was a day of rest. I told him only servile work was forbidden and did he think taking me around the countryside was that? He had no answer.

We slowly drove toward our little house in the woods. It was late afternoon, and we were thinking about our supper. I had leftover chicken in the icebox and Mrs. Bennett had given me home-made pickles and bread and cake. I did not even know where to shop. When I shared that thought with my new husband, he shook his head and said he worked for farmers and could get fresh vegetables, milk and eggs, and could we live on that? We had water from the pump and a stove. The man was somewhat limited in his knowledge of cooking, but he had always lived at home.

When we arrived back at the house, I got out and went inside while William went to stable the horse. I took the chicken out and sliced it and added some bread to the plates, which I set on our table covered with a cloth, but not the lace one from my mother. That would be for special occasions. The table did look pretty, though. I'd put the flowers from my bouquet in a glass and napkins at each place as I'd been taught with forks to the left and knives to the right. The tea cups I left until we would want them. William had already visited the pump, and I took a pitcher of cold water from the icebox. I thought I would make bread the next day if we had flour.

After supper, I cleaned up the dishes and was surprised at how soon I was done. William did not take a pipe, so he did not go outside to smoke. He did not drink alcohol either. We sat for a while at the kitchen table after supper and talked over the day. He told me he would be up very early the following morning to leave for work. And I said I would make him a breakfast of porridge if he liked and tea, not coffee, though because I had none, nor eggs to make a better morning meal. He said he would go into town after work and get me some things, if I gave him a list in the morning. I think I envied him the trip into town. This living out here would take some getting used to.

We were very easy with each other sitting there in our kitchen, and I liked that. It did feel strange, though, for there to be only two of us at meals. He was used to sitting around the table with his whole family every night, just as I had, years ago in Ireland. As the only maid in the house, though, I had usually eaten my meal alone. We sat and thought about that for a minute, and then both hurried to say how agreeable it was to have just us. We lit the lights when it began to get dark and it was just like the other night except this time, afterwards, we went right to sleep, curled up together. It was lovely to be married, I thought as I drifted off to sleep.

The next morning, we both woke at dawn. My first thought was to the trip I must make outside to the toilet. That done, I put the kettle on and cooked the porridge. After breakfast, I kissed him goodbye and gave him a list. "God bless," he said as he went out the door. It took only a few minutes to clean up the kitchen and wash the few dishes and the pan, and then I had a second cup of tea. The bed had been made as soon as we got out of it and the quilt smoothed down. The curtains were opened to when the sun would come up.

I would bake some bread later. I'd found the flour. And he said we would have milk delivered, so I would wait for that. William said he would bring me a chicken to stew for supper with the onions and carrots he'd promised. I suppose I could eat more chicken. I didn't think we would be getting lamb chops or beefsteaks out here. They'd be expensive, anyhow. He would need sandwiches for work. I looked around to see how I would wash the clothes and checked the shelves for cleaning soap. I thought we could bathe in the tin tub, but it would be an effort to heat the water each time. I would need to get used to the pump outside. But we were living in the country now. Nothing needed scrubbing because the rooms were still so clean. I could thank my sister for that. I dusted a little bit and planned my day. I thought a walk would be nice.

The grass smelled different in Lincoln, I decided, as I walked along the road. I knew there were neighbors about a half-mile away but did not feel like meeting them yet, thinking that could wait for another day. When I got back, the thought came to me that we could have a baby. Well, that was something to think about. I began a letter to my mother. Then I hopped up to start some bread.

The rest of the day went slowly. I tried to sort things but had so little to sort, that was done soon.

Then I rearranged the pots and pans and dishes to my liking again, done too soon. I began to think how my husband might drive me to spend the day with my sister or his mother, but thought it too soon after the wedding to be looking for places to go. Then I thought I would plant a small garden of vegetables and maybe some flowers. My mother had potatoes and carrots, turnips and onions. Next, I wondered about animals in the woods, but the land had been cleared for so long by farmers, I did not think I would see anything bigger than a fox.

I heard William coming down the road at six. He came in smiling. "Ellen, I don't know when I felt so happy about coming home. It is hard to believe we are finally together. It's like a dream come true." He could talk like that sometimes. William washed his hands quickly and then wrapped them around me at the table where I stood slicing bread. He piled carrots, potatoes, and onions on the table, then carried a crock of butter to the icebox. Then he said he would pluck the chicken he had out in the cart, and he thought I could cook it all. And so I did, but not before putting my hands on my hips and asking him if he thought I was the maid which he denied and tried to hug me again, so I went all business and began to chop vegetables, sending him out the door. In an hour, the chicken was nicely simmering in the stew and ready for the potatoes, then carrots and onions, and it smelled good. I got out the bowls and set the table.

Somehow we had decided who sat where our second evening together. He liked the stew and finished his bowl and asked for another. We had cold water to drink, and I liked to eat, too, so we were quiet for a short while. He told me he had worked hard this day but couldn't wait to get home to his new wife.

Mary Anne's baby arrived in August. I was there for the birth. James was beautiful, fair-haired like his brother, At three years old, Walter showed little interest in meeting his little brother when I picked him up that morning where he'd stayed with the neighbors and walked him down the road in his little gown and shoes and socks. He wanted to see Mama.

I stayed for a few days. My sister got her strength back quickly and was up in no time at all. William came most days for supper and held the baby while Walter gave all the news of the day to Uncle. He would march alongside when William walked the fussy baby, still talking. The time went by quickly.

William and I took James, they'd named him, to be baptized while Mary Anne stayed at home with Walter. When we returned, the baby was crying and Mary Anne took him into the bedroom for feeding. I'd set the table for company. Mrs. Bennett came with her daughters, arriving at the same time as Mary Anne's kind neighbors, and I served tea and cake. We had the door open. The men stood outside while we sat inside with the cradle in the kitchen. It was cozy.

Once everyone left, I sorted out the kitchen and prepared to leave. Walter cried, and we promised him a visit soon and left quickly.

On the way home, I told William that we were expecting a baby of our own.

CHAPTER 15

Alice

A DAUGHTER

We rode home, talking all the time about a baby. I took myself inside while William went off to tend to the horse, and I marveled at how neat it was. He had even set the table with teacups. When he came back in, I was at the stove putting the kettle on to boil. William put his arms around me and I turned to embrace him back. He was so pleased with the news and I was so happy with his pleasure.

"You are not to work too hard or walk too far," He told me the next morning. "You have to be careful," he told me firmly. I gave him my attention, then, instead of telling him what I thought of him telling me what to do. I took his words of caution as being his way of wanting me and the baby safe, and so resisted telling him I would take care of myself in my own way. I did not realize, though, that I had my hands on my hips until he started laughing.

"I'll take my walk," I told him, "but come back if I feel tired. Do you want to make your own supper tonight while I rest?" No, he did not.

As time went on, I was beginning to be a little round for the first time in my life. I kept the house tidy, and the garden did well. I learned to make pie from the apples William brought home. On one trip to the store, the shopkeeper's wife told me how to make raspberry preserves, so I did that and we had jars of it on a shelf. It was a lot of work, but I kept going and did the same with peaches. And so the summer finished and fall began.

Fall was beautiful. It's my favorite season. I loved the yellow and orange leaves and how they reflected on the blue of nearby Flint Pond. I wish I could be an artist and paint it. The fall turned to winter, suddenly one cold November afternoon when white flakes began to fall from the sky.

I'd written to my mother, and she was pleased and praying, maybe in that order. I'm not sure. I do remember how my father said he wanted us to stay in Ireland, where he could see his grandchildren. I think of that. Mary Anne's little boys are exceptional. I see them once a week. I remember my first boys, too. I've kept my promise to Benjamin and Randall. I've never forgotten them.

The Bennetts came for dinner one Sunday and brought the cradle. I was thrilled. Mrs. Bennett told me it had held many babies and now it was our turn. It had a little quilt inside of it that she'd embroidered.

Winter. The snow came once again. It was good to have William around and to feel the baby growing inside me. I slept all night and took naps during the day. As Christmas came close, I remembered how William had come and got me last year at the station. It seemed like a long time ago.

All up and down our road, our neighbors seemed to have gone inside until spring. It was hard, even for the children to get to school. There were so many storms. The snow was pretty when it was coming down. I loved it on nights when the snow would stop and the stars would come out and it would be so quiet. If the snow stopped in the day and the sun came out, it would be glistening and fairy-like.

But still, I was sick of being inside. William and I would take walks together down snowy paths on a nice day when the sun came out, but first I would cover myself in shawls with extra socks in my boots and hat on my head. I marveled at my favorite blueberry bushes, all covered in snow. One day, we made it all the way to Flint Pond, and I saw it all covered in ice so that we could walk on it.

On Christmas day, the snow had melted a little, and we took the horse and cart, going early to Mass and then to the Bennetts where they fussed over me and wouldn't even let me dry a dish. Then, while it was still daylight, because the days were short, we went to Mary Anne's where Santa Claus had brought Walter a little iron truck he was in love with and the baby gurgled nicely. We'd already had dinner, but the mince pie went down well. We got back home at dark. Our Christmas day was short. We had only love for each other, no money for gifts. Sometimes I missed my pay when I could make purchases on my own.

We sat together that Christmas night. I'd put candles in the windows for Christmas Eve for the coming of the holy family and we lit them again and sat in darkness for a while.

"Next year," said William with a gentle smile, his arm around me, "we will have our own little baby right in this house with us."

"Yes," I said, "and it seems like a miracle it will be so."

I prayed that night warm in bed, a blessing for all in this house and for our families, especially mine in Ireland, and they seemed a long way away, more so as time went by.

March came, and the snow was gone, although the days were still cold and the nights even more so. The extra blankets remained on the bed. We had arranged for the doctor to come. The jar with money stood on the shelf. I had clean bedding ready. The plan was for our very kind neighbor, Mrs. Flint, to stay with me at the house days when it got close and send her husband for the doctor if William was not home. I could not wait to see our own child in the cradle and glanced over many times during the day, picturing a baby there.

The pains started on the morning of March thirty-first, before William left for work, so he went for Mrs. Flint to sit with me while he went for the doctor. He looked a little pale when he left, and for William, in a hurry. I'd never known such pain, and my whole body felt it. Mrs Flint rubbed my back and by the time William returned with the doctor the pains were very close. Doctor said everything was fine. A few hours later and we had baby Alice. She had a beautiful, round little face, not red and wrinkled like some. She was perfect. The doctor was pleased. William paid him at the door and off he went in his buggy.

It was only afternoon, so Mrs. Flint said she'd be happy to stay so William could go tell my sister, and he did and came back with her a short time later. I heard Mary Anne in the kitchen declaring she would be the first to see her dear little niece.

"She has a look of both you and William," she told us. "She looks like an Alice. Won't my boys be surprised."

William just stood there, very happily watching us. We had a healthy child and my sister approved of her. I thought Alice better than any Christmas present I'd ever had. Now it was time to rest and say a prayer of thanksgiving. Later, I would go through my list of things to do, but not yet. William would ride to his parents now while Mary Anne remained with me because he couldn't wait to share the news. And he would tell them at work that he would be back on the morrow because my sister said Frederick would bring her to spend the day with me and the baby.

Mrs. Flint got up to go, then. I told her I was grateful to her. It had been so good of her to come and stay. I didn't know what we would have done without her. She said it was the neighborly thing to do, and she never got tired of seeing a baby born. That's all. And she was on her way. We'd been lucky to have her.

My sister took care of Alice while I slept. I could hear her murmuring to the baby in the kitchen in her cradle. I floated in and out of sleeping and resting the remainder of the day. I don't believe Mary Anne had had this much time to herself for a long time. She was enjoying that. Also, this was the first girl in the family and would be getting a lot of attention. William came back after a while. Then Mary Anne gave him his instructions for taking care of me and Alice and said Frederick would be here soon to take her home, but she would return the next day. William seemed both relieved we would be alone soon and at the same time happy Mary Anne would be back.

And so the day ended with us in bed with our small daughter. From morning to night I had become a mother and William a father, and now I would write my mother with the news. Our lives had changed again.

The following day, Mary Anne arrived with her boys. I napped most of the afternoon, except for when Mary Anne brought me the baby to feed. When I had my lunch, Walter came and sat on the bed.

"Why is everyone having babies?" he asked between having bites of my sandwich.

"Don't you like babies?" I asked.

"They're all right, but they can't do much."

I did point out that he was a baby once, which seemed to surprise him. Then, not on any subject for long, he jumped down and ran outside again.

When I woke up the last time, Frederick was standing in the kitchen door. I called out to him to come in and see Alice, which he did.

"So," he said. "This is what a little girl looks like." And then he looked over at his wife wrapping up a noisy James for the trip home and his older son jumping up and down and said he thought she was very quiet and pretty. And then they were off, but not before my sister said she would return for one more day. William came back in after seeing them off and after a kiss for me, lifted Alice from her cradle.

"I've never had one of these before," he said quietly. "She's the most beautiful girl I've ever seen, next to her mother, of course," he added with a smile. And the second day ended.

CHAPTER 16

Our Child

In late April it began to get warmer. Alice was almost one month old. I didn't have to bundle her up so much when we went down the road to see Mrs. Flint. Sometimes, I had little daydreams of what it would be like to push her in a buggy down sidewalks and go to the shops instead of being out here on these country roads. A memory came to me of when I was still in service. I would go into town sometimes by myself on a Thursday, get myself a cup of tea and a sweet somewhere. There were so few opportunities when you lived at your job. I still lived at my job, come to think of it.

I did get restless sometimes, and I knew that could lead me to trouble. I remembered the time I went to the dance without William and we had that talk. It seemed like a long time ago. So, I did my work and enjoyed my little daughter and said my prayers.

This was a busy time for farmers, so William came home tired and hungry. I missed sitting and talking together because he fell right into bed each night almost before it was dark.

I do speculate about the Bernstein boys, my first babies. After a year now, that part of my life, in a way, does seem like a story, I tell myself. The older one would be in school now, and the little one still home. Mrs. Bernstein did send me a note and little white shoes when I let her know about Alice.

I looked forward to church on Sundays. We often went to the Bennetts for dinner, and little Alice never got put down the whole time we were there. Even the big boys took their turns carrying her around. They all love babies.

The summer went by fast and it was early September and the days were still warm but the nights cooler. I'd done a fall cleaning of our little house, shaking out our rug and scrubbing all the wooden floors, taking down the curtains and washing them. I watched out my cleaned windows for the leaves to start changing color to red and orange and gold.

Our Alice did very well. She called out to us for attention. Papa got smiles from her even when she'd been cranky. When he came home from work, he washed quickly and took her in his arms where he tickled her gently and made her giggle. I thought of having another, but it hadn't happened yet. At six months, Alice was ready to crawl. She arched her back and swayed back and forth, but had yet to put it all together.

(More than a year later)

Mary Anne had a baby girl. I'd been over there helping her. They named her Louise, a pretty name for another fair-haired child.

My garden had gone over to fall. Nothing to pick. All the apples were in and stored. I like cooking pies and making jam, but it was not enough. I would not be happy until I had a brood of children around me. Alice was one year and eight months. We expected more babies would come. For now, Alice was the center of all our interest. She'd had her first birthday at the end of last March and ran around all day. She had become my little companion, following me around. She played alone, too, sometimes seeming to have little conversations with herself, or maybe she saw someone I didn't. She got her way with her papa, but not so much with me. I wanted her to have manners. I was never, though, harsh with my baby.

The rain was coming down very hard on a cold, late October day. William had gone to work. He said he'd work on mending equipment in the barn or separating seeds for planting next year. I love the wind and the rain because it reminds me of home, but this rain was cold and forced me to think of the coming winter. I had my shawl wrapped around me and Alice all bundled up, taking her morning nap after getting up at dawn.

Well, William surprised me. It seems he has noticed me being a little quiet and told me he thought it would do me good to go visit Mrs. Bernstein in Dorchester.

"Alice is big enough to go with you on the train and we can afford the one trip. Would it please you?" he asked.

I did not know what to say, so just laughed aloud and ran across the kitchen to hug him, making Alice wonder at her mother acting that way. She jumped up to be hugged, too. She was a big girl now, which she delighted in telling us when she wasn't saying, "No."

We decided I should write to Mrs. Bernstein first and go in another week before winter came on again. November could be that way. I had a warm coat and Mary Anne, God bless her, had made a little coat for Alice, and she had tiny mittens and a matching bonnet for her head.

Mrs Bernstein wrote back right away to say she would be delighted to see me and Alice and to let her know the day and plan to stay for lunch. So I did write back to her, making it Monday next. William took Alice to the station one day, so she could wave at the train. He reasoned she would not be so afraid if she first heard the noise and knew it to be all right.

That November morning, William drove us to South Lincoln Station. Alice was all right with the noise of the arriving train, but did hold on to her father. I climbed up on the step. She was entirely surprised when the door opened and William handed her up to me. Then she was not at all happy when William did not climb up too. It was too much for her, so I hustled us on quickly and got a seat by the window where she could wave. She cried, "Papa." but then the train got moving and I was able to distract her as the trees and houses seemed to fly by. She quickly became interested and began to talk and point at things. Each time the train stopped, though, she was ready to get off until we reached North Union Station and then she did not want to get off at all.

We walked into the morning crowds in the station and she stared, never having seen that many people together in one place in her very short life. Getting the streetcar didn't take long at all, and soon we were arriving in Dorchester and we got off at Washington Street and walked over to Shafter Street. I can't express how that felt to me except that I was returning from another life altogether, not just from another place.

I went right to the back door and Kathleen opened it, smiling, while she us let in. She admired Alice and told me quickly how much she loved being in this house. I heard voices and two big boys rushed into the kitchen and then stopped quickly, maybe from seeing Alice or not knowing what to say to me. So, I held out my hands, and they came right over.

"You are so big!" I said just like grown-ups everywhere, and they nodded just like children everywhere. It did not take long for Randall, the younger, to start asking questions.

"Who is that?" he asked, pointing at Alice.

"It's Alice, and she is Ellen's baby. Don't you remember Mama telling us?" Benjamin reminded him in his big brother way.

Randall observed she was a girl. Alice, who had been a bit surprised by the size of the boys but loved other children, began to trot around the kitchen naming things and looking at the boys. I reached over and took her coat and hat off. Then, I heard Mrs. Bernstein's voice as she came into the kitchen all smiles.

After a happy glance at me, she asked, "Who is this?" looking at Alice and much to my surprise, Alice managed to say her name quite clearly and allowed herself to be picked up. So then Mrs. Bernstein asked Kathleen to make tea and invited me to follow her into the sewing room and the boys came too.

"We'll have sandwiches," she said in that definite way she has and led us in. I had taken off my coat and hat by then and saw the room looked exactly the same. I was comfortable because this was where we always had our talks. I told her and the boys all about my new home and they wanted to hear about their friend, William.

Lunch went by fast and more tea followed. Alice was delighted as the boys brought her toys and played with her. They even chased her when she found her way to Kathleen in the kitchen and back. I thanked them for giving her all that attention. They did seem to be enjoying themselves. She never got cross, but after a while climbed into my lap and fell asleep there.

At that point, Mrs. Bernstein asked the boys to leave for a while the grownups visited and assured them they'd be allowed back soon. We drank more tea, and she asked me about my life and complimented me on what a good mother I was. I told her I'd learned from her and the care of the little boys. We were easy together, and the time went by quickly.

Then Alice woke up and Mrs. Bernstein reach behind her for a package which she put in Alice's small hands. Well, Alice had never had a package before and we had to help her tear the paper off and inside was a baby doll all dressed up. She didn't know what to do at first and I showed her how to hug it and she did, looking pleased with the same look William gets when he is happy. She managed to say something at my bidding that sounded like thank you. But the hug she gave Mrs. Bernstein was even better. The boys came back and Alice saw that as another opportunity to play. Then, after one more cup of tea and Kathleen joining us for that, it was time to go. I knew I would come back again. Kathleen offered to walk me to the streetcar with the boys and off we went. The last thing I saw was them waving at us as the streetcar clattered away.

This time, Alice understood about the train and when I said, "Papa," she began to hurry on her little legs in the station and dropped her doll and had to be picked up, both her and her treasure because there were just too many people about. I could not help thinking about all my previous trips out to Lincoln by myself. What had not changed was that William would be there waiting. Alice fell asleep on the train and was still asleep when it stopped at South Lincoln Station. I looked out and saw William standing there. I stood on the step and he came right over and took our sleeping girl from me and put her on his shoulder, and then he helped me down with the other hand.

He led the way to the cart and got us both on before turning to say, "I am so glad to see you. I had no idea what it would be like thinking of you and Alice miles away from me in Dorchester."

"I missed you, too," I answered as he handed the baby to me. "But we had a wonderful time, and it was such a plan you made and the boys said to say, 'hello' to you. I've stored up the whole day in my head and will tell you all about it while we have supper."

Then Alice woke up and began to tell Papa about her day and showed him the baby doll and I had more to say as I thought of it and he laughed and said, "Now I know what it is to have two women talking to me at once." Then he laughed again because small Alice had even reached over to take him by the chin to make sure he was paying attention. What a day it had been. I was almost ready to tell William what I had softly murmured to Mrs. Bernstein before we left. We were having another baby.

The next day after our trip, Alice said, "train," and went to get her hat and coat.

I told her. "Some other time."

She was insistent. I distracted her with her new dolly, which I dressed up. After that, she clearly said, "Dolly, go on the train." That kept up until lunch, after which I put her in for her nap. I don't think she will forget the trip.

CHAPTER 17

My Sister Bridget (1915)

Bridget is coming! We've been writing back and forth, letters coming almost every week from Ireland. The girl has a lot of ideas. As big sisters, we thought we'd set her up, having her stay with us in Lincoln until she got a position. We'd allowed ourselves to think, Mary Anne and I, that we could find her a place out here in the country, or at least in Boston where she would be near our friends. The Rafterys were sure to welcome her. Well, one of her ideas was to go to New York.

"I've heard there are lots of Irish in New York," she'd written.

"There are lots of Irish in Boston," Mary Anne had written back.

Then we'd heard from our other sister, Kate. "Bridget has written me about a position she knows of as waitress at a hotel here in New York."

It seemed Bridget had some very modern ideas. She did not want to work in service in a house. We were astonished. It had never occurred to us she would not go into service. We could only imagine what our mother was thinking and could not believe our father knew anything about it.

We made plans. The letters continued to fly between us and Kate in New York. Kate had paid Bridget's passage and for a train ticket to New York from Boston where her ship would come in. We supposed Bridget also had some small savings. We were not willing to let our little sister not see us first. So, we pooled our money for a round-trip ticket between Boston and Lincoln. We were her family. After that, she could see Kate in New York.

Bridget wrote back and agreed to our plan. She enclosed her schedule. Her ship would arrive in Boston Harbor on the second of April. William said he would check first in the papers and then meet her at the dock and bring her to us by train. We were over the moon with anticipation. Bridget would only stay a few days, she said. She had a starting date at her job at the hotel. She'd learned of it from a friend in Mullingar who worked there. We would have liked to have her longer, but sensed she was as stubborn as we are. I tried to remember her. She had been a little girl of eight when we left. The last words we'd heard from her had been, "They'll be back in two weeks." We hadn't been.

The day she arrived was bright and sunny, maybe a little cold. William went off very early in the morning. He knew where to go. We waited all day. I suppose we were a little nervous about meeting this girl we did not really know at all. By noon, just when we had given up and thought we must wait til supper, the cart came down the road. A very pretty girl was sitting perched up between William and his brother Francis, who had picked them up at the station. She was small like us and in a neat dress and shawl, her brown hair done up on her head. She had a huge smile on her face.

We all rushed out, children included, and Mary Anne with Louise in her arms. Bridget jumped quickly down from her seat and ran to us. We were all laughing and crying at once. It was like a found piece of home. She was our last link to our parents, and she'd been with them and the rest of the family in Rathcaled, just before leaving to sail from Queenstown. She did not seem a bit tired nor shy, either.

"I am so happy to be here. It seems ages since I left Ireland. Mother and Father send their love. I have letters from them and gifts too." She sounded like home. She looked straight at Alice and said how pretty she was. And then to the boys, how big and handsome. She then reached over and touched Louise's head. I knew she'd grown from a child, and now we saw a young lady. But to her, we must seem like somehow beloved strangers, so changed we were from the girls who had left Ireland.

She bounced into the house with William following with her bag. The tea went on and she quickly pulled small gifts out, one for each child; a dolly for Alice and wooden toys for the boys. They did not go running into the yard like they usually did when there was company. They seemed mesmerized by her voice and manner, and besides, she kept pulling them over to her and telling them how wonderful to see them, finally. They could not get enough of her attention. Even the baby reached out to her and had to be held. She is a lovely girl, our sister.

The days flew by. She stayed with William and me. We had a little extra room we used for storage and we'd fit a borrowed cot into it and I'd made it nice with a pillow and cover and it gave her a little privacy. But she kept popping out to see us. At one point, she observed I was expecting again.

"In the summer," I told her.

"Lovely," she said.

We had only three days, and she seemed determined to get to know her sisters again. The first day, Mary Anne was dropped off early in the morning. I made tea, and we three talked at length, mostly about home because we wanted to know about family. It was as if we could see them through her and she was good at making pictures for us. Our father was aging, she said, before our mother, who was quite a bit younger than him. But he still went to the forge every day, and it was still a popular business in Rathcaled. The boys were all working and Rose was still at school for a bit longer. Bridget fondly called her a "homebody." She was happiest at home and would never come over, but that was good my sister stated because there would be someone left to take care of our parents. We had to agree, but it made us feel bad. It caused us to think more of the consequence of our leaving. So many had done this, we agreed, but still it was hard. We'd never thought, back then, of our parents getting old.

The second day, we went to Mary Anne's house, and she fixed us a lunch of jam sandwiches and we made a picnic of it which pleased the children who ran around afterwards while Bridget chased them. She did agree that the countryside was like that of our Ireland, all green. She wanted to know if we would ever leave here. We looked at each other, Mary Anne and I, and told her the truth. In America, people moved around when there were better prospects and both our husbands wanted to work farms, so yes, we would be moving. It might take some time, though. She nodded, coming from a very small country where people stayed on their bit of land if they had any and often remained close to home, unless they emigrated. She said that the schoolteacher had a group of lads who were interested in Irish independence and had secret meetings. It was exciting, she said, to hear of it. She thought it likely that Ireland would gain its independence from Britain soon. We were happy to know this.

Bridget's last day was Sunday. We were all invited to the Bennetts for dinner after Mass. She was a big success, charming them as she had everyone else, especially the Bennett boys who were fascinated with this beautiful girl full of talk and laughter. Mrs. Bennett said she looked like us and certainly had the same sound to her words. She was delighted to meet her. I knew it was beyond her how a girl that young could go to work in New York City, but she said to me later that she was glad Kate was there to watch her. I had the thought that no one would actually be telling Bridget what to do. She was ready for adventure, and that was all there was to it.

So, we got her home by early evening, and she packed her bag for the next day. William had gone over how she should change trains in Boston to go to New York. She would have to find her way back to South Station.

"I have a tongue in my head, Willow," she said mischievously, "And I will ask direction but not of any strange men," that for my benefit. "Yes, I have my ticket," she told us, and "Yes, I know Kate will be meeting me at the station." The smile never left her face. I sighed.

Early the next morning, she said her goodbyes. She cried a little then and so did I. We held onto each other, just for a minute, and then she picked Alice up for a quick hug and climbed up beside William for the ride to the station. She was gone in an instant, only the sound of the cart lasting until they turned the corner. She'd made me weary and happy and sad all at once. It was both good and bad to have her bring Ireland back to us in such a way, but I'd not have wanted to miss it, this visit. I wished her well. Somehow, I thought Bridget would be fine. We would be here after all and there would letters, this time not all the way from Ireland. I said a prayer and got busy, but I thought of her many times that day. God Bless.

CHAPTER 18

Spring and Summer

July 12, 1915

Spring came. Mrs. Bennett told me this time she thought I was carrying a boy. William got a new job at the grain store in town. I was so excited. It was still hard work, but my husband is strong. It paid a bit more than farm work, and that was good. He lifted large bags of grain all day and loaded them onto carts or lugged them into the store.

March arrived and Alice's second birthday. I made her a little cake. Grandmother came over with a pretty tea set that had belonged to her girls. Alice loved it and sat having tea and conversation with her dolls. She also sang "Happy Birthday" to herself for days.

It was a pleasant summer that followed. I felt both big and healthy. Alice herself was growing like a weed. Mrs. Bennett had given me some more of Florence's outgrown dresses and I was grateful, but sometimes I wished I could put her into a little pair of pants to play outside in the garden where she got so dirty. I even thought of myself in modest trousers when I took my walks. I don't believe William would have been scandalized, surprised maybe.

Well, July Fourth came, but no baby yet. We drove to town to see the parade, which was fun. I tapped my toes to the music. Alice didn't seem to mind the heat, but I did. We didn't stay long. I needed to get home and sit. William even had me lie down to nap, which I tried to do. I was getting impatient with family, myself and even this baby who wouldn't come yet. I felt cross.

We decided Alice wasn't old enough for the evening fireworks. We did go to the Bennetts because my husband would not leave me alone at home to sulk. They had peach ice cream, and that was a treat. Mrs. Bennett had taken one look at me, given me a seat, and had me put my feet up. I sat there and ate my ice cream and felt better. She thought it would be another week.

I'd never been so uncomfortable in my life. Alice flitted around the house all day because I kept her in so I wouldn't have to chase her. William was hanging laundry, and we were eating a lot of warmed over or cold meals. My stomach didn't like tea at this point, so I drank lots of water and that sent me to the chamber pot. But still I looked forward to the baby. The cradle was all ready. Alice had taken to putting her dolls in there, and once in a while herself. The money for the doctor was in the jar. I hoped it would be quick, this birth. Mrs. Bennett assured me it would probably be shorter with the second one.

On the morning of the eleventh of July, I heard a carriage coming down the road. It was Mrs. Bennett arriving for an unexpected visit. Her son, Francis, had driven her over. I let her right in. We sat together at the table. I was glad I'd cleaned a bit that morning. She went right to the point.

"Ellen," she said firmly. "I think you should come to my house and stay until this baby comes. It will make things easier with Alice. The girls will mind her. I don't like you alone here all day. My sister Tressie always came and stayed with me. I had help. I want you to tell Willow when he comes home tonight and come right over tomorrow morning. We can make room. I'll just shift the children around."

Well, I didn't know what to say, so I just cried. It was such a relief. I'd never been like that, not ever, so it surprised me. She just patted my hand and scooped up Alice, who was looking a bit concerned, and said she'd have her lunch with us and then go home. Francis had retreated to the garden. He seemed to be examining trees, or maybe the sky. We gave him Alice, and he piggy-backed her around the yard. Lunch was prepared, and I was served.

I told William that night, "Your mother was by this morning." His brows went up at that. An unannounced visit from his mother?

"She wants me to come stay until after the baby comes."

"We'll go first thing tomorrow morning," he said immediately. He seemed relieved. So William drove us the next day. It was the twelfth of July and it was going to be a hot day. I didn't tell him but I felt different, like something had shifted inside, like just before I had Alice, but my pains hadn't started yet.

William helped me down and Alice ran ahead of us into the house where we could hear the girls welcoming her. Mrs. Bennett came right out on the porch and took my arm. It was decided I should go to bed. William was told to come back from work at noon. That surprised me, but I stayed silent. Two of the boys had been moved out of their bedroom and the big double bed was freshly made up. I did not mind being put to bed in the morning, contrary to how I would usually feel about that.

William gave me a kiss and left. "I'll be back soon. My mother will take good care of you." And with that, he was gone. I just lay there enjoying the comfort. I'd thought I might feel awkward having someone wait on me, but I'd been feeling so miserable, it was all right. I could hear Alice's voice somewhere in the house. I slept. Later, I sat up and drank some water. I was listening to to the sounds of the household; water coming to a boil, the plop-plop of something dropped in a pot, voices of children, then quick footsteps. Mrs. Bennett appeared in the doorway.

"You look much more relaxed, Ellen. I know your time is near now. I could tell when you arrived earlier. I've sent word for Doctor to come this afternoon and Willow back at noon, as you know." And then she called into the kitchen and her sister Tressie came in. Everyone loved Tressie. She'd never married and was always around for all family events. She was a small lady, not much taller than me, and always had a smile on her face. She loved children and right now she would talk about our Alice.

"She is an energetic little girl you have. She'll be a great help to you later. You and Willow have done a good job. Amelia tells me all about her." Then she turned her attention to me. "Now, if you'd like to come sit in the rocking chair in the kitchen, the time will go faster for you. You can rest and also get up and walk when you want to. That will be good for you. Amelia thinks it will begin soon."

So I trundled off to the kitchen. The door was open, letting in a breeze, and the oven was off on this hot day. I didn't want any lunch, but Alice was brought in and put on a chair. She enjoyed a few bites of her sandwich while talking away at everybody. Her Aunt Martha had a job, but the other girls were home and had taken over Alice.

And then I felt my first pain. I hid it from the children, but the women noticed and went into action. I could tell Mrs. Bennett was checking things off in her mind. The younger boys had been sent fishing for the day with lunches. The girls were getting Alice ready to go pick berries in the woods. They were fastening a little straw hat on her head. They brought her over to say goodbye to me. Then they were out the door with instructions to visit their neighbor after berrying until someone fetched them home.

I had another pain and another. This wasn't going to take long, I thought as they got me ready to go back to bed. Just then, William came in and helped me into the bedroom. A short time later, the doctor arrived. It seemed that if Mrs. Bennett gave you instructions to come, you came. She and Aunt Tressie spent time in the room with me and the doctor. William was sent to the hall several times but never stayed. I kept hearing his voice.

A few hours later and we had a little boy. Our William was small and round like his sister, with the same dark hair. He seemed to rest just a minute or two, before beginning to cry loudly. I'd never heard such noise from a newborn. They cleaned and then handed him over to me and he began to nurse a little, which seemed to calm him. The doctor called him fine and healthy. The baby fell asleep then, so I could study his little face. William had brought the cradle over that morning but his family would not put him down, as he was passed from one arm to another, as each arrived home from work. His Aunt Martha declared he was a beautiful baby and said she would know, being the oldest.

Grandfather held him briefly while smiling at his proud son. And then Billy's papa would not put him down at all. William had a tear, whether because the birth was over or because he had a boy, I did not know. After a while, everyone left us alone. The women shooed every-one out. They needed to manage the rest of the day. Aunt Tressie, before she left, said to us in a low voice, "Felicitations, Ellen and William."

William cradled his son in his arms, saying softly, "Well, Billy, won't we have fun together."

CHAPTER 19

Billy

William did go have his supper while I had soup on a tray. When the baby cried again, he came quickly from the kitchen to hand him over to me from the cradle. I fell asleep after feeding. It was a while later when I awoke to see William in the doorway, holding a sleepy Alice. I reached over and brought her into bed beside me. She was damp and smelling of soap. She closed her eyes as I pulled her in. Papa reached in after a few minutes and lifted her off the bed.

"She's so tired from her day, but she had a good time with the girls. When they brought her back, she still had blueberry smeared on her chin. I think tomorrow will be soon enough for her to see the baby."

I agreed. "Where will she sleep?"

"With her aunts," he laughed. "Nestled in like a kitten. They have it all planned. My mother will listen in for her in the night. They're right in the room next to them." He went on, "I'll sleep here with you if you think there's room with you and Billy."

I laughed. "He's very small but makes his presence known. We'll share the bed."

Billy cried every couple of hours through the night. William would hand him over and after, we'd all fall back asleep again. We were both weary after that night, and William had to get up for work.

"I'll go tell Mary Anne during my lunchtime," he told me quietly. Billy was sleeping. I thought I could rest a little longer, but Billy disagreed. After I fed him, Mrs. Bennett appeared and took him to change his diaper. She thought we could bathe him later if I wanted. I agreed. It was only dawn, but I heard Alice.

Papa brought Alice in and she climbed into bed with me, but only for a few minutes before slipping to the floor and running to the cradle.

"Baby Billy," came out of her mouth.

I thought someone must have called him that in front of her.

"Your new baby brother," I instructed her, and gestured to William to take him out of his cradle and hand him to me. I knew he might wake up and scream, but I wanted Alice to get used to him. I sat up in bed, holding Billy. Alice climbed up beside us. I unwrapped him enough for her to touch his hands and feet and then his head, very gently, showing her how. And then Billy opened his eyes. But instead of crying right away, he seemed to look at her.

Alice's face lit up, and she said, "Hello, Billy," in that bright voice she has. Then came the crying, and Alice did exactly what I do when she's upset. She patted him and told him he would be all right and not to cry. But when that didn't work, she looked over at me.

"He's hungry," I told her. "And he's a baby, so that's how he tells me. He'll be all right."

She seemed to accept that, and Papa carried her off to her breakfast, leaving Billy to me.

A while later, after William had gone to work, Grandmother came in with Alice to bring me a tray for breakfast, which she put on a little table where I could reach it.

"Alice helped me with this," she told me with a smile. "I'm letting the girls sleep a little longer this morning. The buttered toast seemed a bit torn." I thanked my daughter, and she nodded. Her interest was still on the baby.

"He's sleeping," she observed. Then, "I want to hold him." My Alice was always direct.

Grandmother pulled a chair over, lifted the baby out and sat down, pulling Alice over to sit with her. Alice put her small arms around her brother. I got to eat my breakfast. I was surprised she didn't tire of it right away. She was studying him. I wondered what was going through her head.

This time when he cried, Alice just said calmly, "He's just hungry, Mama." Grandmother laughed at her tone. Alice stayed when I started to nurse. I told her it was milk.

"Why doesn't he drink from a cup?" was her response.

"He's too little," I told her.

She accepted that. Grandmother then told her to go wake her aunts. Like my mother, she was not much for letting the young ones stay in bed too long. Alice went skipping out of the room.

"She's been wonderful," Mrs. Bennett told me. "She really is a happy child. Today the girls are going to walk to a friend's house. They'll bring her back for lunch. I'm thinking I might put her in for a nap then. I so enjoy having you here. Tressie will be over later. She can't stay away from a baby."

"Your whole family loves babies," I said with a big smile.

"Oh, yes, I suppose we do. Good thing, too, with this brood." She paused. "You will rest today. I've sent a note with William for your sister to come over and visit in a few days, and bring her little ones. Sisters need to be together at times like this."

I thanked her for that. I had a feeling I was going to get to know Mrs. Bennett a lot better during this visit. Then it was time for Billy's bath. The day was warm but not hot. We unwrapped him and lay him on his little blanket on the bed. He didn't like being unwrapped and set up a cry, so I picked him up and held him close while Grandmother poured warm water into a little basin. Then, as I held him, she handed me the wet cloth, and I gently patted him all over. That, he tolerated, and then I rubbed him dry with another soft cloth and diapered him and put him into his little gown. He seemed content and fell back to sleep. I knew that wouldn't last.

We stayed a week. Alice was in her glory she would run to greet her uncles and aunt as they came home from work, then Grandfather, and at last, Papa. I spent my days mostly in the kitchen now. Billy was beside me in his cradle. But I would be sent off to nap in the afternoon after I'd fed him. I would wake up listening to the sounds of the household.

We drank tea and coffee in the afternoons with cake or pie. I loved it. Aunt Tressie would join us most days. She liked her coffee strong with cream and sugar. Both women would talk about the small village of Harbour Bouche where they came from in Canada. It sounded not unlike the Irish village of Ballynacargy nearest to our small town land of Rathcaled, but colder, much colder! They both came here speaking French, but their English was perfect, with only a small difference in how they said some words.

Some afternoons, the girls would be permitted to go out, leaving Alice to us. I would have both of them in my lap in the rocker until Alice would get restless and climb down. I noticed that my girl did exactly what she was told when Grandmother spoke to her in her quiet tone. "Amelia" as I had been asked to call her, would follow an instruction for Alice with a hug or a smile. "I like her spirit," she would tell me.

After a few days, our Billy's eyes seem to be open more and more, and he even appeared to be looking around at times. He did feed more frequently than his sister had, as a new baby. He was demanding that way. But he would sleep too.

One day, Mary Anne and her children came. It had all been arranged, so I was listening for the cart. Frederick brought her in the early morning. He helped her down with Baby Louise. The boys were not shy and made their hello's to the grown-ups. They were taken outside by the girls who had decided to keep them in the yard where there was a swing and a ball to throw around. They'd bring them in for lunch later. Louise stayed with us. She was crawling everywhere and pulling herself up.

Mary Anne went right to the cradle and lifted the baby out. "He looks like both of you, with William's black hair and your eyes," she declared.

Billy was looking up at her, his eyes getting wider. I knew that meant a cry was coming. To Billy, being awake meant he was hungry. I took him to the rocker for his feeding. Amelia left us to our tea and bread and butter while she went off to do some chores. She promised to sit down with us for lunch and said Tressie would be coming over.

Mary Anne said I looked well. "I wish I had a mother-in-law who lived close by like yours and she's so nice." I knew she meant it, too. Maybe she was a little jealous?

Amelia, on one of her trips to the kitchen, picked up a willing Baby Louise and took her off to give us some peace. She thought she'd take her to the porch and let her watch the children for a little while. You could tell she'd handled many babies as she went off murmuring to Louise. Lunch was a soup made that same morning and we all sat around the table. The children behaved well with a few looks from us. As a treat, Amelia had made cookies. Louise did take a nap, all bundled up on a bed near where we could hear her. Tressie stayed well past lunch, holding Billy when she could. And even following Louise on her little trips around the kitchen. I don't know when I'd had a more enjoyable afternoon. Too soon, it was time for them to go. Frederick patiently put everyone onto the cart and off they went. Alice was a little sad when her playmates left and tired. I rocked her to sleep.

I did no cooking or cleaning or laundry all that week. I was feeling strong again. Billy seemed to be looking at faces. Grandfather sang songs to Alice in the evening, after he'd had his pipe outside, and before she was put to bed. It made me think of my father and how we'd told him he would be so proud of us in America.

"I want to be proud of my daughters and see my grandchildren right here in Ireland," had been his answer to that. Here, he had another grandchild, and I didn't even have the money to send pictures of our darlings. It made me want to cry. I knew it was because I had just given birth. It had been the same with Alice. I sighed and thought again how happiness and sadness always came together. I would be writing the letter to them soon. I could picture them opening it and telling the family about a new little boy in America.

Sunday was set for the Christening and we would go home that evening. I both wanted to go and wanted to stay. I thought Amelia would miss us. We had become so much closer. She liked having us in the house for all we were so crowded and made extra work. I did wonder at how Alice would feel about going home.

A thunderstorm had come in on Saturday night, and Sunday was nice, not so hot for all it being July. That afternoon, William, dressed in his shirt and tie, climbed into the cart. Billy's godmother, his Aunt Martha, held him. Uncle Stephen climbed in alongside as godfather for the ride to church where our son would be baptized as William John Bennett. They returned in an hour. William reported, "He stayed quiet at first, but when Father poured the water on him, he objected and cried, louder than any of the other infants."

"He did look sweet, though, in his little dress and bonnet," offered his godmother, "And he was definitely the most handsome."

I laughed and took my now screaming infant into the bedroom to change and feed him. Alice was covering her ears. Mary Anne and her family arrived after that. Amelia had covered the big table with food and we all went in to eat it. Mr. Bennett poured out his homemade wine, and we all laughed and talked. Billy got handed around. I'd wrapped him in a new blanket over his dress and taken his bonnet off. He seemed content. Alice ran around with her cousins. Aunt Tressie took Billy from me and then Grandmother took her turn, walking him around. I was so grateful to Amelia for having us come and stay.

I had packed the night before, so, as the afternoon was coming to an end, I sent William to get our bags. Alice gave him a funny look, as though to wonder why on earth, we would need them. She also eyed Uncle Stephen carrying the cradle out to the cart. She was not going to take this easy, I could tell.

Amelia helped. "Alice," she said in a very matter-of-fact tone. "You'll be going home now with Mama and Papa and Billy. Uncle Stephen will drive me over one day next week to see you. Now, give me a kiss before you go."

Alice obediently trotted over to Grandmother and then around to everyone at the table to say her goodbyes. But then she stood on the porch and her eyes filled with tears. So, I handed the baby over to William and picked my big girl up and she put her head down on my shoulder like when she was tiny. Everyone called out their goodbyes and their God-blesses, and off we went, Alice in the middle while I held Billy close.

William had been to the house, and all was clean and neat. We'd been given a basket of food with milk, eggs, and butter. Billy was beginning to squirm, so I knew I'd be feeding him soon. Alice looked ready for bed, but I thought it best to keep her up for a while. It would take time getting used to her new brother, but she did have her strong and healthy mother back again. We would be going out to the garden the next day to play. Soon, we would walk down the road to see Mrs. Flint and show off Billy. The trips to Mary Anne's would start again, and Amelia had promised a visit. There was much to look forward to.

Alice fell asleep over her cup of milk and her papa took her off to bed. I put Billy in his cradle, now next to our bed and hoped for a little quiet. Back in the kitchen, William and I sat alone at the table having tea. The quiet was both welcome and strange after the noise of a large family. He told me how he had seen how close I had become to his mother and how it pleased him. It made me happy, too.

"I want a big family, too," I said to him across the table as I slowly stirred my tea.

"It's what we agreed on," he said with a warm smile. "and we are on the way."

Well, we sat there, too tired to get up to go to bed until Billy summoned us with his cry. And that's how the day ended.

CHAPTER 20

Dover

CHANGES

With all these children, now, between Mary Anne and me, we were always busy. Still, we made the time to see each other, as we had done since we were both in service. I wrote to Mrs. Bernstein about Billy. She sent me a lovely note and another pair of little white shoes. William wanted to save some more money, We paid rent for the house. I kept a garden for vegetables, and we had chickens, and we bought a little meat at the town market. I stretched it out with stews served with bread and butter. I canned vegetables and made jam in the summer. I didn't know how we could save anymore. I made our clothes. I spent no money.

Baby Billy watched everything. I knew if he could talk, he'd be asking questions. Alice did, and I tried to have answers for her. "After winter is spring," I told her. "Then it will be your birthday again and you will be a big girl of three years of age." She held up three fingers to show me she understood.

Mary Anne had been quiet. She was quite tired from her three children, but I thought it was more than that. I was thinking she knew something about moving. She hadn't said anything to me yet. William had told me nothing.

One Saturday evening, after both children had been put to bed, we had a talk. I started it by asking him very directly. "Are we going to be moving?"

He looked at me like he didn't want to talk about it.

"Well?" I was being sharp with him. "I need to know whatever you know. Is there a plan?" We'd always made our plans together.

"I didn't want to upset you before I knew what was going to happen," he said unhappily.

There were no smiles between us.

"Dover," he said finally.

I knew nothing of Dover and told him so.

"Fred is looking for a farm to manage. There are lots of farms in that area. He's looked in Dover because there's more money to hire men to run their farms." He took a gulp of tea, maybe, for once, thinking he might like something stronger.

"Does Mary Anne know?" I asked him. This with a glare to my eyes.

"She just found out," he told me. "Nothing is arranged yet, but they could be moving soon. Frederick has a couple of possibilities." And then he paused. "I have a chance of a job in Dover."

I had angry tears. He pulled me over to him. I resisted a little, then sat rather stiffly but close enough.

"We can do better," he told me. "I want to give you more."

"I do understand," was my response. "But you have left me out of it and we always plan everything together."

I was full of talk now. I needed to tell him everything on my mind. "You don't know what it is to leave everyone behind."

He looked at me and said, "But it's not like Ireland. You've told me what that was like. Dover is not that far. We can be back here in a few hours."

"What do you really know about Dover?" I asked my husband.

William had the name of a farm in Dover. He'd seen an advertisement in the paper. He pulled it out of his pocket to show me. William, it seemed, saw our future in a piece of paper. The owner was a wealthy businessman in the city who wanted someone to work his farm. It was called the Pierce Estate. There was a small house and barns. The owner had a big house on the property. The position would be available in the spring.

My husband said he'd had this paper for several days now and had been waiting to show it to me. So, that made me feel better, still mad though, he'd not done it right away. It was time for me to be practical. I settled down and read it.

"You should write to this man," I said firmly. "You need to know and I need time to get used to it if need be. It does seem like an opportunity."

"That's only fair," he said back. The relief showed in his face.

But I didn't let him off too easily. I told him he would be taking me to see my sister the next day. I allowed hope in. "Maybe we could be living close to each other in Dover, my sister and me?" This was possible, although I knew Fred had more than one opportunity in that area.

The next morning, we surprised Mary Anne. I went inside where Louise was toddling around, still in her little nightgown. Mary Anne was clean and neat herself, her hair up and an apron over her clothes. We looked at each other as William drove away.

I did not let her get started with the baby or tea. I just had one word, "Dover." She kept her face straight. My sister, like me, preferred to be in control. I, for once, kept quiet. We stood like that for about a minute. It felt like more.

Finally, she burst out. "I only just found out and it isn't sure. Frank," They had begun calling him Frank sometimes instead of Frederick. "Frank is going to look into it, this farm. It's what we want. I've been wanting to tell you, but I'm not entirely happy."

It sounded more normal, that flood of words. But I wasn't smiling yet. I still had crying coming up inside of me. I took a breath and scooped up Louise, just to give myself something to hold while I settled. I took the better view of things. "Why didn't you tell me? William just told me last night that there are jobs in and near Dover. He has a possibility. I forced it out of him."

She fell on that. "So it will be all right."

Then we both paused because nothing was for sure here. We'd both be daft to believe that.

Well, the worst was over. Louise called to be put down. Billy began to smile and gurgle from the cradle in the kitchen where I'd placed him when I came in. And his aunt ran over to pick him up. So we could breathe again.

And the Flood girls began to move forward. We spun our tales of being together in Dover. We admired all Billy's new tricks; blowing bubbles and punching the air with his small fists. We watched Alice and James run around in circles until we finally took them outside in the garden where the warm sun made us feel good.

When William came in the late afternoon, he looked relieved to see our calm and happy faces. He did pick Alice and James up, though, and looked at us from behind them, at first, to determine our moods.

On the ride home, I chatted easily about the day, but I did not want him to think that all was forgotten, not between me and Mary Anne or us. I'd forgiven William, but I would not forget. I was like that.

We were a family. We would be all right. I was trying to look at moving to Dover as an adventure. I would be a farmer's wife. What would it pay, I wondered? Would we still pay rent? Would there be chickens, horses, cows, crops? Things to ask William when he got a response. I turned to tell all this to William in bed beside me, but he was already asleep.

Frederick got word he had a job on a dairy farm in Westwood. Not his first choice, but a good start, they thought. She told me right away, this time, when she knew. We both talked and cried a little about it. We could travel between Dover and Westwood, but it would not be minutes away like now. They got ready to move. Each time, now, when I went over there, I thought how it was coming to an end.

Next, William got a response from Mr. Pierce, who had put out the advertisement. He wanted William to meet with him in Dover. He said he'd looked over his letters of recommendation and all, and he thought he might suit. He enclosed train tickets for Mr. Bennett, who would be met at the station in Dover and taken to the farm where he would be interviewed. William had never had an interview. He has always gotten jobs by word of mouth. I got his suit out and pressed it as well as his shirt and added his tie. My husband would look nice, I told myself, and he already knew how to talk.

He left very early that morning to the train station with his brother, Francis. He would have to switch trains in Boston, a long trip. We waved goodbye, Alice and me. It was a long day waiting, but he finally arrived home in late afternoon, after we'd made dozens of trips to the front porch to look for him. I heard the wagon and Francis delivered a smiling William. Francis went along back home. I was sure he would tell the family all about it.

William told it in his own way. "Mr. Pierce was very businesslike. He sat with me, first in his office in the big house, and asked me all sorts of questions about running a farm. He asked me, in detail about planting, dairy, farm animals, and keeping books. The maid brought us coffee. Imagine that."

"I liked your letter," Mr. Pierce told me. "It seems you have experience and work hard and it is apparent you like the farm life."

"Then he asked me about you. 'Did my wife know how to churn butter, cook, keep a garden and all?' I assured him she did. Then we crossed over to the farm where I had a tour from the present farm manager."

At this point, he got up and started to walk around the kitchen. He was that excited.

"The foreman he has now, is getting old and wants to move to town. He showed me around. There's a nice cottage and two big barns. Ellen, the house has an indoor bathroom and electricity and even a telephone!"

I looked at him in disbelief. "This a story you are telling me, William. You must be teasing me."

"No, it's true. I couldn't wait to tell you."

I sat there for a minute in contemplation of these marvels. I was smiling away. Then it hit me that he'd put the cart before the horse. "Do you have the job?"

"Yes, my Ellen, I do." And he picked me up and swung me around, much to Alice's pleasure, and she had to be swung too. Even Billy was giggling from his cradle. What a night this was. I could not hear enough of it.

He went on to tell me about Mr. Pierce's collection of old carriages he kept in one of the barns. It would be part of William's job to take one out each week and drive it to town, and there was a church nearby in Medfield.

Finally, things settled down enough for me to put supper on the table. He talked through the whole meal, adding details of his day as he remembered them. After we put the children to bed, we kept on talking. We decided Mary Anne and Frederick should come to supper on Saturday, so we could all talk about Dover and Westwood. The next day we would go to the Bennetts. He would want to talk to his family. On Saturday, William got off early from the grain store, so he picked up Mary Anne, so Frederick could just come straight to us. We had an early supper.

At the end of that evening, it looked like this. Frederick would move his family to Westwood in March, directly to the farm he'd be managing. William's job in Dover started in April. We would also move in March and rent a house in town for a few weeks. William could take a job as a farm hand until starting work at Pierce Farm. We had enough money saved to get by for a short time. William thought, once on the farm, he could earn extra income in addition to his salary. We all nodded. It was a good plan. The next day, after church, we would go see the Bennetts. Willow, their oldest son, would be the first to leave Lincoln.

William gave his notice at the grain store. They wished him luck, and he came home with his last pay envelope. He'd rented a house on Centre Street in Dover. It would mean living in the middle of town for a about a month until the move to Pierce Farm. He would look around when we got there for work as a farm laborer. He thought someone would need him.

It was so hard to leave. One day, it seemed, it was still weeks away and then the day was there itself. There was not much left in our little house. It had all been put on the cart the night before. Mary Anne and her family had left weeks ago. I had not heard from her.

The Bennetts had put on a big dinner for us; a roast, pies, homemade wine and all. But instead of welcoming me to the family, they were saying goodbye. And that was very hard. I am not good at farewells.

This time, it was me who had stood on the front porch, not my little daughter, with my own eyes filled with tears. Amelia helped by not saying much, just hugging me and sending me to William, who was already sitting in the cart with the children. Their grandfather had carried Alice and Billy out. William's brother Robert was driving because our wagon stood at home loaded with our belongings. I sat up, holding a wiggling Billy in my lap. Alice, who had been told all about the move, sensed the mood of the grown-ups. She sat quietly with wide eyes. She was almost three years of age and Billy would be a year old when summer came again. Everyone called out their goodbyes.

So, next was moving day. I looked at our little house for the last time. I'd not planted anything this year. There were a few old plants pushing up. I'd said goodbye several days ago to Mrs. Flint down the road. I would miss Lincoln. But there was something in me that loved an adventure, and that feeling carried me away from Lincoln and toward our new home. We left early in the morning and William said we would be there by noon. Some of the trip would be on dirt roads with spring mud. We were headed to the town center, so that would be paved. He'd arranged a place to keep the horse and cart until we went to the farm. We would sell them later for cash. I did like the idea of living in town, even if only for a short time.

The trip took hours, but the children were good, both of them. Alice looked all around. William and I talked, and the baby slept sometimes. We were comfortable. I did not know exactly what to expect, so when we arrived on Centre Street, it was pleasing to see all the houses close together. William had told me we would be in the center of town. I would look forward to walking to the shops. I knew when we arrived, it would take time to arrange our furniture and make it home, but I'd done that before. It was just a new place to put in order. William had been instructed to get the key from the landlady, and so we stopped first at a big white house. He went to the door while I remained behind with the children, although Alice wanted to go with Papa. In a few minutes, he came out with a smile and a bag of cookies. Our landlady called out they were for the children. That was a nice start. I called out a thank you.

I did chores while the baby napped. I placed our jar of money on a shelf, then looked around for a broom. After a quick neatening, I unpacked our dishes and pans and found room for them. We had eggs and potatoes for tonight. I would have William bring wood in from the pile outside. I ran out quickly to both inspect and use the outhouse. It was fine. I could not help but think of the indoor bathroom of our next move.

That evening, I lit the gas lamps. It always seemed to me that in a new place, it was important to make the gloom of evening darkness depart by making it light. William was not gone long and was delighted to tell me he had been told of a nearby farm that might need a laborer, so he would go there in the morning. He was happy with eggs for supper. Amelia had sent a loaf of bread too, so we made ourselves full and the children went to bed without any trouble. I made sure Alice had her dollies, and Billy could sleep anywhere. Our first night in Dover was fine. I sent William off the next morning, after coffee and a breakfast of porridge and bread.

We walked to the store that morning. Billy, I carried on my hip, and Alice held my hand like a good girl. She was not always so agreeable about holding on, but this day, it being all new to her, she was more biddable. The shopkeeper greeted us. "You must be the Bennetts. Your husband was in yesterday and I told him about a job. I understand he is to take over Pierce Farm next month. He seems a strong young man. He told me he had a wife and family." Then Mrs. Smith, our landlady, came over to greet us and nicely took Billy, who was squirming to be let down.

I took some butter and a bit of ham along with a bundle of carrots and more potatoes; also flour, coffee, sugar, and eggs. I handed Mr. Andrew some change I'd taken from our jar and thought how I must make it last. He said his boy would deliver the order after school. Mrs. Smith handed the baby back to me and I made our thank you's and off we went. She had asked me if everything was satisfactory, and when I said it was a nice house, she seemed pleased. "Your husband has already paid the first week's rent," she told me. I was adding things up as I walked home and it seemed if we were careful and William brought some money home we would be fine. It was good not to have too many worries. We were sure of the farm, and that was the best part.

Our second night in our new home, William was too tired to do much talking but pleased, in all, with his workday. He ate and then slept, so I sat up and read my book. The children slept again all night. I'd decided they were good travelers like me. The next few days were the same. William did bring home a chicken, and I made it last several days. We had a small icebox and the ice man came just like when I was in Dorchester. We also had a milkman, so important for the children. Billy was now on a cup, but I still warmed his milk in a pan first. We walked every day down the road and to the post office. On the third day, I was rewarded with a letter from Mary Anne, but she said she would not come this Sunday because the children had all been sick and herself, too. She promised she would be there on the Sunday after. They were happy on the dairy farm, she said. She enclosed her love to me and William and the children and said how much she missed us.

Well, when I told William, he said, right away, we could take a ride on Sunday after Mass to Pierce Farm. "We'll be welcome," he told me, "and you can take a look around. I'm sure you'll love it."

He was so happy with his plan. It made me almost glad Mary Anne would have to come another time. Medfield, he explained to me, was right next door to Dover, and that's where the Catholic church was located. He knew he could find the way, and then to Pierce Farm in Dover. He thought we would be making many Sunday trips, but in one of Mr. Pierce's old carriages, "in style," he called it. Sure, I'd be looking forward to that.

Sunday, the sun was out and although it was still cool, we were comfortable in coats and shawls. The pretty church is called Saint Edward the Confessor. The priest welcomed us. It is a small congregation, not so many Catholics in town. They came from all over. The children behaved, and we went down Farm Road to Smith Street, where the farm was. The first thing I saw was a big house set back from the road by a lawn. But across the road was the cottage, just as William had described it. And next to it, two large barns. A man came out the door and waved at us.

"Well, you must be Mrs. Bennett and the little Bennetts," Mr. Norton said with a smile. "Come on in," he said politely. He had white hair and suspenders. I thanked him and we got the children down.

I was enchanted by what I saw next. The inside was so cozy. There was even a storm porch and two floors. The second floor had bedrooms, and the promised bathroom. On the first floor was a real parlor with a door. I could see us sitting there in the evening. Imagine. Next we went outside to the barns. Alice and Billy met the cows, a new thing for them, and the horse. Chickens ran around in the yard. The other barn had the old horse carriages, some of them on the second floor. They could be taken down with a sort of rope elevator, it was explained. I would leave all that to my husband. Our new friend had started the plowing, and he and William talked farming. He also said he had sometimes shot a pheasant for supper during the season, so I knew William's shotgun would be put to use. It would be a whole new kind of life for me.

We drove back to town all pleased with ourselves and had our dinner.

"William, I am so happy with this. We were right to come."

We were in a good and wonderful mood that afternoon, and I did not think any argument would ever take away what we had together. We went to bed that night very pleased with each other. Maybe we would be having another baby sooner than later. In my head, as I went about my work the next few days, I described the farm and all its marvels to my family in Ireland as well as to my sisters in New York. It did occur to me that I'd not had a letter from my younger sister, Bridget in a while. I wondered at that.

CHAPTER 21

Dover Beginnings

PIERCE FARM AND OTHER MATTERS

This time, we packed the cart after breakfast on the morning of our move. We were only going a short distance. We were excited. The sorrow of leaving our lives and family in Lincoln had begun to fade a little. I'd not had trouble with the decision to depart Lincoln, just with the leave-taking itself. I'd seen Mary Anne and her family, who had come to church from Westwood one Sunday. We'd all had dinner together at our house. The talking had gone on all afternoon. My sister and I had made a plan to go visit them on the dairy farm. But I had not told William about it yet. After all, he was just starting his job and my work on Pierce Farm was beginning. I would wait awhile.

After a short ride, we arrived. Mr. Norton was standing by the door waiting for us. This time he was dressed in a nice shirt and pants and had next to him a suitcase.

"I've left you some of the furniture and rugs," he told us. "I won't need them in rented rooms in town. I've already moved my things." He introduced a friend from town.

Mr. Norton seemed happy enough, and in no time at all, he was riding down the road toward town. We waved. I'd made sure he knew he could come and visit. William had spent some time with him during the last couple of weeks and learned enough to know how to get started. The plowing was done and planting was next. He knew all about the cows. I knew about chickens. Keeping house was easy. I looked with eagerness at the woods and wondered about walks and berry-picking. I felt a little like I had when I moved to Lincoln as a newlywed, as though I was on vacation in the country. Of course, now I had two young ones to look after and, God willing, more on the way. We would be some distance from their grandparents now. But the Bennetts had promised to come out sometime. I had so much to do. It was already middle of the morning and nothing much accomplished.

As I took the children into the house, I thought it would be much harder to watch Alice and soon, Billy, as he got going. Just outside the door was a magical place to play and explore, as well as many opportunities to get into trouble. Alice already wanted to go visit the kitties in the barn. There would have to be rules now if I wanted her to be able to play outside. Even the chickens could be bothersome to such a small one. As the children got bigger, though, they would be used to living on the farm. That was the life we'd chosen for our family. William had gone out to the meadow to see the cows and had taken Alice with him. I knew she'd be safe with her father. Billy crawled around inside. He seemed to be calling, "Papa." Soon, Alice wouldn't be able to get out without her little brother, once he started walking and talking.

The first day went by quickly. William put the furniture together. I made the beds. We had a small lunch, and I planned a big supper. I did get out with the children in the afternoon. We went right to the woods. I was like a child myself. We found early violets and Alice picked a small bouquet. Billy was getting heavy on my hip, though. I was glad he would be walking soon. We found a lovely spot with soft, velvety moss and I did set him down there for a bit, watching that he not eat any. I gave him words, like "soft" and "pretty" but he persisted in pulling at it with his small fingers. Then he started to crawl away, so I had to pick him up again.

William had been happily mucking out the barn. I say happy because even that chore had him in smiles. He was singing, too. The beds were made and the children napping. I thought I should cook something nice for the first night in our new home. This felt permanent to me. We would raise our family here. I let myself think it would be easy, even though I knew better. I saw only joy on this beautiful spring afternoon. The cloth went on the table and the Saint Bridget cross over the door. Stew tonight and fresh bread and even a cake for dessert if I could handle it. It had not taken long to put the kitchen together.

While the children were still napping, I put the bread out to rise. Then, I took myself into the parlor and opened the curtains to the sun. There were two big armchairs in pretty good condition, a divan and a rug. It needed dusting. I thought William and I should sit there in the evenings, talking and perhaps reading. Later, when the children were bigger, we could play checkers and I could read to them and tell them stories. I knew farm families went to bed early, too. And then I remembered Mrs. Bernstein's piano and how she played it when I was busy with chores in the kitchen. I had so enjoyed listening. And then I had the fine idea that maybe Alice could learn to play the piano. Well, I did put that thought away at the back of my mind.

When the children woke up, I got to work on supper. William was walking the farm, looking at all of it. He expected Mr. Pierce would make an appearance some day soon. I'd not met him yet. William was interested in taking one of the carriages down for our trip to church the next Sunday.

"Do you think I should wear my best clothes?" I queried him with a smile. "Will I be the lady and her children inside, while you play coachman high up on the outside seat?"

He laughed at me. "You've not seen yet how elegant the carriages are, Ellen. You will indeed feel like a lady."

I looked at him closely. "Do you remember when we went out walking together the first time, and you took me into Boston?" He nodded. "I told you what a nice time I was having, and you said that was how you treated a lady."

"I was serious, Ellen."

ELLEN FLOOD - 127

"And you always walked on the curbside. Also, you never failed to take me all the way back to my job in Dorchester before getting the train home yourself."

We both got quiet for a few minutes over these memories.

The days took on a routine that first week. We rose early and William milked the cows before breakfast. Then we both did chores, and I cared for Alice and Billy. Papa always made a point of taking Alice somewhere different on the farm each day. Billy would get his walk around the barnyard with Papa after supper. We would all go to bed tired from the fresh air and sleep well.

Then one day, the first letter came from my sister Kate in New York City. The address was her housekeeping job. It was mostly about our little sister Bridget at her waitress job in the hotel.

> Dear Ellen, I hope you and William and the children are keeping well. The farm sounds lovely. I know you will both work hard. It is good, I think, to bring your family up in the country. I am mainly writing to you about our Bridget. It seems she has met a young man. His name is Martin. He comes from Cambridge, Massachusetts, but his parents came from Ireland. I have not yet determined from what county. He is ten years older than her. He is a waiter at the same hotel. He lives in a house with other boarders. Martin has been married before. His wife died several years ago. They had married very young. There were no children. I have met him several times after Mass on Sunday. (Yes, she still goes.) He is agreeable. Bridget is a good girl, but she is also very young and alone in New York, except for me, and I work all the time. Martin is nice, but I am concerned that she is not chaperoned at all. She lives at the hotel and no one is watching her comings and goings. It would be different if she had gone into service with a family like we did. I have talked to her about being careful, but she doesn't want to listen. She knows it all. I am worried and running out of patience with her. I've told her to write to you and Mary Anne to tell you both about her beau.

Love, Kate

I put the letter down right away and took a breath. I had waited until the house was quiet. Well, this news would not be going to the parents in Ireland. That was sure. I pictured her gallivanting around the city with her beau. Then I thought of me and William. But I'd had a house to go back to and someone checking on me and Mrs. Bernstein had met William. I thought of how astonishingly pretty my little sister is, especially when she smiles and how she would be excited by her romance and not entirely silly, but maybe a bit heedless. Perhaps Kate was just going too far with her worries. It was normal, after all, to find a beau and spend time with him. The part that concerned me was her being alone with him with no one expecting her back, except for work. I did not imagine her employers at the hotel concerned themselves with anything except her being on time. I wondered about talking to William about Bridget. Surely, he would have something to offer. Did this Martin treat her like a lady?

William said right away that Bridget needed to be independent of her sisters. But when I pushed, he admitted to being a little worried himself. He thought he would like to meet her young man. I suppose he was thinking of his sisters, but they were still at home under supervision. Well, I didn't think Bridget would be bringing him all that distance just to meet us, so something had to be done. William left me to write to her, after cautioning me not to be too heavy. "The last thing a young girl wants is interference. I do remember a very independent girl, you know. I married her." And with that, he sped away with both children to the barn. "To feed the cats their milk," he said. It had become a daily event.

I wrote immediately to Mary Anne. I wanted her opinion on things. Kate had written to her, too. But before I could compose the letter to Bridget, I got one from her.

Dear Ellen, Kate told me I should write. I've been very busy at my job. I still like the hotel. I've met a young man. His name is Martin. His parents come from Ireland and he grew up in Cambridge. We spend time together when we are both off work. He's teaching me about the city. It's nice to have a beau. I see Kate sometimes after Mass. I know she has told you about Martin. I hope you and William and the children are fine and happy on the farm in Dover. It is difficult to get the time to get out to see you.

Love, Bridget.

I didn't think that was much of a letter. I already knew more about Martin from Kate. I would talk to Mary Anne when we saw each other on Sunday after Mass. I suppose I had some idea of getting Bridget to come stay with us for a while, or at least for a visit. I really wanted to talk to her in person. I didn't know quite what to think of Martin being much older than her and married before.

"Mr. Pierce owned the property on Farm Street in Dover. It was called the Pierce Estate. He lived in the big house when he came to the country. A Boston businessman, he brought clients out and they would be sent home with fresh produce, butter and eggs. Pa worked for him as foreman and we lived in the cottage. There were two barns. One had cows, the other Mr. Pierce's collection of antique horse carriages, which he wanted to display. They came down on rope elevators. Every Sunday, Pa had orders to take a carriage out and we went to Saint Edward's Church in Medfield, Pa sitting outside on the driver's seat, Ma and us on the inside. Pa was always out in the rain. The carriages were all very fancy, covered with oilcloth with windows in the back and kerosene lamps. Pa would take the same shortcut every Sunday, through a farm where no cars were allowed, saving about five miles. Pa and the farmer would always have the same joke. The

old man would say to Pa, 'Do you think it's going to rain?' And we would all laugh."

"I have an idea of what the house looked like. My earliest memory of the cottage is in the cellar where I first learned how to spell s-t-o-v-e. It was printed on a carton on top of the furnace, really, it said "stove lining" and it was my first spelling lesson."

~Bill Bennett, Age 90

CHAPTER 22

Life in Dover (1917)

I lost the baby. It was early days and still a dream, but I felt so sad. We had the doctor from town when the pains came, but, really, there was nothing he could do. William made me comfortable. I was up and around the next day. My husband tried to make things easy for me but I didn't need much help and when I saw him looking so sad, I just felt worse. I think it is better we find a way past this. The only one I let know about it was Mary Anne in a letter. I told her not to come. I did carry the pain around in my heart, though. But the doctor saw nothing wrong, so our family could still grow.

June came, then July. Summer days on the farm are long and pleasurable except for the heat and the bugs. Our cottage was near the woods. We could take relief, though, under the trees and at the brook. I would take the children there to wet their feet. Usually, they would get wet all over. I would take their two little wet bodies back for their naps. I insisted on naps. Every day. We had a screen door that helped keep some of the bugs out.

I tended the garden daily; rows of pole beans, beets, carrots, onions and, of course, potatoes. We ate all our vegetables yellow with butter. That was another chore, churning the butter. I would wait until the heat of the day had begun to diminish before my outdoor job, weeding. The children would be near me. Soon, William would come in with the cows for their five o'clock milking. Then we would all go in for supper and then, early to bed.

The children go barefoot in the summer. I go without stockings and have not worn corsets since I worked as a maid in Dorchester. That's five years now. It seems, now, like another life. I do sew every day. There are some things can be done sitting down. I walk, if not to the brook, then into the shady woods where we pick wildflowers. I don't know all their names. William told me about black-eyed Susans and lady slippers found in the deeper woods. I have found where the blueberries grow.

Now, every Sunday, we go to church in one of Mr. Pierce's very fancy old carriages. The seats are covered in oilcloth. There are windows in the back and kerosene lamps. The children and I sit back in comfort with a top over us, while William sits up high. He takes a shortcut across farm-land where cars are not allowed. After Mass, we get an ice cream cone in town. The children love that. I think it will be one of their memories as they get older; the carriage ride to church and the treat every Sunday. I am expecting again. I am feeling fine and refuse to worry. Anyway, I have too much on my mind with Bridget.

Our Kate called me one afternoon on the telephone we have in the kitchen. I will never forget the sound of her voice after the operator put her through. When she gave me her news, I did hope that no one was listening in.

"Ellen?" I heard, "Is that you?" Her voice was loud. I could not believe I was speaking to my sister all the way in New York City.

"It's Kate. My employers said I could call. I told them to take it out of my pay."

I didn't care about that. I just wanted to know what was wrong. And then, as though it was simply a social call, she added, "Are you keeping well?" Well, I just wanted her to get to the point. "It's marvelous," she continued, still on her subject. "I just gave your number to the operator and there you were!"

I couldn't take anymore.

"Kate, why have you called?"

Then there was a short silence. I was afraid we'd been disconnected and I might have to call the operator myself.

"It's about our Bridget. She came to see me last week. She's expecting a baby."

I felt my mouth go dry. All I could think of was Kate's words. I could hear my children's voices
in the background.

"Is she all right" I asked.

"Yes, Bridget is fine and healthy."

"Are they getting married?"

"Yes, they are, Ellen. What did you think?"

"I want her to come to us." That was immediate, that thought, I didn't have to think of it at all. "You have your work, Kate."

Again, a short silence. I waited.

"Bridget may have other ideas about where she has this baby, Ellen," said Kate. "Be prepared for that. We're to meet after Mass on Sunday. We'll go have tea."

I didn't know what she meant by "other ideas" and told her so.

She didn't respond to that. "I will write you after I see her and Martin on Sunday. Wait for my letter before you write to Bridget and then hold your tongue. She needs us now, even if she doesn't entirely know it. She's young, you know. But do talk to Mary Anne."

So then we said our goodbyes. I didn't want this call to cost her too much. But I knew we both had more we could have said. I was in a state. Kate was right about waiting to write to Bridget. I would not wait, though, to tell William. I told him when he came in for supper.

"Kate told me Bridget is expecting a baby." I told him.

His eyes opened wide at that. The children were busy with their play.

"Martin will do the right thing." said William. I saw that it was a statement, in no way a question.

"I know he will," I told him. "But no real plan has been made yet. Bridget has only just told Kate."

At that, he looked around. "When did you get the letter?"

"Kate called me on the telephone," I answered him.

He looked amazed but quickly moved back to the subject of Bridget. "She can stay here, you know," he told me.

"Yes, but plans have not been made yet. Kate promised to let us know more in a letter next week."

William nodded, but I could tell the news had just knocked all other concerns out of his mind, like a stone dropped into a calm pond.

I wrote a letter to Mary Anne. I didn't want to wait to talk to her until Sunday after church.

Dear Mary Anne. I hope you are all well. Kate called me from New York yesterday. Imagine the shock when her voice came on. Well, it's all about our Bridget. It seems that she and Martin have put the cart before the horse. She is expecting a baby. She went to see Kate at her work. There are no plans made yet except that they will get married. I would like Bridget to come to us. William, of course, is fine with it. But Kate cautions that Bridget may have her own plans. Martin will make her a good husband. Kate will write to me next week.

Love, Your sister, Ellen

I waited for Kate's letter and it came mid week after me watching the mailbox for several days.

Dear Ellen, Bridget and Martin will get married in November. I have already taken her to the doctor. She is not that far along yet. I have urged them to come to you in Dover, where they can get married around family. I would come, too. Martin's parents are only in Cambridge and could travel out. She is thinking about it. I am keeping an eye on her. Bridget is very independent, as I don't have to tell you.

Love, Your sister, Catherine

I shared Kate's letter with Mary Anne.

Each month Bridget would write to both of us about her health. One day, this letter came.

Dear Ellen, I am hoping you can share this letter with Mary Anne. We will come to you to be married early in November. I will stop working at the hotel then. I am in good health but feeling tired all the time. I rest when I can. The weather has been nice. We go walking, Martin and me. He takes good care of me. I wish I could sew better and my knitting is worse. Anyway, I can't be making little things when it is still a secret. I've only told my good friend Mary, and she'll tell no one.

Your loving sister, Bridget

I wrote to Bridget. We wanted the date they would be coming to us, so we could arrange to publish their notice of intent to marry here in Dover. Then the church needed to be informed. I'd have no trouble with Father about that. He knew us well enough.

Dear Ellen, I am so excited. We will arrive on the first of November. Kate and I will come out to you in Dover and Martin will go to his parents in Cambridge. I know the wedding is on the third. We will all be so happy. I can't wait to see you all. Your little sister is getting married!"

Love, Bridget

Why would Bridget being so perfectly happy make me a little grumpy?

On the day of their wedding, of course, the weather was beautiful, even for November, almost balmy. Bridget looked lovely and Martin very handsome. He is much older than her. Maybe that is a good thing. They stood before the priest at St. Edwards and said their vows. William and I were witnesses. Then we came back to the house where Mary Ann and Kate had set up the refreshments. We toasted them with last summer's dandelion wine. Everyone was pleased with how things had turned out. A baby is always a blessing. The next morning they were off back to New York where Martin had taken rooms for them, not far from his work at the hotel.

In February, William and I welcomed another little girl into the family. We called her Genevieve. I believe we will call her Jenny, for short. I wrote to the parents. They did know we would be greeting another little baby in the spring. Bridget had written to them about her marriage to Martin.

We heard today. I knew when the telephone rang, it must be Kate. "Bridget has a little girl, Margaret. I think that's after Martin's mother," I had to sit down. I felt both relief and joy and like crying. Kate, too, had a happy tear in her voice. I stood on the front steps to call William from the barn. Alice and Billy were now five and three years of age. And our baby was five months of age.

We heard from Bridget. She and Martin have decided to move to Dover, at least for the time being. They have some small savings. It was Martin's intention to get work on a farm. I immediately wrote back to her after William did a little searching, with the information there was a house down the road from us where they took boarders. William thought he could get Martin work on a dairy farm.

Bridget is coming!

CHAPTER 23

Dover Spring-Summer-Fall (1919)

That spring, the birds were back singing, and winter was not coming back. The days were longer. We would be welcoming a new baby soon. But this year, my pregnancy was giving me a little trouble. I did not feel myself. I was uncomfortable and very tired. Of course, I did have the care of three young ones and Jenny was still a baby. William helped and Alice did her best, but she was only just turned six years old herself. She could be counted on to watch her sister for short periods of time, which was good because Jenny did get around. I needed to know where Billy was all the time because he had the run of the farm with some rules which he was known to break, going too far, for instance, without telling me. I would panic if I couldn't locate him, even for a few minutes. He would always answer eventually.

One afternoon, after a particularly miserable day, William came in and found me crying, which was not like me at all. The children were wide-eyed. William fixed eggs that night for supper and sent me to bed early, doing the cleaning up himself. The next day, I felt a bit better. Alice never left my side, and even Billy was more in evidence than usual. I finally sent him out to play.

Well, William wrote to his mother without telling me. When her letter came back, he shared it with me.

My Dear Willow, Of course, Ellen and the children can come to us near when the baby is due in May. We will get Doctor White, the same as when Billy was born. I will be so happy to have the children around and their grandfather will, too. Also, your Aunt Tressie is delighted. We will get to see another grandchild born in this house. Show this letter to Ellen. Give her my love. I am concerned for her health. Write again, but I expect to see you in a few weeks.

Love, Mother

I cried a little with relief. A few weeks later, I packed us up, and we all got into a buggy for the trip to Lincoln. A while later and we were all piling out to a big welcome. I was told to rest, and I did, helping with small chores, though, because I am not one to recline. Alice remembered the house very well, and she and Billy ran around. I put them in charge of their small sister and they did a good job.

Aunt Tressie came to visit. We gave her Jenny. She was also happy to welcome another baby.

George was born on May 28, just a week after we arrived in Lincoln. The doctor came. I found a way to phone William at the farm to let him know the baby had arrived. William arrived the same day, after our friend, the grocer promised him a few days of feeding and milking the cows. William and I held our George all that night. He was little with soft, black hair that I hoped would curl. I forget each time how tiny a new baby is. He made our Jenny look immense. Alice was very pleased. She wanted to hold him all the time and watched me give him a bath in the kitchen sink. She handed me the towel and then watched me diaper him. She laughed when he wet straight up in the air before I could catch him with a diaper.

After a few days, we went home. As Amelia handed me the baby, I gave her a big look of gratitude. Every baby should have such a beginning, and every family such a welcome. I felt myself again, in control even with this small brood of children. William just looked pleased.

It had all gone his way. Aunt Tressie loved George. It seemed that whenever I was not holding him, she was. Tressie told me this little boy seemed special to her. She thought she'd seen him smile, even though he was just days old.

Jenny didn't care much about the baby. She noticed when he cried, though, I'd put her in with Alice. George had the cradle in our room and Billy his own room for a while. We had a simple Baptism at the church and coffee and sweets afterward at our home. Bridget was the godmother and William's friend Eddie, the godfather.

Billy wanted his new brother to be big enough to play with him. I told him it will take a long time. Another year after this one, and Billy would go to school. Unlike his sister, he was not interested in writing his name when I provided pencil and paper, although he liked words and numbers. He had too many things to do. I supposed the teacher would tame him.

Sometimes we had company. William's brothers came sometimes by horse and wagon, and most times with the older folks. I loved that. Those were special occasions. They could be a loud bunch, his brothers. They were big now, young men, all of them. The older girls had beaus and didn't always come, except for Florence, who was still too young. The men would walk the farm with "Willow," commenting on crops and livestock. Billy would go with the men, sometimes getting a ride back on someone's shoulders. I hoped they knew he listened to every word they said, storing it away for later.

Alice would stay at the house with us. She liked spending time with her young Aunt Florence. The babies would be admired, and each spent a lot of time in someone's lap. George remained special to Aunt Tressie, who would cuddle him as he seemed to be listening to her. Jenny would be bursting with excitement. She was delighted with her grandparents, who paid her lots of attention. All the Bennetts loved babies, including the men, who would jiggle one in their arms while pacing back and forth or toss one gently in the air. The little ones went right to sleep after the company left, all worn out.

I hardly remembered the summer, it went by so fast, so busy I was with a new baby and tired from the heat and all the activity now with the other children to look out for. They were good, but Billy needed watching and Jenny must be supervised, and Alice was very creative in her projects, busy all the time. William was always helping, but he had the farm chores, too. I fell into bed each night and went right to sleep after my long days, sometimes even before I said my prayers. Alice started school in September. She was six years old. Four-year-old Billy had helped milk the cows early that morning, his first time. He got some attention for that. George was just four months of age. He was round and jolly and watched everything. I was still nursing him, but he'd started on food. Jenny was one year and seven months. She just whirled happily around all day, but Alice was our star. On that first day, we all stood at the end of the lane waiting for the school barge to come. Alice wore a pretty blue dress and new shoes and carried a bag with her lunch in it. She had never been away from me all day. Finally, we heard the wagon come down the road and it stopped right at the end of our path. The driver smiled and asked, "Does Alice Bennett lived here?" Alice was astonished. Her father lifted her up. She quickly took her seat next to another girl and waved goodbye.

We watched it roll away. It was a big wagon with bench seats, so all the scholars sat facing each other. The driver was up high. It was pulled by two horses. I wondered how the wagon would make the corners. William pointed out how it was made about the same width of a buggy. Then I wondered how it would get through the snow. "Different barges," he informed me, "like big hay wagons, but with runners."

Then, Billy turned to me where I stood holding the baby, and asked, "When will Alice be back?"

I stood there with the baby and signaled to William to chase his small daughter who was running away from us.

"After lunch, Billy, in the afternoon."

I eyed William.

"Billy," I said, "I think Papa could use some extra help today." I looked over at William, who had returned with a squirming Jenny. He nodded.

"Come with me, Billy. I need help today" Billy looked very pleased. "First you'll help me see to the cows in the pasture, check some fences, and after lunch, we'll muck out the barn." I could tell by the look on Billy's face, these were all unexpected treats. So, Billy spent the whole morning with his father doing chores, which I suppose took longer with the lad just having turned four years of age. He was a fast learner, though, and strong though small.

At lunch, Billy made a big show of scrubbing his hands at the sink just like William and drying them on the towel put there for that purpose. I set out the bowls of stew.

"He worked hard," William told me with a big smile. "We are going to work on the milking. One cow seems to like to fool around." William's expression told me there would be a story about that later, just for me. The hours after lunch until Alice returned home went rather quickly. I was busy with the baking while the babies napped. Billy did help his father muck out the barn. They cleaned up again. At three o'clock, we heard a wagon coming. We all rushed down the path. William carried his two youngest. Jenny kept calling out, "Alice!, Alice!" The barge stopped and Alice hopped down from the open door, waving away at the other girl she'd sat with and calling "goodbye" to the driver. She rushed over to us. I could tell she was very tired, but still excited from her day.

"I love school." Those were the first words out of her mouth. William and I both grinned at that. Alice continued. "I have a pencil and crayons at school, and a book to read." She paused. "You have to be quiet and listen to the teacher. Some of the children are big, too." Then she looked directly at Billy. "We have milk and graham crackers in the morning. The milk comes in little bottles with straws, and we each get two crackers." That got her little brother's attention. "We have recess. That's when you go outside to play. We have swings. We eat our lunch there, too." She screwed up her face. "I expect not when it rains or snows. But there's a stove in the room to keep us warm. The teacher writes on a blackboard with chalk." Billy had no understanding of that at all.

"Alice will explain it all to us," I announced, "But now we are going to have milk and cake and tea for us." Billy was off like a shot. He knew we usually had bread and butter. This day was a good one, even if his sister had gone off to school and left him.

"I helped Papa," we heard him say as they ran together into the house. "I milked a cow!"

"We only kept cows for milking. One cow, a wise guy, would grab the top of my head. Pa would have to take care of the milking. We had supper after the milking, which was the most important thing."

~Bill Bennett, Age 90

CHAPTER 24

Year of Winter Census and Summer Storm (1920)

Woodrow Wilson was president. The war was over two years now. William had had to register for the draft but had not been called, nor had Martin or Frederick. There were four children in our family.

He came and took the census one cold day in January. I sent Billy to go get his father in the barn. I had the census-taker sit down at the table and after he removed his coat, poured him a cup of coffee. I heard William come in, stomping his feet on the storm porch. The children were gathered around, very attentive to this official-looking man in our house, wearing a tie, addressing me as Mrs. Bennett. I sat with a staring baby in my lap, while the man got his papers in order. He carefully placed an ink bottle on the table and took pen in hand. William sat at the other end of the table.

"We'll start with Mr. Bennett, full name, age, and place of birth, please."

"William John Bennett, age twenty-nine, born in Braintree, Massachusetts," said William quickly.

"I'm William, too," chirped up Billy.

I shushed our son with a finger to my lip.

"Your parents, sir, and places of birth."

"William Henry Bennett and Amelia Delory, born in Nova Scotia."

I saw him write, "Canada."

"Do they speak English?"

"Yes."

"What is your occupation?"

"Farm overseer."

"Is that for a private family?"

"Yes, I work for Mr. Pierce."

Then it was my turn.

"Your full name, please, age, and place of birth."

"Ellen Flood, age thirty-two, born in Rathcaled, County Westmeath, Ireland." Alice noted that bit of information.

I saw that he just wrote "Ireland."

I went on because I knew what he wanted. "My parents are John Flood and Anne McCormick, speak English and live in Ireland."

"When did you emigrate?"

"1904." That went onto the page, too.

"Are you a citizen?"

"Yes."

"When were you naturalized?" was the next question.

"I became a citizen in 1912 when I married." That was easy to answer.

He didn't ask for my occupation. I suppose because he saw the children all around us. That would be my occupation, that and house-keeping.

Next came the names and ages of the children. He looked around a bit wearily, and I poured him some more coffee.

I took some pride that they were all born American citizens.

"Alice is six," I told him, "William is four, Genevieve is," I thought for a minute, "one year and eleven months, and George is eight months of age."

The man took out a small leather book and determined that William had paid his poll tax. He prepared to leave after putting the papers into a bag. Then he turned to me and asked if I had a sister two houses away, named "Bessie," married to Martin Donlon.

"Yes," I replied, and then a bit of wickedness got into me. "But her birth name is Bridget."

He looked a little surprised. "But she goes by Bessie now, so that's what I put down for the census. It is very important to give the correct information." I let him know I agreed. William was shaking his head at me. Our census taker said no more about it.

In February, we celebrated Jenny's second birthday. I don't want to say she is a wild girl, but she does run around with her brother Billy a lot. He gets her going, but she also has her own ways of getting into trouble. She would turn the house into a trash heap if I let her have her way entirely. She entertains us, though. She's a happy child. Alice came home with red paper hearts from school and told us all about the glories of Valentine's Day. She cut out lots of hearts for us. I was picking up scraps of paper for days. I can't wait for the spring when they can go out.

Alice turned seven years old the end of March. She announced that she was almost in second grade, a big girl now. Billy looked a bit jealous. He has another year before he even starts school.

I got my wish for spring. The warm May days were marvelous. After these harsh winters, spring with its budding green leaves and flowers is so welcome. And it comes before the punishing heat of summer. Our little George turned a year old at the end of May, right near the anniversary of our marriage. We were wedded for eight years, William and me.

Summer came with the fourth of July, which was rather quiet on the farm. We had no fireworks, but one hot summer night thunderstorms moved in. I sat at the kitchen table with my holy candle and my book, and rosary, to keep my mind off the terrible crashes as the storm came right over us. Lightening was making the whole sky as bright as daylight. I could clearly see the farmyard, and hear the noise of the thunder, one boom, right after another. The children were asleep. William had gone up to bed. I'd appointed myself guardian of the house. I did not know how he could sleep through it.

I said a prayer and just then an ungodly crash of thunder came, so loud, I jumped up. I thought lightening must have struck very close. There was a loud crack and I saw flames. I could clearly tell one of the barns was on fire. I screamed for William, who was already on the way downstairs with the baby in his arms and the other children tumbling down the stairs behind him. He handed George to me and ran out the door. I grabbed Jenny under my other arm. Alice and Billy followed me out the door. We all ran quickly in our bare feet and nightclothes away from the house.

William shouted to me to get the children to Mr. Pierce's big house for safety. The cows were already out and he was leading our horse out of the barn. "I don't know when the fire brigade will get here," he shouted. A few minutes later, the rain started to come down hard. Billy called out he was drowning as we ran through the pounding rain. Lights had come on at the house, so they knew we were coming. I looked back to see that the other barn did not seem to be on fire, but the first one was still burning despite the rain.

I went into the house with the children. Some of the staff was there, and the children were welcomed and wrapped in blankets. Soon they were being spoiled with attention and milk and cookies. But I stood at the door, hugging George in my arms and watching William. I wished he wouldn't stay so close to the burning barn. He moved away just as wood began to crash down. He saw me standing there. "All the animals are out," he yelled across the road. "Tell Alice I saved the kittens." His voice was hoarse.

Finally, they sounded the fire horn. It seemed like a long time before the engine came. Men jumped out, but it was too late to save the barn. It was gone. They sprayed water out of the hoses on the remaining fire and then embers. There was no use for the long wooden ladders. Our cottage, though, was intact, and the other barn. It was a long night before William would let us go back home. We knew how lucky we were that the house had not been struck and the fire had not spread. The firefighters stayed all night. Back home, I made them tea and coffee and in the end, gave them breakfast. They had worked hard. In the morning William called Mr. Pierce. It was not the barn with the old carriages that had burned down, and so the animals were moved in there. I don't think I caught my breath for days.

The children just saw it as an adventure. The men came back the next day and helped William clear the rubble. A few days later, Billy was riding his prized metal car up and down the cement floor, all that was left of that barn. We would smell smoke for weeks. These things happen in the country, I know. Mr. Pierce will come for an inspection, but will probably not rebuild the barn we lost. I will never forget that night. We could have lost our family. I do not dwell on it though. I've said my prayers of thanksgiving. William, too, is grateful it was not worse.

"The barn burned down one night when it was struck with lightening. The firemen could see the fire but waited until the call came in to know what country road to go down—a volunteer fire department. A wrong road in the country could have left them miles from where they wanted to be. That night they brought us kids up to the mansion in the heavy rain and I remember calling out, 'I'm drowning.' They spoiled us with milk and cookies. After the barn burnt down, the cows were simply moved to the other barn. It was never rebuilt. I drove a toy car with ropes attached to the axle up and down the empty cement corridors where there had once been cows and horses. I backed my car into the driveway like a truck driver."

~Bill Bennett, Age 90

CHAPTER 25

Fall-Winter (1920)

Alice was breathless with anticipation on this first day of school. We had managed to find her a small book bag which she grasped tightly in one hand. She left for school on what they call a "motorized barge." No more horse-drawn wagons. William said it was a Ford Model T. So, we no longer listened for the clop-clop of horses. Instead, we had our ears open to the sound of a motor car. We watched Alice squeeze in next to a friend on one of the long bench seats. A few lucky children sat up front with the driver. And much to my surprise and relief, because some of the boys and girls seemed quite big, an adult rode as monitor. It was a nice day, so the canvas window curtains were rolled up. I suppose they fasten them down in wet or cold weather. We waved goodbye. Billy looked jealous. I'd send him if I could, but then his papa would miss his worker. Alice came home in the afternoon quite full of herself as she sat herself down at the table to do her homework. Billy looked at that and stomped off outside, saying he had important things to do.

The Norfolk Hunt Club was right next door to our farm. Billy could see it from his bedroom window. The day of the hunt, we stood in front of our cottage and watched the men in their red coats fly by us on their powerful horses. I had to admit it was a beautiful sight. Billy was the most enthralled by the proceeding. I think he pictured himself riding like them. He wondered about the fox, though. His father would not tell him. Once a year, the club put on a spread for all the farmers to thank them for letting them ride across their fields. Tables were set up in a field nearby and all the food was free which delighted, especially, the children. They ran around all day. I noted Bridget's daughter, Margaret, running with her cousins.

I see the day clearly in my memory. I stroll with my babies and take the opportunity to talk to other women. William chats with the other farmers. Wooden huts are set up, one for "sweet cider" and the other for "hard cider." I treat myself to a little of the last and enjoy it immensely. It is a cool fall day outside when the sun shines on all like a final blessing before winter. I drink in the fresh air, feeling happy inside and pleased with my life. I store it away for later that day and its feelings.

Winter was hard and long. William went out in the dark morning to feed the cows and most times, Billy went with him, sometimes walking on the crust of the snow. They let the cows out even when there is lots of snow on the ground because they need exercise. The cows don't mind it, trudging through the snow. Sometimes the silly animals lay down in the snow. Of course, they were back in the warm barn by nightfall.

By early December, I'd formed all my ideas for Christmas. Alice and Billy knew enough to be excited. The others, still babies, picked up on the happy mood. I sang all day, lots of Irish carols and ballads. William would join in. George was toddling around now. Jenny had to be watched constantly that she not discover the hiding places for the few gifts we had for them. She was cunning, that one. Meanwhile, I put my plans into execution. For the girls, I sewed cloth bodies for the doll heads we sent for from Sears and Roebuck. Also, we had an iron car for Billy. He was fascinated by anything that had wheels. William had made George a small wooden wagon, the wheels from the catalog. George was a sweet baby, seldom crying, almost always smiling. Of course, we spoiled him. We'd been blessed with healthy children. I knew it was not always so.

The day before Christmas, William took Alice and Billy into the woods to pick out our Christmas tree and came back with some gar-land, too, for draping around the house. I wasn't particular about the tree, but each year it was a good one. On the evening of Christmas Eve, we would light the little candles on the tree. And in each window, too, a candle to light the way of the Holy Family. There were buckets of water everywhere. Billy said with awe, "The candles never go on fire."

We put them to bed early. When they got up in the morning, I gave them their breakfast in the kitchen. The parlor door was shut tight. Pa had something to do in the barn. Then we heard a door bang and William came back. He opened the door and Santa Claus had come! The gifts were under the tree.

We went to Mass. The church was all decorated and full of strong, soaring organ music and the sound of joyful voices. Our Christmas morning was full of joy and resplendent with all the beauty of this sacred day. Bridget came over with Martin and their little Margaret for dinner. We had our meal and sat at the table a long time, the grown-ups, while the children ran around us. Then we had music. William played the harmonica and we sang and danced. I will always have a picture in my mind of George banging his little feet to the music and turning around and around until he fell down like a little drunk and was carried off to bed. We were blessed.

"A lady drove us to school in a beach wagon with a bunch of other kids. There weren't many ladies driving back then, so this lady, she was ahead of her time."

"The Norfolk Hunt Club was right next door to the farm. Once a year, men in red coats would ride through all the farms, like a steeplechase, jumping the walls and chasing the fox. Pa would never tell me if the dogs were allowed to catch the fox or not. Once a year, to thank the farmers for permitting them to ride over their fields, the hunt club would put on a spread. Tables would be set up in a field and all the food was free which delighted all the farm kids in the area. Two wooden huts would be set up; one would say 'hard cider' and the other 'sweet cider.'"

"In the winter, the weather seemed hard and long and it was dark in the mornings when Pa and I went out. Pa let the cows out even when there was snow on the ground because they needed exercise and they didn't mind it, trudging through the snow. Some of them even lay down in the snow. They stayed in the warm barn at night."

"I remember Christmas. I went with Pa to pick out the Christmas tree. It was on the property. And we would pick garland too, green, to be draped around the house. The tree had real candles the size of birthday candles. And they didn't go on fire. On Christmas Eve we would have candles in all the windows and water buckets everywhere. We would go to bed early and in the morning, the parlor door would open and Santa Claus had come. The gifts, they would be under the tree. The biggest present I ever got was an iron truck that I could play around with. The girls got dolls that my mother made, sewing heads from Sears and Roebuck onto rag doll bodies."

~Bill Bennett, at age 90

CHAPTER 26

George

OUR CHILDREN

January went by quickly, and now we found ourselves in the month of February. I was weary of being in the house. The morning began with steady snow. I opened my kitchen door. By noon, the snow was blowing sideways like flocks of tiny birds thrust through the air, caught in the wind.

Another day and the storm still raged outside. Snow was stuck to the windowpanes. Morning light. The children were still sleeping. William came in from the barn. We were having a quiet breakfast together. I heard stirrings upstairs. Billy would be first down. He doesn't like to miss anything. We sipped our tea. The snow made the kitchen bright. The grocer wouldn't get out for days, but we had enough.

I shared some memories with William. We laughed at the story of my first time ice-skating with his sister's borrowed skates. I fell down and lost my dignity but learned to skate in one day. It was like dancing.

We sat together comfortably. He reached out a hand to touch my face. Then Billy came scrambling down the stairs and George called from his crib. Our quiet time was done.

The children got sick with colds. They got better and had begun to run around the house.

George, though, was still quiet, and he developed a troubling cough and a bit of a fever. I'd been sitting with him in my lap most of the day. He was not yet two years of age. We'd warmed up soup now, for supper, three nights in a row. Jenny had run a fever one night and kept me up, but it was gone by morning. I was up with George every night. I'd not been able to keep his fever down. I didn't like his breathing or his cough.

William called the doctor. He came in the afternoon. George didn't even show much interest, listless, he was. Doctor said we should keep him warm, give him water to drink, and take him into the bathroom with a pot of boiling water. The steam would help him breathe. It helped a little. But he did not get better.

Billy would eye me sometimes. He was not used to not getting any of my attention. Alice minded Jenny. William kept to the house. I would only take a short nap while his papa held the baby. One day ran into the other. George got no better. Bridget came over to help me. The baby took no notice when we changed him from one lap to the other. She almost cried to see him so sick. I could not waste my time with tears.

I prayed to the Blessed Virgin Mary. One day, Mary Anne appeared. Bridget had called her. Only a week had gone by since George took sick. It seemed longer. The doctor came again. He looked very concerned after listening to the baby's chest. Doctor handed the baby to me and took William over to the table. I saw my husband shake his head, first, no and then yes. I knew it wasn't good. The crying stuck in my throat and the tears started in my eyes. My sisters looked the same.

William called me over after letting the doctor out.

"Ellen, Doctor says tonight there will be the crisis. We should do what we've been doing, but George is very sick. There is no medicine to help him. We should just stay with him and keep him comfortable. And pray," he added.

I did not want to hear this. I wanted to scream. The children stood hushed in the kitchen. They sensed that something was happening in this house and it had to do with our baby. They looked scared, and I could not help them.

My sisters stayed the night. We took turns holding George. William held him high on his shoulder to try to help him breathe. We wanted to breathe for him. We died a little each time he coughed. The night was long, but it was the last night George would be with us. William and I were both holding him when he passed. It was the worst moment of my life. I could hear the sound of my sisters praying. The others were asleep upstairs. They would not know until morning that their little brother was gone.

We would not put him down. His little body was quiet now, and he was gone to God. I knew that and had to accept it. Finally, William went upstairs and brought down his little crib, and we laid him in it with a blanket. I wanted him warm, and we stayed with him all night because he could not be alone.

In the morning the children came down. We explained how their little brother had been too sick to stay with us and had gone to God. He looked asleep. Alice went over to kiss him goodbye. Billy just stood there shocked. Papa's arm went around him. I picked up my Jenny and hugged her. She was the baby now.

Bridget went home, taking the children with her, and sent her husband Martin over. William knew what to do. He called the priest, who came right over to bless our baby. Then the men gathered quietly and talked. I could not hear all they said, but I did hear "burial." We had no money for a burial plot. We were a young family and had never thought of death. I went over to them. Father said we could bury George on the land of Medfield State Hospital, on the hill nearby, where, he knew, other babies were buried. Tomorrow he would say a Mass of the Angels.

Father gave us a few minutes to gather ourselves and then he prayed, all of us kneeling and making the sign of the cross at the end. Later that morning, I heard a cart outside. A knock on the door and a man's voice and William went outside with him. I heard them unload something and saw William carrying it to the barn. The cart left and William came in. "Ellen," he said, and his words choked a little. "The undertaker from town has brought us a coffin for George." I started to cry and so did William. It was a final, needful thing and a very kind gesture, but it sent us into new grief. Then our friend, Mr. Norton, arrived from town and busied himself with the cows. He came to the door before leaving and promised he would be back in the morning to do the chores.

People came quietly in to see us during that day. Bridget and Mary Anne and their families were there. My sisters served food and some drink. There is no jollity at a child's wake. The next morning, our family went in the first carriage with my sisters. The men followed in the cart with the casket. William carried the tiny box into church and we followed him in. I remember little of the Mass, but that Father wore white vestments. As we left, the bells did not toll, but rang in melody. We drove to the hill where George would remain forever. It was cold but not snowing, and not dark yet. That night, my eyes would keep going to the window, blackness behind it, and my baby on the hill.

We were changed after that. George's passing made us different. We would never expect all good things again. When you love a child and that child is taken, life is never the same.

The children tried comforting us in their own ways. Alice seemed to grow older overnight. Billy helped keep Jenny out of trouble. They were quieter than usual. Billy broke down in tears one day, confessing he'd been jealous of all the attention George was getting when he was sick. So, I had a crying little boy to comfort. My sisters came, bringing their children, making a full house, but at night, we were, again, left to ourselves.

Alice went back to school. I had a note from her teacher saying how sorry she was. My sister, Kate, in New York said she would arrange a visit soon. Her voice had faltered and stopped on the telephone. I told her it was all right, that I understood. My mother sent such a letter to me, I wept all day. My father was heartbroken at the news. They prayed for us. Our old priest in Emper, said a Mass for George Bennett and sent a note and a holy card. Billy perked up gradually, but I'd see him looking sad sometimes. This was the first sorrow in the children's lives.

A few weeks passed. Amelia and Aunt Tressie Bennett arrived one day with the girls. They were so kind. After we got over the initial sadness of their visit, we talked naturally about our loss. Aunt Tressie who had said small George was special, even as an infant, led the way, in the cold, up the hill to the little grave. I was ready. When we came back, we had hot tea to warm us.

It's been a long winter. I feel frigid when I open the door. The snow stands firm, hard and icy. Our George is buried under it. I cannot conceive of a spring without our baby who left us in this cold, white winter. How can spring come now, all warm, green and sunny? There will always be a winter in my mind. My little one only saw one spring.

"When I was four years old, my little brother died. George was just a baby, but I remember playing with him. When he got sick, I was jealous of the attention he was getting. I felt guilty after. He had pneumonia and when the crisis came, he died. There were no miracle drugs back then."

~Bill Bennett, at age 90

CHAPTER 27

Come Spring

"Come spring," announced Alice, "I will be eight years old." And then she looked over at me with a side-glance, because she sees my sadness. It had not yet been two months since we lost George.

I hugged her and called her "my big girl." March was cold and rainy. My mother sent me a letter with a pressed shamrock inside of it for Saint Patrick's. It brightened my day. In Ireland, we would go to church. Here, I say a quick prayer and tell the children all about the saint and the meaning of the shamrock. I hold it in my hand for them to see. This precious one in its letter goes safely on the shelf. We had a cake for Alice's birthday on thirty-first March, as we always do.

Early in April, I sent Alice and Billy across the way to the large, green lawn in front of Mr. Pierce's big house. They picked dandelions for the wine William would make for his brothers when they came to visit. William became more like his father every day. I would look out the window from time to time to see them; Alice in her little straw hat and Billy bending down to pull his socks up. They made a picture. I noticed them glancing at the road sometimes, as though they were watching for vehicles of one kind or another. After a while, they came running home with a basket full of dandelions. I noticed them looking out at the road.

"What's wrong?" I asked.

They looked at each other. Alice spoke first. "It pro-b-shun," she said. I had her say it again, but still I did not understand. Billy looked at her as she said it. I asked her to explain. "It means it's against the law to make wine," she answered. I hadn't known she was aware of Prohibition. Billy shook his head in agreement.

"We kept watching for the police because we could get arrested," he said solemnly. "Papa is going to make wine."

I knew I couldn't laugh because they were, in a sense, right, but I also knew no one was going to come after us for our bit of home-made wine.

I made up my mind. "First, you will not be arrested," I said. They looked relieved at that. "And it's only a bit of wine and we're not selling it." They nodded. "You can talk to Papa about it." That seemed to satisfy them for the time being.

William looked surprised when they informed him of his breaking of the law, but kept from laughing, which made me proud. He rubbed his head and after about a minute, told them they should not worry. He would never let them be taken, and anyway children could not be arrested. He would take responsibility for the small amount of wine he made. Also, he would tell the uncles not to tell anyone when they went back home to Lincoln. So, that seemed to satisfy them, although I could tell Billy had more questions but was not asking them then.

Late April. Jenny, three years of age, does not understand where George was gone. The others tell her he's gone to heaven. I told them we would go pick wildflowers in the woods soon and put them on the grave. Billy and Alice liked the idea. "It might make us feel better," they told us. In a shady place on the hill, lily-of-the-valley had grown all over, showing their delicate white flowers and broad green leaves. Pink blossoms decorated the apple trees. William had marked the grave with a small wall of stones. We found some wild daisies and put them there.

May came, the month of our Blessed Mother. It is George's birthday. It would have been his second. The children picked sweet-smelling white lilacs, and we put them with water into one of my big glass canning jars. Papa climbed with us up the hill to place the flowers on the grave. It was sad, but still. It was a beautiful day, and we'd not miss him so much if we'd not loved him so.

I remember that day well. I look up at the blue sky and think of him. Jenny is singing. She says she is singing a song for her little brother. We smile. She likes that and gives us a dance, and we can't help laughing. Alice and Billy look at us in such a pleased way, it makes us realize how hard it's been on them. I propose cake and they run down the hill to the cottage. I give one last look, and we follow them down. I think something passed by that day. I don't know what. It was a feeling I had.

That summer, not a day passed that I didn't look up at the hill, now green, quite bathed in sun. I thought we would wear a path going up. One day, Jenny ran ahead on her small legs and for a few minutes, I could not find her. She was out of my sight and I called out her name, until Alice found her in a wild blueberry bush off the path, where she was picking and gobbling berries, her small face stained blue. I grabbed her tight. That was one change since George died, I was more fearful about my children.

Alice and Billy went picking blueberries from the high bushes in the woods behind the house. They were easy to pick. Some went for blueberry pie. They sold the rest, door to door, earning a little money which they kept in a dish. I let them spend their coins at the Grange Fair. We all went together. I had asked Billy what he was going to spend his money on. "Sweets," he said with some excitement. "I love cupcakes!" He is his father's son.

One day that summer, a farmer came around to our door. It seemed a doctor had been hired to take out the tonsils of all the farm children in our area. Evidently, fortunate children in the city had this done. It was modern, we were told, and free. We were given a date to bring the children to Mr. Pierce's big house, where the operations would be performed. William and I had several evening discussions and decided it was the right thing to do.

We told Alice and Billy they would be having their tonsils out, so they wouldn't get any more sore throats. Jenny was too young. They would go to sleep and when they woke up, we told them, their tonsils would be out, and they would have ice cream. Their father had already churned it, and it rested in the icebox. That morning, we walked them across the road. The doctor was in one room and there was a nurse at the door, in starched white cap and apron. No one smiled. All the parents were nervous.

Alice and Billy held our hands tight. When their turns came, they marched right in.

While we waited, we saw other children carried out, looking pale and sick. We worried. When Alice came out, she looked the same as them, and Billy, too. We carried them home. Their legs would not hold them up, and we put them right to bed. Their throats hurt bad, they told us, and they didn't like the ether. It made them sick. We took turns sitting up with them all that night. They were not ready for ice cream until the next day when I gave them nothing but ice cream, all they wanted. They soon got over it, but I didn't. I wondered if they would really not have any more sore throats. It bothered me for a long time.

It was a grand day when both Alice and Billy went off to school in September. They were ready early, both of them combed and washed and in their new school clothes. I'd had to make Alice new dresses and Billy had two new shirts and short pants. They ran to the car that took them to school and scrambled on. I stood there watching as they left. The quiet didn't last. Jenny was around me all day and asking, in her high voice, "When will Alice and Billy be home?"

William and I both looked around the house at the same moment for Jenny at lunch time, did not see her, and raced outside, calling her name. We found her headed to the bus stop. She looked so small. Jenny had a little bag in her hand and told us, "I'm going to school." I quickly carried her right to the house where I put her in the corner where she stayed, despite her papa giving me unhappy looks while glancing over at his darling younger daughter. I would not have her do that again.

Her brother and sister made their triumphant return in the afternoon after Jenny's nap. She was delirious with joy. They did play with her for a while. But, Alice, it seemed, had lots of homework. Billy claimed to have none, and we accepted that for now. He just wanted to get outside. That afternoon, Billy brought the cows in as usual, but this time, one young cow had become a bull, and chased him all the way in. I heard Billy running and shouting, and so did William, who ran the young bull into the barn where he tied him up. Billy was fine, just scared. So it was a memorable day for him. He boasted to his sisters at supper how fast he was to outrun a bull. Mr. Pierce arranged to sell the bull. We only had cows for milking.

As fall moved toward winter, I could not help thinking of the last holidays we had with our George. In my mind, I see a tiny boy dancing to the music from his father's harmonica. I see us all sitting around and clapping for our little performer. He was a happy child. I will never forget him. In my dreams, I still put him to bed at night upstairs in his crib. It is too soon for me to think of having another baby. William has said nothing about it. It could happen, though.

"Alice and I were sent to pick dandelions on the lawn of the big house. Pa would be making wine for his brothers when they came to visit. We kept watching the road because we thought we could get arrested because it was Prohibition. It was 1922."

"I also remember the Grange Fair. The whole family would go and we got to spend the money we earned picking and selling blueberries. We went into the wood behind the cottage and picked high bush blueberries, easy to pick. My mother made blueberry pie, and that was good, too. We also picked wild berries, but I don't remember taking them home. We ate them. I spent most of my blueberry money on sweets at the fair. Cupcakes were my favorite."

"A doctor was hired to take out the tonsils of all the farm children in the area. Operations were performed at the big house. They used ether. I remember spinning wheels. I suppose the doctor was a surgeon. I hope he was. I remember being carried home to the cottage. Not having any sore

throats after having your tonsils out is a lot of baloney. I had lots of sore throats."

"Cows were called bossies but one time, by surprise, a cow turned out to be a bull. The bull chased me all the way in. Next morning, someone came out and cut off his horns and put a ring in his nose. The bull was sold."

~Bill Bennett at age 90

CHAPTER 28

November Adventures

TRAVELERS

I sat in my chair in our little cottage parlor on the evening of All Saints' Day, wrapped in a shawl against the evening chill, with my stocking feet tucked under me. I had some sewing in my lap, but really no desire to work. William in the opposite chair seemed very interested in the newspaper that sometimes came with our grocery order. Finally, he got up and came over, the paper folded so he could show me something. He held it out and pointed to a notice with his finger. It seemed the S.S. Majestic, the largest passenger ship in the world, was coming to Boston in a little over two weeks. It was going into dry dock for repairs. It would remain there for three days and people could view it. "If you get there early enough," William said, "you could even see it come in. I thought I could spare the time to take Billy to see it."

Well, that was a lot to take in.

I thought quickly.

"It's not that I don't want Billy to have this treat, William," I told him. "But what about me and the girls?"

"You know I can't take young girls with me," he answered. "What would I do when they needed to go to the bathroom? There will be no facilities for women and girls. And Jenny is too small to go such a distance in a buggy? And, you don't really want to go?" He looked concerned. Well, I had sworn I would never again go near a big ship after the ride over fresh from Ireland to America, over eighteen years ago now. No, I didn't want to go.

But I was not ready to give in, not entirely. I quickly told him what I had been thinking recently. "I want to go see Mrs. Bernstein in Dorchester. I've not been since Alice was a baby and it's not the same, writing letters. You are not the only one who wants to get off the farm, William."

I think I surprised him a little bit. After all, he'd made a plan, but he recovered quickly and gave me one of his smiles. "I have no reason not to want you to go. We can manage the money for one trip. I can take you to the station one morning and pick you up in the late afternoon. Billy can stay with me." The man thought quickly.

So, William planned the day of their visit to the S.S. Majestic, and I wrote to Mrs. Bernstein about visiting two weeks hence. She wrote back days later to say she was happy and surprised, and would be delighted to see me again, and my girls, and to give her the day and time. I decided I would go on Monday, the thirteenth, two days before William's trip to Boston with Billy, when the ship was to come in. That meant both children would miss a day of school that week. But we both thought it important that our children learn about new things. We were modern that way.

A few nights later, we explained things to the children. First, Pa talked about the biggest ship in the world coming into Boston. Alice and Billy knew about Boston, little Jenny, nothing at all. Then he said he would be taking Billy to see it. "A long trip," he said, "in horse and buggy." Alice looked disappointed at that. There was no mention of her going. Billy, though, had gleaming eyes. So, I took over.

I looked right at Alice and said, "We will be going to Boston, too, on the train, a few days before, just you and Jenny and me." Alice's eyes lit up at the thought of going on the train to the city. She had no memory of going there before, although she'd been told of it. Jenny was only four and Alice was now nine years of age. The children knew I had come to America from Ireland with their Aunt Mary Anne. They knew I had worked as a maid for the Bernstein family in Dorchester until I married. Those little boys would be big boys in high school now.

Billy required more information from Pa. "A big ship is coming to Boston, Billy and you and I are going to see it in about two weeks. I've always been interested in boats and ships and I saw this in the paper. We will go and come back in one day, just like when your mother and your sisters go to Dorchester." Billy's eyes got wide at that. "The S.S. Majestic is the biggest ship in the world," Pa added. Never having seen a ship, our son had no ideas about them at all. I could see his father would be educating him.

William picked up a train schedule at Dover Station for me, at the little depot in the center of town. He made a point of taking Alice with him. When they returned a short time later, she flew in with the paper timetable. Papa had shown her how to read it. Well, it seemed we could leave at eight in the morning, getting an early start with the people going into work in the city. I would figure out the rest of it. Couldn't I just open my mouth and ask if I needed help? I would have enough coins with me to pay for the streetcars. The train tickets would be round trip. We could get them that morning.

I spent the next week sewing new dresses for my girls and lengthening their winter coats, perhaps a bit too warm with the mild weather we'd been having, but best to be prepared. I had my Sunday dress and a serviceable coat and gloves. I had my hat. I suppose they still wore hats in Boston? Our shoes were fine, and would get a good polish the night before we left.

The day came soon enough. We were all up at the dawn. Billy looked a bit forlorn, his eyes going over to his sisters. Jenny was jumping for joy. Alice looked almost ladylike in her best clothes. William rushed us into the buggy for the ride to the station. He did not want us to miss that train. I'd given the time for our return. I felt a little flustered, but didn't show that to the girls.

We all stood on the platform, our little group amongst all those people who rode the train every day. I had our tickets clasped in one hand. The girls leaned against me. As the train pulled in, whistle blowing, I thought Papa might have one of his girls at home, Jenny was so affected by the noise. I thought the train must seem to her, like a big mechanical monster with the steam coming out of it. I think she feared climbing into it. But she observed nobody else seemed worried. So, she pulled herself together and took my hand. Then, Alice surprised me by going over and giving her little brother a hug. He gave her one back, not their usual way. Papa wrapped his arms around both of his girls, and gave me a peck on the cheek, and up we went. I hurried us to a seat, and we waved out the window until we couldn't see them anymore. Jenny almost had tears, but soon was looking out the window, with her sister, at the woods and the little town centers, as we flew on toward Boston. The wheels went clackity-clack over the tracks, in a rhythm, like music, all the same. The engine rumbled. It was quiet inside with the windows closed to the cool November morning. But when the doors would open at a station we would hear the whistle and see the swish of the steam. My daughters looked out the windows with contentment. I found myself feeling very happy. Next, South Station.

At South Station, the doors opened and everyone rushed off. I sat with the girls for a few minutes, to let the crowd go, and then we walked down the aisle to the door where a nice porter lifted each little girl down, and then took my hand while I managed my skirt on the stairs. I thought to go right to the ticket desk to ask about streetcars. My city self was back. At that moment, as we left the platform and went into the center of the station, both girls reacted. Alice said, "This is the most beautiful place I have ever seen!" Her little sister, on the other hand, took my hand, looked up, and informed me in loud tones that she had to go to the bathroom. So, that was the first thing we did. As we entered that marble palace, Alice had her next, "most beautiful" moment. I thought this would keep up all day. I took care of Jenny, sent Alice in. When she came out, I told them, "Stand right there where I can see your feet and hold hands," and thus made my own visit. They did what they were told. When I came out, an old woman told me what nice and obedient girls I had. I said, "Thank you."

When we came out again into the grand station, our eyes went up to the ceiling. I saw white panels, each formed in a square, and then there were beams, too, and all of it together made it beautiful. I continued to look heavenward until Jenny took us back to earth by pointing out the pattern of little pieces on the floor. The word came to me, "mosaic." We were fascinated.

We looked around then and saw all the concessions. I loved the bouquets of flowers. There were tall stacks of fruit displayed in all their colors. I pulled their gaze away from the confections, knowing I had no money for candy. I exclaimed on the shiny granite of the walls and after that, the huge space. And did they know it went up for five stories?

People were bustling all around. The noise was tremendous. I pointed out the red caps hauling trunks and valises to and from the trains. Alice declared that when she grew up, she would travel by train and bring a big trunk and a valise. She thought she would travel to New York and stay with her Aunt Kate. Jenny said she'd go, too. I had a sudden memory of traveling all the way from Ireland with one small bag. Jenny was looking at the shoe-cleaning and polishing chair with a small lad not much bigger than her brother, briskly shining a gentleman's shoes. I explained. She looked down at her own tiny shoes and I said I thought I could manage to shine her shoes at home.

The ticket agent told me to walk downtown and get the train to the elevated at Washington Street, which would take us to Dudley Station, where I would get the streetcar to Grove Hall. I'd not planned on taking the El. It was new to me and I had a brief moment of regret or maybe panic. I'd made a plan to directly take the streetcar all the way to Dorchester and I don't like to change a plan, once made, but I told myself I could do this. We would be fine.

We crossed the busy street under the Atlantic Avenue Elevated to Summer Street, where we would begin our walk downtown. But first, I had them stand on the sidewalk and look at South Station with the big clock on top and the columns and huge arched openings. I wanted my daughters to get a sense of the size and grandeur of the railroad station. The girls were astonished by all the other big buildings and remarked on the noise. City streets were not in their experience. Jenny never let go of my hand and Alice stayed right by me. Jenny pulled back each time before we crossed a street. Alice waited for me and looked both ways, as I had instructed her. Jordan Marsh was still there where it had stood in my memory for years. Alice pronounced each store window "beautiful." I remembered all those years ago going in town with my friends on our maid's day out, passing through the big brass-trimmed door of Jordan Marsh and being called "ladies," although we had little to spend. I didn't have time to take the girls in now, as I was on a quest to get us to Dorchester, but I told myself there would be another time.

The man at South Station had told me to go downstairs to the Washington Street Tunnel at Summer and Winter Street. He said I was to stand on the Winter platform because that was southbound and would take us to Dudley. Downstairs, I checked my purse for coins. William had had me take extra from the jar. "Just in case," he'd said. I handed over my ten cent fare. I understood the streetcar to be five cents.

It was very noisy below, and Jenny covered her ears. I kept them away from the edge, but they could still look down into the depth from where we stand. A train came in on the other side, the northbound Summer platform first, making a great grinding noise as it came to a stop. Jenny looked like she might be losing her nerve, so I held her closer. I told them the people on the opposite platform were going somewhere else. I think this all was a little beyond Jenny.

It was not long before our train pulled in and we climbed on. At that point, Alice was talking about how exciting it was, but Jenny has been shocked into silence as the train moved out and up onto the tracks of the "El," as they call it. I think we were all amazed. Up so high, we could see the tracks ahead, winding before us. Below, we saw the tops of buildings and even into the high windows of people's homes.

I knew we had only two stops before Dudley Station; Dover and Northampton. I'd seen the map. Dover Station had a wooden platform like an island in the air, a noisy one. We were up above Washington Street. The girls were looking down from the windows. I showed them Holy Cross Cathedral across from the train, all gray and magnificent.

I'd been there once, long ago. It was Good Friday, and I'd gone with friends to say prayers. The inside was massive.

Northampton Station was next. After that, we saw the switching tower just before Dudley. They called it a pagoda because of its curved roof. Inside we could see a man sitting on a stool. Then, the train screeched around the grand curve into Dudley Station where we got off. The station is a twist of trains going and coming overhead. Below, the streetcars leave to go all over suburbs like Roxbury and Dorchester. The station itself is modern and majestic. Mahogany trim in the waiting room and windows with diamond shapes in them, and shiny brass trim everywhere. We looked up at ceilings that seemed to leap upwards, with hanging lights, and then glanced down at long, long platforms. Alice pronounced it "beautiful." Birds were swooping and chirping inside where they'd flown in from both open ends. That's when the bird poop landed on my hat, making both my girls laugh. I grumpily took out my handkerchief and wiped at it. So much for looking my best.

We found our streetcar right on ground level, paid our five cent fare and climbed on. I checked with the conductor that it was the right one and off we went. There were sights familiar to me, as we went down Washington Street, but there were also many more shops and buildings than before. I got the girls up from our seats well before our stop. It tickled me to hear Alice thank the conductor as we were getting off. He had a smile for her. It was pleasant hearing the trolley bells ring as we walked along. I remembered the sound well. A few short blocks and we were in the neighborhood, all neat houses and small front yards and then twenty-three Shafter Street, looking the same. We went around to the kitchen door, not out of any sense of place but because it was the way I always went in. For a moment, my thoughts had left my girls, and I looked quickly over at them. Alice had her company face on, while Jenny was looking a little tired and flushed from our rush to Dorchester. It was a lot for her to take in, and now another new experience. She had little understanding of who these people were, but she had not a shy bone in her body and would do fine.

A young girl answered the door right away. Had I ever been that young? I knew Kathleen had left to get married a few years ago, and, of course, Mrs. Bernstein had hired another Irish girl. Her name was Mary. She told me she came from County Galway, so nice to hear a voice so recently come from Ireland. She was pretty and friendly, and I hoped she was paying attention to what one could accomplish in America. I thought I might have a word later. Smiles all around and then, as if all that time hadn't gone by at all, I heard Mrs. Bernstein's voice calling out as she came into the kitchen from the sewing room.

"Do I hear Ellen? And who has she brought with her?" And with that, there she was, dressed neatly and nicely as usual, smiling and speaking in that clear, quiet voice I remembered. She took my hands in hers and we said a lot just by looking at each other. Old friends are like that. The girls remained quiet and attentive. Then she turned to them and said, "And who are these young ladies?"

It was my Jenny who answered first. "I'm Jenny and I'm four." And when that went well as Mrs. Bernstein seemed to be listening carefully. She added, "We came on the streetcar and before that, two trains, a big one and then one up high, from a long way away and it's taken all morning." And then, she added, "This is my sister Alice." And all that done, she began to take her coat off.

"I'm pleased to meet you, Mrs. Bernstein," offered Alice.

"And I am delighted to meet you both," said Mrs. Bernstein, reaching out to shake Alice's hand, and then Jenny's who had just taken herself out of her coat.

So, we all stood around, smiling while Mary put on the kettle for tea. I quickly looked around the kitchen and saw she was keeping it neat and it looked like a fresh cloth on the table. In my mind's eye, I saw William sitting there, eating his cake after he'd brought me back from a Sunday afternoon. I eyed the staircase to my old room. So many things had happened since then. Jenny didn't let it stay quiet for long. She announced she had to go to the bathroom, always a necessity with my youngest daughter, She sailed off with Mary upstairs. She came down a short time later to tell her sister she'd seen Mama's old bedroom and did she know Mama really lived here before, and it was a pretty room, too.

Mrs. Bernstein had made plans. Mary would bring us all tea in the sewing room and she would get to know the girls a little bit. I hoped they would remember their manners. Then, she continued, "With your permission, Ellen, Mary will take them for a walk to the park, it being a mild day, so you and I can have a visit, it being so long since we've had anything but letters between us." I nodded at that. The girls looked excited. They'd never been to a park before.

Mrs. Bernstein continued, "And then we'll all have lunch together." She looked over at me. "And we'll have a visitor who may surprise you, Ellen."

Tea went very well. Nothing spilled, napkins used and please and thank you offered. Mrs. Bernstein asked questions of the girls, and they were happy to reply. Jenny talked about the kittens in the barn. It seemed Alice had much to say about school and how she was a good speller and liked books. And then she mentioned her brother, Billy. At that, Jenny chirped up.

"We had another brother, George, but he went to heaven and we miss him." And then she went back to her bread and jam.

Mrs. Bernstein looked over at me. Of course, she'd known because I'd written her. Her expression told me we'd be talking about it later, as well as about happier times.

A few minutes later, Mary came in to get the girls and in a short time, had them all organized and out the door after their goodbyes. I had asked Mary to please keep an extra eye on Jenny, who could be very quick. Mary said she would. I was sure they would do fine. I turned to Mrs. Bernstein.

CHAPTER 29

Our Visit

Mrs. Bernstein poured fresh tea. "Your girls sound a bit like you, Ellen. And the older one, Alice, has your ways, I think. She would be your dependable child, but able to speak up for herself. The little one is, I believe, an original." I laughed when she said that.

Mrs Bernstein gave a sigh. "Ellen, I must talk to you about your little George. I was so upset when I got your letter. I cannot imagine what that was like, losing a child. I picture him as a miniature William with dark curly hair and a big smile."

"He was a sweet boy, and as you guessed, looked a lot like my William. For a while, after he died, I had trouble saying his name because his end would come into my mind, not his life. It will be two years next February." I stopped for a minute. "When George got so sick, my sisters came to stay and we were all there when he passed." At that point, both our eyes filled with tears, and our napkins were put to use drying our eyes. I went on. "He's buried up on the hill, but I really hold him in my heart. He only saw one spring." Mrs. Bernstein nodded, and her feelings showed in her eyes. I thought, then, that I might want to share my secret with her before the end of this visit.

Another sip of tea. "Ellen, I really think you should call me Anna."

Well, I didn't know what to do with that at first, but I thought, just for a minute, and decided I would like it and told her, "Yes, if you would like me to, but it won't be easy." I smiled, because it did feel right after all these years to call my friend by her first name as she did me.

We moved on. "I want to know about my boys," I told her. "Will I see them later?"

"They will make a point of coming right home from school this afternoon. They are not quite young men yet, but large boys. Benjamin, at fifteen, is the more serious one. He has made his Bar Mitzvah and did a fine job of learning the Hebrew. We were very proud of him. Randall is thirteen and a half. He's more lively, has lots of friends, and I need to keep track of him. They are both good students. They sometimes bring you up and always talk about you when I've shared parts of your letters. In their memories, Ellen is always singing to them in the kitchen or telling them stories. You had a nice way with them. I always trusted you."

"They were my first babies, Anna." I think I must had a funny look on my face when I said her first name because she laughed at me. "They taught me what to do. I learned patience because I always wanted to do things fast and you can't always do that with children. I loved them. I always listened to you. The first time I went off to Lincoln, you told me to remember I was in charge of myself and when you expected me back. Of course, when I returned that Sunday evening, you guessed at what had happened, but you were nice enough to wait until I told you of our betrothal, but you did tease me a little bit."

"You were different, Ellen, not quite the girl who had left on the train two days before. It only followed you would marry William. I did hope it would not be for a while, though, and that's how it turned out. I let you keep your secret until you were ready. That's what happens when you take a young and pretty girl on, and she meets a handsome young man."

"I found you polite, Ellen, but I could tell your feelings from your face, such as when Cousin Beatrice was rude to you at tea one particular afternoon. I watched to see how you would react. You were not demeaned but handled her quite well with a promise of 'fresh tea presently.' You used good grammar, showed nice form, and did not display the embarrassment my cousin was looking for. I thought to myself that time that this young girl from Ireland would go far."

"I remember the day well, Anna. It was early in my time here and I was determined to make the tea party nice for you. So, I had to think quickly about the fresh tea and decided right then how to handle it, and I was quite proud of myself. I wanted to please you, but not give in entirely to Cousin Beatrice. You were so calm, too. I learned from that, to ignore things sometimes. You did it so well, talking about the weather." She smiled at that.

"Now, I have a surprise for you, Ellen, and I think I'll tell you about it now. I told someone you were coming today and she asked to be invited, too. Who do you suppose that could be?"

I started to shake my head that I had no idea, when something struck me. "Not Cousin Beatrice!"

She laughed at me. "Beatrice told me she would like to see you again, to see how you turned out. She's gotten it into her mind that maybe you've made a good life for yourself, despite being Irish and a maid. And, you may have discovered she has a special feeling for children and I've told her all about yours. Don't be surprised if she comes bearing gifts."

That's when the girls came running in, all excited by their trip to the park. Jenny showed me a tiny red spot on her hand where she'd fallen because she was running. Alice reported. "I've never seen so many automobiles, and the city is so exciting! There is a statue in the park and a fountain where Mary says water comes out in the summer."

Jenny loved the babies. "Babies get pushed in carriages," she told me, "so we looked at all the pretty babies." She thought for a minute. "I like the automobiles too, and I want Papa to get one. We can go to church in it." That being settled, she said she wanted to go home now if that was all right. "I miss Papa and Billy," she said sadly.

"Wouldn't you like to have lunch first, Jenny, and then in the afternoon you can go back home?" asked Mrs. Bernstein. Jenny, after thinking for a minute, responded that she thought she could just stay long enough for lunch, so Mary took both girls upstairs to wash. They were back down in no time at all, rushing down the stairs in a way I remember the boys doing when they were small. At that point, the doorbell rang, and I heard Mary's steps as she went to the front door. I was a bit nervous, I suppose, but mostly I was curious as to how it would go, me and Cousin Beatrice at lunch together.

And then she appeared. Mary had taken her coat, but she still wore her fashionable hat, making Jenny stare. I prayed she would not ask why. I remembered the ladies all wearing their hats at afternoon tea. Alice stood right up. She might not have formal manners, but I had taught them to stand up for grownups, and Jenny scrambled up too. I was proud of them. Cousin Beatrice spared no time at all in first greeting her cousin and then me. "How are you, Ellen?" she said clearly. She extended her hand. I thought she must have practiced this before coming. She shook my hand! So, I remembered my manners and said how nice it was to see her after all this time. She nodded.

Then she changed her attention to the girls who were still standing. This time it was Alice who took the lead. "I am pleased to meet you," then stopped because she did not know her name.

"You can call me Miss Beatrice," she told her. "I knew your mother when she was much younger."

"Hello, Miss Beatrice." This came from my younger daughter. She had decided she was in the presence of someone important like Mrs. Bernstein, but maybe different, too. She kept looking at the hat, a small pretty one with a half-veil.

"And what are your names, young ladies?"

They were both able to answer, quietly for them. Then they seemed to be waiting for this grownup to do or say something else to them, but instead she turned to us and asked if we would be going into lunch. "I have something for each of the girls but would like to wait until after we've eaten."

The girls looked at her in awe. Jenny started to say something, but I silenced her with a look. "What did you get me," was not allowed, ever.

I wondered how the girls would do in the dining room, but Mrs. Bernstein kept things going while the girls did their best with their soup and then the little sandwiches and drank their milk. I kept the conversation going with talk of the farm and the beauty of the countryside, and Cousin Beatrice asked questions about William and our son. "Do you miss the city?" she asked, and when I said that I did, I noticed Alice looking over with some interest. I don't think she'd ever thought about that. Jenny was very focused on eating her sandwich because dessert had been mentioned and she knew the rule.

"Your daughters have very nice manners," Cousin Beatrice observed, and then she actually smiled at them. I'd never found her to be one who smiled easily, so I thought we must have made a good impression. That pleased me. And then Jenny looked over and asked Miss Beatrice why she wore her hat in the house. We held our breaths. She looked right at Jenny and said, "When I lunch with my friends at such a pretty table, I dress up and wear my hat. Is that all right, young lady?" Jenny shook her head, yes, and told Miss Beatrice that she thought it was a very nice hat, and that was that. Anna and I breathed again.

There was ice cream for dessert. Both girls cleaned their dishes and Mary was directed to bring more, which she did, vanilla. When we were finished, Anna suggested we go to the parlor and visit. Once we were all seated and it was funny to see my girls' legs stick straight out from their chairs, Miss Beatrice announced she had a gift for each girl and called them over to her. They went. She pulled two prettily wrapped packages out of her shopping bag and handed them over.

They both said, "thank you," and looked over to me to see if it was all right to open them. I nodded, and they pulled the paper off each small box, and inside the tissue paper was a small purse and cotton gloves, pink for Jenny and yellow for Alice. They'd never had anything like that. Alice was the first to say how much she liked them. Then, Jenny put the purse handle over her small arm and with some little difficulty pulled the gloves on and began to dance around the room. "Look inside the purse," directed Miss Beatrice, and they did, their eyes getting round as they each found five shiny pennies. And then, Jenny discovered in the bottom of the gift box, another something wrapped in tissue, a tiny china doll. Alice quickly found hers, too. Jenny squealed with delight. Alice smiled her thanks. Miss Beatrice looked pleased.

"When Anna told me you were coming, I knew I wanted to see you again. I know I could be difficult, but I came to like you." Now, I was the one in awe.

So the girls went off to the kitchen to visit with Mary, who promised us some more tea presently. And we talked, in a way not unlike how I do with my sisters. It was a strange afternoon that way. I told them I had dreams for my children, that William and I would do our best to make sure they would go forward in school and life.

And then the boys arrived. I could hear them in the kitchen, their voices friendly and the higher voices of the girls, and then there they were at the door. I stood right up, and after a minute, decided to hug them both. Benjamin laughed because he was taller than me, and Randall announced that he planned to be taller than his brother some day. No strangeness between us at all. That was when Mary brought more tea and cake for the boys who, she said, were always hungry. I watched them with their dark eyes and their mother's smile as they ate their way through cake, and big glasses of milk for both of them. It did occur to me that someday my own children would be big like them and tried to picture Billy taller than me.

Benjamin asked Alice what grade she was in and said he remembered third grade very well because that's when he began to love to read. Jenny declared she was ready to go to school now, but the school wouldn't have her, which made us all laugh a little. Randall told Jenny that if he could decide, he would say she could go to school. So, that made her feel better. We all laughed and talked together. The boys were fond of their Cousin Beatrice, I could tell, and included her in their conversation. The girls were fascinated by tales of sports and going about the city. It was like I'd never been a maid in this house. Who would have known it would turn out like this? I stored it all away to tell William at home and with that, realized it was getting late and we would have to go.

The boys instantly said they would go with us on the streetcar to Dudley Station and make sure we got on the El. I had a memory of two small boys being walked to the streetcar stop to say goodbye on our last long ago visit. Cousin Beatrice got up, saying she did not know when she'd had a more delightful afternoon. I went right over and took her hand. "I am so glad you came today," and using the name she'd given to my daughters, added, "Miss Beatrice." She smiled at that. Then I turned. "Thank you for being so good to us," and I added, "Anna." She was busy tucking three small packages into the shopping bag. "Books for each of them, Billy, too." This had been an afternoon of surprises.

And then, just before leaving, I whispered into Anna's ear. "I'm expecting a baby this summer."

She said to me quietly, "Write to me soon."

The boys grabbed their coats. The girls made their goodbyes, first to Mrs. Bernstein, and then to their new friend, Miss Beatrice, who suddenly pulled them toward her and asked for a hug which they happily gave her. I thought I saw a tear in her eye, but who knows. Coats on and gifts in the nice paper shopping bag, we were on our way. The girls chattered at the big boys all the way to the streetcar.

Benjamin lifted Jenny on and Randall took Alice's hand. I think it was a look of adoration she gave him. I decided to call them the charming Bernstein boys. At the El, Benjamin carried Jenny up the stairs when he saw how tired she was. Randall again took Alice by the hand. I thought she might start calling him beautiful, too. The train came quickly, and we paid our fare. As we left the station, the boys were waving. The girls just looked overcome, as though they could not understand all of what had happened in this one day. They leaned on me and I turned my mind to getting home again.

CHAPTER 30

Home from Dorchester

It was an easy ride on the El to Washington Street Station, where the train went down into the tunnel. Then we climbed up onto the street. I buttoned up their coats against the cold. It was crowded, with many men and women getting off work. Everyone walked fast and hard to make their connections. Some ladies, I thought, must be done with a day's shopping in the department stores, because they were carrying full shopping bags. I briefly envied them the funds that would permit that, but it passed quickly, that thought. I kept my little daughters close to me for the walk to South Station. We hurried in with a crowd of people, all determined to get their train home. I checked the board for our departure and determined, thankfully, that we had time enough to breathe. Some nice woman slid over on a wooden bench to make room for us, so I was able to let our shopping bag rest on the floor.

The girls were quiet. It was just becoming dusk on this November afternoon. It gave me a bit of a strange feeling. I'd not been so far away from home in the evening in a long time. I was feeling joy at being only a train ride from Dover and maybe feeling some nerves because it was getting dark. And then, suddenly, all the lights came on in South Station. It was wondrous, all those electric bulbs. I could see it in the eyes of the children. Alice murmured another "beautiful." I shared their delight. I started to hum a tune. The girls looked very contented. I suppose I did too, back in the days when I was in the care of my mother.

As the time came closer, I pulled my bag to me, then stood up and hooked the handle over my arm, ticket clasped in my hand. "Alice, you will walk right beside me while I hold Jenny's hand." Alice looked agreeable to that, but then she reached over and took the shopping bag from me, saying it would leave me free to hold the tickets with that hand.

"I know the track number," she announced, "and I see it over there." I thanked her, and we went off in that direction. Some day, she'll do this all by herself, I supposed. That thought gave me pleasure. Independent daughters are a very good thing. I would have to tell her father what a good little traveler Alice already was. It was a very tired Jenny who held onto my hand all the way down the platform, no tears, though. I was determined to get a seat, so we walked quickly, keeping up with the crowd. We were handed up the steps. A gentleman stepped aside to let us go down the aisle ahead of him, I smiled my thanks. We dropped into a seat. I sighed in relief. Nothing to do now, but go home on the train.

The train moved slowly through the city lights. Alice loved the lights. I thought I might have a city girl. And then, after some time, going faster, the train made its way into beginning darkness. At each brightly lighted station, people got off. Alice wondered aloud how people could live in so many different places. Then, she looked at me and asked, "How will Papa know what time to come and get us?" Her little sister looked up at that. She had heard, "Papa."

"The train gets in at 4:45," I told her. "Remember the timetable?" She sighed with what seemed like relief, not the usual thing for my Alice. I thought maybe she'd had enough adventure for one day.

My little one just murmured "Papa" from where she'd curled up against me.

It didn't take long before we pulled into Dover Station. Such excitement! I hurried them off the seat and down the aisle to the door where we were helped down. Two figures came rushing over and the girls left me and ran over to them. Papa and Billy were smiling all over. Our day was done.

William hustled us into the back of the buggy on which he'd lit the lanterns, making it a pretty sight. My husband climbed up high and Billy surprised me by climbing inside with me and the girls. He managed to sit beside me where I held a sleepy Jenny in my lap.

"We made supper," he announced. "Pa made chicken and gravy and potatoes. We'll warm it all up when we get home." He seemed surprised that his father could cook. Actually, I was, too. He'd only ever managed eggs before. I wondered at the state of my kitchen. And then Billy, looking at me, said, "I missed you, Ma." I pulled him over for a hug, which he did not seem to mind at all.

Minutes later, we pulled up in front of our cottage. William had left a light on and it looked so inviting. It was hard to realize we'd been only gone for a day. The table was set for supper. The kitchen was warm and, to my surprise, clean and neat. I put a still sleepy Jenny down in her chair and went over to the stove to check on the chicken which was cut up and resting on a warm plate in the oven while the gravy sat on a burner and the mashed potatoes in a bowl with a cloth over it. He'd opened a jar of green beans. Bread and butter were on the table. Billy grinned at my surprise and pleasure. William, when he came in a few minutes later, said, "So, let's have supper and hear about your day."

Jenny was first, "We got surprises from Miss Beatrice; gloves and purses and a doll and five pennies!" Billy looked over at the mention of coins. The other stuff did not interest him.

William gave me a funny look at the mention of Miss Beatrice and I sent him a look back that said, "Later."

Alice then reminded me that Mrs. Bernstein had put books in the bag for each of them. "You, too, Billy," she said. I noted how nice she was being to her brother. Maybe we should go away more often.

"We'll look at the books after supper," I told them. The girls talked about seeing Mama's old room, and how nice everyone was to them, and they'd been to a park. Jenny told her papa he should get an automobile to go to church, bringing a smile from William.

"Do you think your pennies will pay for it?" Papa asked.

"Maybe," said his youngest daughter, "if Alice puts hers in, too." Alice looked ready to tell her how an automobile would cost more than pennies, but I stopped her with a look.

After supper, the girls flew to the shopping bag to pull out their gifts. Papa was very impressed with what little ladies they looked when they paraded back and forth, purses over their arms and gloves on. Jenny ruined the effect by running over to her father and throwing herself into his lap. Billy didn't think much of it at all, but kept quiet. After a short time, I went over and pulled out the three wrapped books.

"Billy should be first," I said, and handed over his package, which he opened quickly. On the cover it said, *The Story of King Arthur and his Knights*. We studied the picture together. This time I would be the one educating our son. "It's about knights. They were soldiers from long ago who fought with swords. They served King Arthur." I remembered the stories from school. He found more pictures inside, shiny ones. He was pleased.

Next was Jenny and hers was a picture book, *The Tale of Peter Rabbit*. I knew we would have fun reading that to her. "A picture on every page," I told her "It's about a bunny like the ones we see around here." She sat on the floor to hold it, already turning the pages.

Alice opened *Anne of Green Gables*. I was so pleased Anna had remembered. A neighbor girl had loaned it to me long ago, and I'd read it over and over, just romantic enough for a young girl. Perfect. Alice was a good reader and would have no trouble at all. Perhaps I would read it again.

"Peter Rabbit tomorrow," I announced, "after supper." Then, to Billy, "I'll get you started on King Arthur tonight at bedtime and Alice can read to Papa." I wanted them to love books like I do.

It was Jenny to bed first. The child was mostly asleep already. "Alice, get your school clothes ready and get into your nightclothes, and Billy the same." William went over to carry Jenny up to bed. He seemed happy to have me in charge again, so Jenny fell asleep right away. Alice sat down at the kitchen table to read the first chapter to her papa about the orphan girl with the red hair arriving on the train. He told her he liked the story too, before sending her up to bed.

I sat on the bed with Billy and gave him King Arthur and his knights with armor and swords. I could see his imagination working away. It would not surprise me if a wooden sword would be in the making and the farmyard become a battleground. We would have to watch the poor animals.

All settled down early and a short time later, it was our bedtime. In bed, I gave William the full report. He chuckled at Miss Beatrice joining us for lunch. "You don't know your own charm," he said. I told him how well-behaved the girls were the whole day and how the Bernstein boys had grown. And how my good friend Mrs. Bernstein told me to call her Anna. He smiled at that. Then I went on to describe South Station and the elevated, neither of which he'd experienced. And then I told him what a good traveler his older daughter was. "She's planning a trip to New York," I told him, "to visit her Aunt Kate."

"When she's much older," he said quickly. I agreed to that.

"I missed you," William said, "and Billy did, too. He'd never come home from school just to me before. He made me go to the station before your train was due. He could not contain himself. I don't think he was entirely convinced you would be on that train."

"Well, in two days' time, you'll be off yourself and Billy will have his turn," I stated. "And Billy will get to see some of the city and I'll miss you, too. Are you sure you know the way? How early will you leave? Are you certain of where the ship comes in?"

He laughed at all my questions. "It will be fine, Ellen. I know the way and Billy's old enough to go. We'll leave about five o'clock in the morning and return by afternoon in time for the milking. I have it all figured out. He'll never forget it. He can tell his children some day that he saw the biggest ship in the world."

I laughed at him. "You want to see it too, big boy that you are." And then he pulled me into an embrace that lasted a while. I decided to tell him my big news on his return from Boston. It would make us both happy then, to think of it, another baby.

Finally, we fell asleep, but not before I first ran through the day I'd had. I did let a little worry into my mind about their trip in just two days. Just before I fell asleep, it occurred to me that I hadn't observed any anxiety in my husband before our trip. But I supposed us to be different in that way. William just takes what comes. I think longer about things. I thanked God for putting a blessing on my day and then I went to sleep.

CHAPTER 31

The Biggest Ship in the World

The night before Billy left with Pa to go see the Majestic in Boston, he slept in his clothes. William was up to feed and milk the cows at 4 am. Billy was up, too. I fed him, made coffee for my husband and cooked eggs, which he swallowed down quickly and then was out to the barn to hitch up the horse. I wrapped Billy in all the warm clothes I could find. When William came in, I handed him a blanket and a large paper sack of sandwiches. William already had the feed bag and pail for water. The hanging lantern was lit on the buggy because it was still dark.

I'd never seen either of them, man or boy, so excited. They couldn't wait to get started. I could only smile and wring my hands at the same time. I waved them out of the farmyard and stood there until I couldn't see them anymore, or hear the clop of the horse. Then I turned back to the house. The girls were still in bed. I sat quietly and drank my tea until the morning light came. I did not feel so fearful of their safety when it was daylight. And William had promised to be home before dark.

I closed my eyes for a moment and remembered my one and only sea voyage.

It was a big ship, the Aurania, in the year 1904. I sound like an old lady, but it does seem a very long time ago. I was eighteen years of age. Passage cost me and Mary Anne twenty-five American dollars. We traveled with a friend, Bridget Raftery, also from Rathcaled. We had saved up from our jobs in the shops. We were ten days in steerage class, the lowest deck near the engines.

That day of our voyage, we got on in Queenstown where we'd traveled from Mullingar, scared and giddy girls that we were. Downstairs were our assigned berths. My sister and I had upper and lower bunks, with me in the upper. We had mattresses stuffed with hay. I worried, right away, about vermin, but none were in our sacks, at least, although we could hear rustling somewhere at night. We had life preservers for pillows.

We were not seasick and made friends with some of the other girls. Bridget Raftery, I've not seen her in years. I heard she got married. Each morning when I woke up, I would have to remind myself of where I was. They served us meals from a big tank. We each had a pail and knife, fork and spoon. It was not nice, that sort of dining, but we ate because we were hungry. Then we washed our things as well as we could. There was not much to do, so we told stories and sang. Someone had a fiddle, and we danced some nights. I don't remember being tired at all. There was a boy. I've not forgotten him. His name was Patrick and I thought I liked him, but he was staying in New York and that seemed a long way from Boston, so I didn't encourage him. Anyway, I had Sean at home. Mary Anne was keeping an eye on us.

After ten days, we docked at Hoboken, New Jersey. Part of me could not wait to get off the boat while the other part of me had got used to life on board. They rushed us steerage passengers off and onto a crowded ferryboat that took us to Ellis Island. We had landing cards pinned to our clothes and held onto medical inspection cards. I had my first doubt that I might not stay in America. I couldn't breathe. Mary Anne seemed to be the same as me, but she held it in better. I was terrified. What if we were separated? Off the ferryboat, we were herded into an immense hall to begin what they told us was inspection. Nobody had told us about that. It took hours. We passed the physical, healthy Irish country girls that we were. I could breathe again. Then we had vaccinations.

They stung. Next, they marked our coats with chalk. I tried not to feel demeaned. It was just the way they did things, I told myself.

We went upstairs to the clerk and answered his questions and showed him that we each had what amounted to three dollars in British coin. Then, we changed it at the currency exchange to pay for the train to Boston. We were directed down the stairs on the immediate right for the train station. The center stairs were for detention, they told us. I felt bad for those people. On the ground floor, you could have your baggage shipped, but we only had, each of us, one small bag and we carried it the whole time. We had hours until our train to Boston, so we went to look at the restaurant. Lunch was eleven cents for beef stew, boiled potatoes, and something they called pickled herring. We did not know when we would eat again because the food on the train could be quite dear, so in we went, holding our bags firm against our skirts as we ate. We got tea, too.

Several hours later, we were on the train to Boston. That took the rest of the day and we were in a great mood. Bridget had let her cousins know when we would be arriving and they were there to greet us at the station. That's how I got to Dorchester and found a job there. The children already know about that. It was the trip I was remembering on the boat. Enough of memories.

I kept busy all that day. In the afternoon, the girls started to look for them, running to the road to see if the buggy was coming. At last, about four o'clock, we heard the clop of the horse and down the lane they came. I threw my dishtowel on the table and ran out. The girls were there before me. Father and son sat up high on the seat and looked just as excited as they had that morning when they left. Neither looked the least bit tired. Billy was the first to climb down. He was holding two small paper bags of candy. The two of them could find sweets anywhere. He handed them off to his sisters and ran to me.

"Ma, the ship was huge. We got to the pier in time to see it dock there. I never saw so many people in one place. Pa pushed me in front. We saw it coming. When it came closer, it was bigger and higher than anything, bigger than the buildings. We looked little next to it. We waved at the men standing on the decks. The United States Marines were there, too, in their uniforms. Pa said they were watching to see boys out of school, but then he said it was really to keep order. A man told us the Majestic was as big as four hundred houses!" He stopped for breath. "And there was a lot to see after that. A band played, and the soldiers saluted the captain of the ship. I wonder what it would be like to be a sailor." I looked at the small boy before me and was glad there would be many years before he left his mother. Alice was listening, but Jenny was more interested in her candy.

William came in from the barn and sent Billy out for the cows. The girls wandered off, too. He looked at me. "I think he's still too excited to be tired. It will hit him later. I'm so glad we went. You know, they will be grown before we know it." That, of course, made me think of what I had to tell him this night. William continued. "Billy is very smart, you know, and asks a lot of questions. He wanted to know how the boat went. I just gave him a short explanation of steam travel. He takes everything in. He was quite a sight, one of the few children on the dock. He wants to see the open ocean. "

"I can tell him about that," I responded. "I stood on a ship's deck and watched it."

And then Billy and his sisters came in and we prepared for supper. I'd made a nice stew. Billy wanted to keep talking about his day. "It was really cold on the dock and windy. There was a little place for hot coffee and Pa got me one, too, with lots of milk and sugar, and we drank it from mugs standing up. Then we went to get a good place to watch. It was getting crowded and then someone yelled it was coming. We could see the smokestacks and people started cheering. When it got close, the big hull was pushing the water. It was churning white. And then, there it was right in front of us, the biggest ship in the world!"

He stopped at that point to make sure we all understood the drama of it. "Pa showed me the picture on the side of the ship that showed it was owned by the White Star Line, a white star in a red square. There were all small round windows and two tall masts and triangle flags up and down, flapping in the wind. Sailors were standing on the decks.

And on the side, it said, HMS Majestic. The British flag was in the front." I made a face at that. "And it took only five days to come over from England to New York." Then Billy recited the facts. "The Majestic is more than nine hundred feet long and weighs sixty-four tons and has nine decks." He looked over at his father. "It came in on the flood tide before high water, right, Pa?" William nodded. "And it was in dry dock for repairs," he added. Then he ran out of breath and got back to eating his supper.

But after just a few minutes, Billy looked up from his supper. "We ate our sandwiches on the dock after we went to the hitching post and gave the horse water and tied on his feedbag. We stayed there on the dock for a long time and kept looking at the ship. Pa had me count the nine decks. More people came to see the ship. And then Pa said it was time to go home, so we hitched up the horse and came away, but I kept looking back at the ship. I almost remembered the whole way home because of how the city streets, and how the buildings looked. It was nice, though, when we were in the country and near to Dover again."

Then he and Alice had a discussion about ships and trains, her new specialty. "I would rather go on a train. I'm going to New York some day." She flounced just a little bit. William and I were enjoying this conversation between brother and sister.

"Well," countered Billy, "I would rather go to New York on a big ship."

"That would cost too much money, Billy," she said in her big sister way.

"Then I would get a job on the ship to pay for it," he said just as importantly. Alice had no answer for that. I had pie for dessert and Billy put his attention back to eating. William and I smiled at each other.

Billy went up to bed that night without any urging at all. When I went up to read to him, he was already asleep. I straightened out the downstairs and got myself ready for bed. William had a few more things to say about his day with Billy. "It was very cold on the dock, so I did wrap him in the blanket you sent. He didn't complain. He was just taking everything in. And when he saw the ship coming, he just got so excited! I think he was stunned at the size. He will always remember this day." I agreed with that. I felt proud of our son, and of my husband for giving him this experience.

As William turned to me after climbing into bed himself, I said I had something to tell him. He didn't look exactly worried. I think he knew right away from my tone, what was coming. "We're going to have another baby, William." That's all it took for him to wrap his arms around me and start chuckling.

"I knew you had something on your mind, Ellen," he said gleefully. And then in a more sober tone, "Will it be too soon for you after the loss of our George?"

"No," I told him. "We will still hold George in our hearts, but this will be another one for us to love." And so we went to sleep, each in our own dreams, but also folded together in this new one. I did thank the Blessed Mother for their safe trip.

"Another time, Pa took me to Boston in a horse and buggy to see the biggest passenger ship in the world, the Majestic. Hitching posts were still everywhere. We had a feedbag, a canvas bag of oats, and carried a pail to fill with water. I never thought I'd ride in a big ship in WWII, the Aquitania, which had been made over into a troop transport."

~William Bennett at age 90

CHAPTER 32

Dover Time

FAMILY

Winter arrived one early December day when the sky turned gray, the wind picked up and a blizzard came in. We were not prepared. The children were in school. It was still afternoon and already getting dark. I remembered back in Dorchester, my first northeaster, when I thought I would go out with my friends that evening until the shopkeeper told me I would get lost in the drifts. I was a girl then, with a girl's thoughts. This time, my children were out there in the snow.

I worried about Alice and Billy. It was still snowing and the skies dark. I wrapped up in coat and shawl and walked down the path to wait for the car. William let me go and stayed with Jenny. I was down there for a while, imagining all kinds of things. They were so late, nearly suppertime. Finally, I saw headlights through the blowing snow, and then heard the big car slowly coming down the road. It stopped. Alice and Billy jumped out and ran to me.

"We were skidding and sliding," said Billy, "and went off the road! The big boys had to push us back on." Alice shook her head at him. At almost ten, she knew better than to worry me. I said a quick prayer for the other children not home yet. We walked up the path with my arms around them. Jenny was jumping up and down inside the door. I got out of my frozen over-clothes and put supper on the table.

I'd earlier considered telling William to walk toward town and see if they were stuck on some snowy road in the woods somewhere. Now, I could relax. I expected there would be no school the next day. There was good sledding on the hill, once the digging out and the chores were done. I thought of my baby up there. The thought came to me that I will always have to live here on this farm, until I die, because George is buried here. I felt a shiver. Then the new baby moved inside me.

We managed to buy them a board game for Christmas this year, and I sewed clothes for the girls, and knitted hats for all three. Jenny had doll dishes. Alice her own little wooden box for her things, like a jewelry box, which her papa made for her, painted and glossy. Aunt Kate sent her a small bracelet. I got her a comb and brush, too. I sewed a new dolly for Jenny. Billy got little metal trucks. Christmas was, as usual, magical and quick.

This time, January and February went by fast. Alice noticed me growing larger, and we had a talk about it. I'd not wanted her to notice. Billy said nothing. Jenny is still a baby herself. It was February again. I don't dwell on losing George. I'd rather remember my youngest boy when he was fine and healthy. Our Jenny turned five.

Early in March, Mr. Pierce instructed William to go to a big farm auction in our area to buy equipment for the farm, and Pa decided to take Billy with him. Billy was beside himself with joy. I packed them a bag lunch that Saturday morning after milking, and off they went in the horse and cart, Billy perched up on the high seat next to his father.

They were back in time for chores, just as the girls and I were returning from Bridget's where we spent the day. I had wanted to do something special for them, so we had made cookies in my sister's kitchen and had a tea party. It was nice. Some of the cookies we saved, but not very many.

William unloaded the cart of leather harness and a pile of metal plow parts. I had no notion of their use. Billy could not wait to present his sisters with two small paper bags of candy. They whooped at that.

"Billy ate his already," commented his papa with a grin, "and washed it down with sweet cider."

March came and Alice turned ten, "double-digits," she announced. Eight-year-old Billy looked like he would like to achieve that sooner than later. Spring went by and it was early summer.

I was tired as the hot weather began. We had the doctor because my legs had swelled. Doctor said I should rest each day, lying down, he said. Alice took on chores and Billy now owned the vegetable garden. His father told him it was the boy's job on the farm. He did his job, weeding and picking the vegetables when they were ready, the pole beans, and all. I served them yellow with butter.

The children went barefoot in the summer. The soles of their feet got hard and calloused. I wore shoes but no stockings. I had let my skirts out to accommodate the baby. I tried to keep myself neat but felt large and clumsy.

It was June. The time for the baby came closer. The swelling had gone down in my legs. I felt fine. One day, Doctor Mitchell came by. He said he was in the neighborhood. But I think he really came to tell me he thought I should have this baby at Norwood Hospital. William and I were both shocked. It had never occurred to either of us that this baby not be born at home like the others. I instantly thought about the tonsils and how we had thought that was such a good and modern idea.

Doctor saw the look on my face. "I think you and this baby are fine, but I would feel better if you delivered in the hospital. You could have problems again with your legs, when it is time to give birth, and I would not have you at home for that."

Then, he must have known we were thinking of the cost. "I will arrange it all. You will not have to pay beyond my regular fee."

We certainly wanted everything to go well. There was little time to ponder. I was only a few weeks away from when we thought this baby would come. After Doctor left, we went upstairs to the bedroom. We had sent the children out during the visit and now they were busy with chores and Alice had Jenny with her.

"Swollen legs don't seem like much to me," I complained.

"We will take no chances," said my husband firmly. "I will not have anything happen to you or this baby." He continued. "You should go to Mary Anne. Their farm in Westwood is closer to the hospital."

I gave him a look. He gave me one back. I retreated. "I'll write my sister today."

We heard Alice calling upstairs. "Do you want me to set the table and should I turn the potatoes down? Jenny wants you."

So our talk came to an end. I was frightened, I admitted to myself, of the hospital. I was afraid of disease. Also, hospitals offered something called "twilight sleep" during the birth, which was supposed to make you not remember the pain, or something like that. I did not know how I felt about it. I had dearly wanted to have this baby at home. And I disliked our family routine to be disrupted this way. I loved my sister but did not want to stay too long there. She already had four children. That was a lot of work, and I did not like adding to it with mine.

After supper, I sat down to write a letter to Mary Anne. I planned to go see Bridget the next morning, too. I would not have her think that she was not included in my plans. My sister Bridget would be a big help when I came home with the new baby. I thought briefly of leaving small Jenny with her aunt, but then just as quickly thought she should not be separated from her brother and sister.

Two mornings later, the phone rang. Mary Anne was on the line. "Yes, Ellen, of course you can come." That's all she said. I found myself crying just a little bit. My sister paid no attention to that. She was all practical. "I'll expect you in a few days." Then she said, "Goodbye, Ellen" and that was that.

"I went with my father everywhere, so I knew a lot about farming. Sometimes, Mr. Pierce, Pa's boss, if another farm was having an auction, would send him off to buy anything needed. I would go with him with Ma's bag lunch and if I was lucky, I would get some cider. Pa would buy farm equipment. I looked forward to these trips, especially if I got something to eat, too."

"Summers were hot. I did a lot of weeding in the garden. I picked green beans, a hot job, down the rows and watched for beets and carrots to be big enough to pick. At the end of the season, I picked everything. The only boy, I did all the gardening. We went barefoot on the farm. Each foot was one big callous."

~Bill Bennett, age 90

CHAPTER 33

Mary

It was a week before we set out to my sister's house, despite William pushing me to go. I felt no difference that would tell me it was close to my time. The June heat bothered me, but I rested during the hottest time of the day, and the children with me. That made it quiet.

By the beginning of the next week, though, I felt a shifting within me. We packed. I walked over to Bridget's house down the road to let her know we would be leaving the next morning. My little sister, though, was not one to worry. "I'll see you soon enough," she told me, "and with a new little baby."

William and I had explained to the children how we would be going to their aunt's house. They were excited. Alice wondered at my going to the hospital to have this baby. Billy thought it a place to buy babies. Jenny was not interested in babies.

We left in a carriage in the early morning. I gave a glance back at our cottage, standing empty. I pictured William returning alone, later. It was a long ride. William was quiet this morning. The children were not. They chattered about their cousins. It was like a vacation for them.

As we turned down the long road to the farm, three figures appeared, running toward us. It reminded me of years ago when William's little brothers had chased toward us in the buggy, the first time he took me home. These children did not stare, though, and they shouted our names. At five, Jenny was not the youngest. Cousin Eddie was only three years of age. His older brother Jimmy and sister, Louise, pulled him along. Louise lifted Jenny down and Alice and Billy followed. After a minute, little Eddie took Cousin Jenny's hand, and they all ran toward the house. Mary Anne was standing on the porch, smiling.

William helped me down.

"I thought it would be today," said my all-knowing sister. "Come in and have dinner, William, before you have to go back."

The children had all disappeared to the barn where there were new calves. The tea kettle was on. I settled thankfully onto a chair while William brought in the bags.

"Billy will go in with the boys," said my sister. "I gave you the one bed in Louise's room. Jenny can sleep with you, and the big girls on the floor with blankets and pillows. They'll be happy enough. So, there's room."

Dinner was stewed chicken and gravy and potatoes. Billy loved his glass of thick milk. "Like drinking cream," he said. Frederick came in from his work and joined us at the table along with Walter, now a big boy of almost thirteen. He was taller than me. I remembered when he was born. Frederick welcomed us to his home.

Too soon, it was time for my husband to leave. He had already hitched up the horse and was saying his goodbyes. Jenny appeared at that moment. At first, she just looked confused, then asked, "Where is Papa going?"

"He has to go back home for the cows," I told her. "Papa will come back another day."

Jenny's eyes filled with tears. "I don't want Papa to go." Mary Anne went over and picked her up. Eddie's eyes got big, and he went to stand next to his mother.

William stood there at the door, not knowing what to say to comfort his youngest daughter. Billy and Alice didn't look very happy either.

Jenny was crying now. This was new for her, and she didn't know what to do with it. Then, Mary Anne stepped in and, putting Jenny down facing her, looked right into her eyes and said, "Papa is going home and you need to give him a hug. When he comes back, there will be a lovely baby to show him. You are going home again, but not until after the baby comes. Now, go say goodbye."

Jenny did what she was told. The tears hadn't left her face, though. Her brother and sister went over to say goodbye. It had become quite quiet. After hugging each of his children, William gave me a kiss on my forehead, climbed up into the carriage and drove away, giving us a wave.

Their cousins had been watching all this. "Let's go pick strawberries to have with fresh cream for supper," quickly said Louise. "Then we'll show you our woods. Later, when it gets dark, after supper, we'll play games outside until Ma tells us to go in. Maybe we'll find fireflies." They ran off, pulling Jenny by the hand. Now, the child had other things to think about. I looked after them with gratitude.

Mary Anne and I had more tea.

"Are your legs all right?" she asked me.

"They're fine, but Doctor doesn't want me to take any chances."

She nodded at that.

"I'm afraid of the hospital," I told her. "I haven't told anyone else that. There are diseases in the hospital. I so wanted to have this baby at home." I was cross. She knew that and was gentle.

"We want you and this baby to be safe."

"You sound like William," I replied, but I managed a small smile. "You know, sister, we both like to be in charge and my husband took over on this. I didn't like that."

"So, that's part of it," she said thoughtfully. I could tell she understood now. She smiled back at me, but didn't say anything more.

The afternoon went by quickly. Our supper was anything but quiet. The children were hardly ever together like this, and they couldn't stop talking. Mary Anne's children had not only entertained their cousins all day, but had made Jenny so tired, she fell asleep at the table, and her Uncle Frederick carried her up to bed.

The others ran around outside on this warm summer night. We sat on the porch and watched them dart here and there in the dark, calling to each other. Walter sat with us. He did the farm chores every day with his father. He was quiet, too, but listened to everything we said. We could see bats flying in the night. When it was completely dark, we called them in. I sent Billy to wash up, then Alice.

The gas lamp went upstairs, first for the boys, Walter carrying Eddie, then for Louise and Alice who went up obediently. I was last, holding my back, while my sister helped me up the stairs. I put out the lamp as soon as I was undressed and curled up next to the sleeping Jenny. I looked out the window at the unfamiliar darkness. Oh, I would be glad when this was over. I fell asleep before I could say my prayers.

Three days went by. The children were getting used to it. Everyone helped keep track of Jenny, who had discovered kittens in the barn. Eddie had less freedom. We had them play together where we could watch them. Billy went with the boys to herd the cows, morning and evening. We had the big girls helping in the house, but agreed they should have time to be cousins, so we did leave them some free hours. I liked watching them, Louise with her fair hair and Alice with her dark curls. It was nice for each to have a girl near in age to be with.

Then, on the fourth morning, I woke with pains. It was not light out yet. But Mary Anne and Frederick were up, and young Walter. The other children were sleeping. I called down to my sister in the kitchen. She came right up and helped me get dressed. I gave each sleeping girl a quick kiss. Mary Ann got me downstairs. Meanwhile, Frederick had hitched up the buggy.

Mary Anne would be going with us. Walter would be left in charge. He was standing, barely awake, shaking his head, "yes" to every command his mother gave him. Alice and Louise would watch the little ones, she told him, but he should keep an eye on our Billy. He gave me a "Goodbye, Aunt Ellen," I could tell he did not want to think about women having babies.

It was a short ride to the hospital in the early morning light. The summer heat had not come on yet this day. The pains were getting closer, though, so I did not give much thought to the weather. We arrived. I did not want to go into that big brick building. Mary Anne looked at me as though to say "So, now you want to go back?" I let them help me down from the carriage and we walked through the big doors. A nurse dressed in starched white, looked up when we came in and we went right to the desk.

I gave the doctor's name. I was on the list. I had the silly thought that if I hadn't been, I could have gone back home. The pains brought me back to reality. This baby would be coming soon. I still wanted to be at home. But I told myself I was here to have my baby the modern way. And it had stayed in my mind, how I might have complications.

A short walk down the hall and I was put to bed in a room with other ladies, big like me. Some of them were moaning. I heard a baby cry somewhere. The nurses got me undressed and into bedclothes and into bed. I informed them I usually had relatively short labors. The nurse looked at me like they knew more than I did. She checked me over. I had to admit the clean sheets felt nice, and it was good to be lying down. My sister had been sent to the waiting room. I missed her. Before she left, though, she told me Frederick would be calling William soon.

"Oh, William," I thought, "You won't be the first to see this baby."

Everyone was a stranger except Doctor. When he arrived, I almost cried.

He did a quick examination under the sheets.

"You are doing fine," he assured me. "Nurse took your blood pressure and you are all right."

After he left, and because I was hurting and cross and lonely, words just crept into my mind. "Then why am I in this damn hospital!" I hated everything about this place. I felt like they'd taken my sister away when I needed her. I did not like being in a big room with women I did not know. I wanted my husband. I remembered how kind the Bennetts had been to me when I had George. I knew this was not the time to think about him, but my thoughts were all over the place. I felt like an abandoned child, not a grown woman. I cried, but turned away so no one would see or hear me. I was miserable, and it was not just because the pains were getting harder and closer together.

They left me alone for a while, then the nurse came back. She said I'd be getting medicine to help me, "twilight sleep," she called it. She told me the baby was coming. Well, I knew that! The bed had wheels on it and they pushed me down the hall and into a room with bright lights. I looked up and saw Doctor's kind face. Someone told me my husband was in the waiting room. I don't remember anything else but being told I'd had a little girl. I went to sleep again. The next time I woke up, I asked for my baby and my husband and my sister. I was prepared to get out of bed and go find them. They told me my sister had been sent home, but my husband was downstairs.

It must have been the way I looked when I said it. Our baby was brought to me immediately. Finally, I had Mary in my arms. She was beautiful, and quiet for now. I examined her all over. She had a little round face and dark hair. She was a good size, like my other babies. William appeared then, looking worn and pale, but he smiled at me. I handed the baby to her papa. "Say hello to Mary Martha," I told him. And then the nurse left us. He cuddled her gently, touching her soft, dark hair.

"Welcome, Mary Martha," he said softly. Then, turning to me, "I am so glad you are all right, Ellen." He had a little tear in his eyes. He sat on a chair close to the bed and I touched his arm. We sat together like that.

After a while, the nurse came back, and William was told to go. There were special rules about visiting, it seemed, even if you were the father. "Damn hospital," I said to William, after she left us alone for a few minutes. William's eyebrows went up, but I could tell he was trying not to laugh.

"You'll have to confess that," he told me with a twinkle in his eye.

I ignored him, "Find out when I can get out of here."

William said he'd try his best. "They're not holy nuns," I told him. "Don't be afraid of them and talk to Doctor." He nodded.

I was glad he would be staying at Mary Anne's that night because he looked so tired.

I dozed with the baby. The next visit from the nurse was to tell me I'd be going to a ward and the baby would be going to the nursery. I told her that was not how I wanted it. We looked at each other and she sighed and went to get her supervisor, who turned out to be bigger than her and full of herself.

"Mrs. Bennett," she said, "We have rules here. Your baby needs to go to the nursery with the other babies, so you can get some rest."

"I'll get more rest if my baby is with me," I answered, matching her tone. I might be sitting up in bed while she stood over me, but I knew what I wanted and didn't mind saying it.

Again, it must have been how I looked as much as what I said, because she told the other nurse to take me and the baby to the ward. Mary was in a nice little rolling bed, so it was no trouble for them at all. It was late afternoon by then and we napped together until she woke up and I nursed her and there was peace. The other ladies did not quite know what to think. Their infants were brought to them at regular times for feeding. I admired their little ones. There certainly were a lot of them.

They didn't let me get out of bed. I disliked the bedpan but managed it. I looked forward to William coming to see us the next day. I expected I would be awake at least some of the night, feeding our daughter. I would take pains to not to let her cry and disturb the other mothers.

I said a prayer to the Blessed Mother Mary to thank her for a safe delivery.

"We had electricity, not kerosene lamps, like the Naffs on their dairy farm in Westwood. We drank unpasteurized milk there. It was like drinking a glass of light cream. Their cows were inspected monthly. When we stayed over, the lamp would go up the stairs for the boys to go to bed, then the girls, and then the lamp went downstairs."

~Bill Bennett, age 90

CHAPTER 34

Going Home

The next day, very early in the afternoon, William and Mary Anne came to see me during visiting time. I looked up and there they were, standing by my bed. I had tidied myself and felt well, only a little sore and tired. They were peeking around. I told them all the babies had been taken off to the nursery. The nurses said they should not be near people. Nonsense, of course. I was used to everyone holding a new baby. I had already planned to walk down to the nursery with them. I had a robe and slippers on, in some thin material. I told them I would be fine. What a strange thing to put mothers and their new babies in different places.

We were not the only ones traipsing down the hall in search of our infant. We were part of a parade. When we got there, we saw Mary in her little cart. A paper card had her name on it. We admired her through the window. At least her father had held her yesterday. I thought my girl was looking out at me, wanting me like I wanted her. "Get me out of here," she seemed to be saying, her little face all squeezed up for a loud cry, matching my own desperation to be out of the hospital. Mary Anne had her "I'm not going to say anything" face on. They admired our little girl and then walked me back to the room.

"Go right downstairs after this," I told my William, "And ask when I can go home." My sister nodded her head in agreement.

Then Mary Anne added, "Tell them Mrs. Bennett will be coming to her sister's house for a time where she and the baby will be cared for until she goes home."

"Do you have the baby with you at all, Ellen?" said my sister.

"Yes, but only because I insisted on it. She was with me all night. They only came and got her for visiting time." We smiled at each other.

The visit was too short. They left when the nurses indicated it was time. I reminded William that he was going to talk to them at the front desk. And then they were gone, but not before my sister said, "Mary is beautiful and I will tell the children all about their new sister." My heart dropped a little at the mention of our children. I had not even asked how they were, I'd been so concentrated on getting out and then home. I told her quickly to tell them Mama would be back soon. I was especially concerned about our Jenny. My sister said she would talk to them and that they were fine. I imagined I would find out more later.

After a short while, I asked for my baby and got her. Mary came to me screaming. The poor little thing had had to wait for her feeding, and her crying had gotten out of hand. I took a few minutes to calm her, so she would nurse. The other babies mostly came crying, too. It is my belief that new babies should never be allowed to cry. Only a day in this world and made to wait. Madness.

Doctor came in that evening. "Mrs. Bennett, it seems you want to go home."

"Yes, Doctor," I replied, "And I am sure the nurses will express some relief at my going. I am grateful for their care, but I can manage now, with my sister's help."

"Well, your baby is very healthy and you seem fine enough. I would say two days more. We keep new mothers longer in the hospital."

So, the time passed until I was leaving. I put Mary into her little gown, bonnet, and receiving blanket. I got my own clothes on without assistance and just sat on the edge of the bed waiting. I was eager to see my children. I was so eager to leave, I could feel my face flush as I heard their voices coming down the hall.

On the way home, Mary Anne told me how Jenny had run downstairs that morning they took me to the hospital, looking for Mama and been told I had gone to the hospital to have the baby which had no meaning for her at all. She began to cry and surprisingly it was big Cousin Walter who was the only one who could comfort her. He sat her down at the table and said, "Mama will be back in a few days with your new baby and Auntie will take care of you until then. And, Papa will be here later." Well, it seemed the mention of Papa calmed her down. Walter gave her breakfast and then the girls took over.

But when Uncle returned alone, she had a fresh load of tears and it was only when Uncle brought Aunt Mary Anne home that things got better. Papa arrived a few hours later, and then things quieted again until he left for the hospital. Jenny kept to the porch, waiting for Papa and wishing for Mama. She still had no desire for a baby. And her companion, little Eddie, waited with her, having less understanding than she did of babies and hospitals. He only knew she was sad.

As we came up the road to the farm, I saw one small figure running fast towards us. She was moving so fast I was afraid she would fall but she didn't and reached us in no time at all, her voice calling out over and over, "Mama, Mama." William brought the buggy to a stop and reached down and pulled her up and into the carriage where I had the door open. I'd quickly handed the baby over to my sister and reached for Jenny. She burrowed her head into me as though she would never let go. I was almost in tears myself. She never put her head up until we reached the front door and let herself be lifted down. Then waited impatiently while I was helped down and then grabbed my hand and called out, "She's home!" to the others assembled on the porch. Billy gave me a relieved look, and the others looked happy, too. I let Mary Anne bring the baby in and sat in the kitchen with Jenny in my lap.

We could not really interest Jenny in the baby. Billy observed how small Mary was, and the big girls got their turns holding her, and even Billy took his turn. Eddie touched her and when she moved, ran to his mother. We passed the afternoon having tea and this time when William was ready to leave, and we told Jenny how he'd be back in a few days, she seemed to accept it.

The cradle was in the kitchen the rest of the day. The others went off to do chores or play, but Jenny stayed with us, and Cousin Eddie. At bedtime, the children went upstairs to bed, even Jenny with a look from me and a promise I'd be there soon. It wasn't very late at all when I went upstairs, too, Mary Anne carrying the baby and Frederick, the cradle. Jenny was waiting for me awake, her eyes wide. She soon settled down and fell asleep beside me and never even woke up when Mary woke to feed, nor did the other girls, although I heard them grunt in their sleep a little. It was a peaceful night.

Papa arrived back to take me home on the third day. Now it was time for Eddie to be tearful. "I don't want Jenny to go home," he cried to his mother, who comforted him and promised a visit in a few weeks. Billy clambered up on the driver's seat with his father, and the rest of us were arranged inside. I had already thanked Mary Anne for taking care of us and Frederick too, and the older children. I told them I felt so grateful and so lucky to have my family. I didn't cry, although I was a bit close to it.

This time the children were quiet on the ride home, while William told me all about the farm and the neighbors and how Bridget had come over and cleaned the house and made a supper for us and that our niece, Margaret, had missed us. Papa told Billy he'd missed his helper, too. Billy had been quiet during his time away on the dairy farm, and now he seemed to be perking up the closer we got to home. Our family would be together again. I had secretly vowed if God gave us another baby not to have it in the hospital. William would have a big argument on his hands, if he thought otherwise.

As we went up the road, I could see my sister waiting in front of our cottage with small Margaret. As soon as the carriage stopped, the children were down in a flash. And after a greeting to their aunt, Billy was off to the barn and the girls into the house. Bridget came over and took Mary in her arms. "I told you everything would be fine, Ellen," she told me with her wide grin and then looking down at the baby, pronounced her beautiful. We moved into the kitchen where the water was already boiling for tea and I could smell fresh bread. William had placed the cradle there and I could hear the sounds of home again. I was content.

CHAPTER 35

Farm Summer

My memories are so perfect of that summer. I see us all. We are having a lovely June, all green and pretty. Our little daughter, Mary Martha, is enchanting. She opens her eyes and smiles and gurgles in some language only babies know. We have spent all our time admiring her. She will be a little spoiled, I think. She is the family pet. The parents have written to say how pleased they are and how we are in their prayers. I never want to leave home again. The children have settled back in again with play and chores.

Billy turned eight years old in July. Bridget and her girl, and Mary Anne and her children, came to visit, and the children ran all over the place. I went outside to check when it got quiet. I found them all in the barn. I heard, as I was approaching, talk of "playing doctor." I sent them all out of the barn. Billy has only recently realized that the children are his cousins and the lady, Bridget, his aunt and Mary Anne, his other aunt. Children are funny. They can know so much and so little, both at the same time. Billy listens to everything, and he has a lot of questions. I heard him ask his father the other day, "What about the hereafter?"

His pa responded with one of his favorite sayings, "Don't know. Nobody ever came back." I don't know what got him thinking about life after death. I suppose he'd been paying attention at church.

Every Sunday we go to Saint Edward's, in the horse and buggy. Billy and Alice both had some questions about something new the pastor was doing. He passed the basket around himself with a new contraption that looks a bit like a corn popper. William explained it to them. "Father wants more money from the congregation, so the coins land on the screen first where he can see them. People don't drop in so many pennies that way."

August was very hot and uncomfortable. One night in particular, I'd had trouble getting our little Mary to sleep. I rocked her in the chair in the kitchen for a long time until her wide-open eyes had finally closed and her small body settled into mine with regular sleeping breaths. First, I stayed there because I was too tired to get up. Then, I suppose, because I had the feeling this could be my last baby and I would hold her close. Upstairs, later, I checked her in the cradle next to our bed. She was sleeping peacefully. William was asleep next to me, after a long day on the farm. His arm, coming out from under the cover, was tanned brown. We were both different after the loss of George, but Mary was a blessing.

I was tired after a day's housework and being a farmer's wife. Today was laundry day and our beautiful baby was fussy, too. I washed the clothes on the washboard, rinsed, and then ran them through the wringer. After that, I hung them neatly outside on the line. The ironing came later when the baby napped. I had two irons, one on the stove hot, and the other in my hand, going back and forth. I planned my meals and each morning I got the cooking started for the noon meal, which is when William stopped his chores to return to the house. Supper was easier and early because we did not stay up late.

Another day, I took myself down cellar with the intent of doing some canning. I went to look at my supplies and saw empty jars but no elastics. Then I remembered them running around down there one afternoon. I called them. Jenny looked innocent, but when Alice and Billy saw me standing by the jars, they looked guilty. It seems they had taken the elastics and shot them at each other until they broke. So, it was a few days before I could do my canning. I had to get new elastics delivered from the grocer with the rest of our order. They got a talking to, but I suppose it was a bit funny.

Alice was a big help, but I did decide, one day, that she should get some time off and let her walk to her friend's house and spend the afternoon. Billy grumbled about weeding the garden, but I noticed how much he loved his fresh vegetables with butter. Sewing, I did in the evening. I wished we had a radio to listen to.

We ate lettuce from the garden, fresh. I liked to sit on the step, peeling potatoes. We ate a lot of potatoes, just like in Ireland. I shelled green beans, breaking off the two ends or shell peas for supper. Billy liked to sit with me then. He'd tell me what was on his mind. He had a lot of questions. He wanted to know more about heaven. I told him what I'd been taught, that if you lead a good life, that's where you go. "George is in heaven, Ma," he said. I agree. The baby cried, and the conversation ended. Billy ran off to the barn. Sometimes, he went into the woods with sticks and there was the pond he liked. He picked me wildflowers. He'd never gone fishing, though. When he was older, Pa would teach him to fish and to hunt.

Summer evenings we sat in the parlor, which is cooler than the kitchen. William played the harmonica. Billy tried but had yet to get any sounds out. We sang K-K-K-Katy. I still like to sing.

I will always remember these evenings. Some day, a long time from now, they'll all be grown and gone. I tried to form a picture of William and me, old and alone together, but I couldn't. But I did not think I would ever leave the farm. That idea was strong in me. I believed it to be true.

One day when William was plowing, with Billy mounted on our horse, while his pa guided the plow down the rows, the horse stopped suddenly and would go no further. The crops were high by then and nothing could be seen that would stop a horse like that. So William stepped over to look around. And suddenly he saw a woman, crouched down and staying very still, like she was scared, like a rabbit. He called out to me to come, and I ran out in my apron with a dishtowel over my shoulder, drying my hands as I went. He very softly told me to come over and then I saw the woman. I began to murmur to her like I would to a child, seeing she was so frightened. After a few minutes, I held out my hand, and she took it, so cold it was, not like mine on such a warm day. She went with me.

Once in the kitchen, we heard the whistle go. I'd known as soon as I saw her that she was from the Medfield State Hospital. We weren't at all worried. It had happened before, but not on our farm. Sometimes they would run away. So, I made her tea, and the children sat around and watched her. She never said a word, but she ate her cake, too. I think she trusted us. William set off across the field and up the hill, and in a while he came back with a man and a woman, both in white jackets. Our guest smiled at them and accepted the woman's hand, and off they went back to the hospital. It stayed in my mind a long time, how she came to be in a mental hospital and what it was like for her. She seemed to be well-treated, but how could I really know. We gave the children a simple explanation of how people get sick in their minds sometimes and need care. Billy was impressed with how the horse knew to stop and not let the plow hurt her. Animals can be like that, sometimes.

"My friends were mostly my sisters and some girl-cousins who lived nearby. That was my Aunt Bridget and my cousins. I didn't make sense of it at the time. She brought kids. We ran all over the place. One time, we were playing in the barn and we had the idea to play doctor, but Ma must have suspected something because she came out of the house where she was visiting with the aunts, and sent us all out of the barn."

"Pa played the harmonica at night. I couldn't learn how to play the harmonica. He covered the notes he didn't want with his tongue, the others, that he wanted to come out, he left open. I covered all the holes and got no music at all. He cupped the harmonica inside his hand while the family sang, K-K-K-Katy."

"Pa's favorite saying when I asked about the hereafter was "Don't know. No one ever came back." My father's words came out of my mouth later, after I was out of his reach.""

"Ma was a farmer's wife. She did the cooking and took care of us, but she didn't do any farming. She did sewing, too. She wasn't required to do any of the gardening. I was the boy in the family and the girls spent their time with our mother, learning to be housekeepers. It was the only future they had back then."

"Ma canned vegetables. I remember me and my sisters taking the elastics off the empty jars to shoot at each other, leaving Ma short at canning time. I remember jars sitting in pans of water."

"The only time she had to listen was when she sat on the steps snapping beans or shelling peas. I didn't know the right questions to ask."

"We went to Saint Edward's in Medfield in a horse and buggy. The pastor, he passed the surrounding basket. He wanted no pennies in the collection, so he rigged up a box with a screen like a corn popper. That way, he could see what everyone gave. It improved the collection."

"The only horse I ever rode was bareback, hitched to the cultivator, to steer, while Pa plowed from the back between the rows. The cultivator turned the soil over-put the weeds underneath. Sometimes, he would be cutting grass for hay. One time when Pa was plowing, the horse stopped and wouldn't go any further. It turned out that a lady had escaped from Medfield State Hospital. The horse knew she was hiding, They came and got her. That's how I remember that. The inmates would escape sometimes and they would blow the whistle."

"Ma was small with brown hair she wore braided on top of her head. She came from Ireland, she and her sisters, I think from Cork. She was a kitchen canary, a maid in a house, before she married my father. I *suppose she had a brogue, but to me, it was just the way she talked. She said a lot of mother things that sons don't pay much attention to. When Pa was sent to the train station to pick up an Irish maid for the big house, she would tell me to go with him."*

~Bill Bennett, age 90

CHAPTER 36

August

It quickly turned to August, so hot and muggy. The baby stuck to me. I looked forward to September, to the cooler weather and the children all going to school, even Jenny who would be starting grade one. She would still be only be five years old. I sometimes wondered if I should keep her home. But I reasoned that she knew her letters and numbers and had pretty much memorized Peter Rabbit. She learned a lot from her brother and sister and could even spell a few words. She wouldn't be the only young one in her class.

Mr. Pierce decided that he would like William to go to Boston, to Mechanics Hall, which I understood to be a place for shows and performances. I'd seen picture advertisements in the papers. I knew it was near the railroad yards. His boss wanted him to pick up some lumber left over from a convention there. Mr. Pierce had business connections everywhere. William thought he would take Billy. The boy was getting to be big enough to be a help to him at eight years of age. They'd take the cart to bring everything back. Billy, of course, was thrilled with the news. Alice knew, by now, she couldn't go. I could tell she was feeling a little rebellious by looking into her eyes. They show everything, like mine.

I decided she should have time with her friend, Jeanne that day, before summer ended. I called her mother. They had a phone, too, and invited Jeanne to come to us. I would pack them a picnic and send them to pick raspberries. I planned to keep Jenny with me, although she would not like that. I'd give all of them tea in the afternoon, before I sent Jeanne home. Jenny could help me make a cake while the baby napped. I like a plan.

William and Billy left early after milking the cows. I packed them a paper bag of sandwiches as usual. Billy had heard about the cake and hoped they'd be some left. Alice said she doubted it. Billy climbed up beside his father without a word, and off they went. I had no particular worries about this trip. The weather was fine and they'd be back in the afternoon. We waved them away.

Jeanne arrived later that morning. She lived maybe less than a mile's walk away on another farm. I sent them off, so pretty in their summer dresses and straw hats. I remembered a tiny Alice going off with her aunts to pick berries a long time ago. "Be good," I called after them. "Stay away from poison ivy and don't eat all the berries." They laughed. Jenny was standing on the steps beside me, frowning with her small arms crossed in front of her. I knew it was good that she not always get her way. There were no tears today because she'd learned that unless she was hurt, exceedingly tired, or frightened, crying did not get her anywhere. She'd been marched up to bed a few times.

"I'm going out to the barn by myself," she told me sadly, "I'll play with the kittens, then, maybe I'll sit and wait for them to come back."

"You'll have a long wait," I told her, trying not to smile, and watched her trudge away.

Mary gave me an easy morning by taking a long nap after I fed her. I did check on Jenny in the barn and she was playing some kind of game which involved skipping in and out, while singing a song she'd made up. So, she was fine.

Right after lunch, I started the cake. Mary had nicely gone in for another nap. We got the big bowl out and lit the stove. It was not so hot today. We mixed it up, Jenny and me, and then I added the currants. I make a good cake. When it came out of the oven to cool, I heard Mary calling us with little chirps. She was all smiles when I bent to take her out of the cradle. I sometimes thought her smile was a bit like George's had been. There was that much sweetness in it. She was growing so fast. I let Jenny sit in the big chair with the baby in her lap while I cleaned the kitchen. To think Jenny had been my baby not so long ago. I still missed George. Sometimes, in the summer twilight, I could still see him running happily again around the yard and screaming with joy as his sisters and brother chased him. It would make my throat tighten a bit. It was a mix of joy and sadness that came over me when I saw him.

I wondered if William ever saw our George like that. I glimpsed the future sometimes, as well as the past. I never did see myself old.

The girls arrived back in the early afternoon, all flushed and happy as only two ten-year-old girls can be. I wondered how many stories they had told each other and what future plans they'd made. Also, they produced about two cups of raspberries, for which I thanked them. I set the table for tea and cake and we sat around.

Jeanne loved the baby. She was the youngest of her family. I showed her how to hold her and she delighted in making Mary giggle. We all laughed around the table. "Alice and I found a place to put our blanket where it was mossy and cool, Mrs. Bennett," she told me. "We took turns reading our favorite parts from Anne of Green Gables."

Jenny ran to get Peter Rabbit. "I can read it," she said brightly. And she did. She had memorized it.

"Good job," we told her, and then it was time for Jeanne to go. I told Alice she could walk her as far as the meadow and reminded Jeanne to go right home. Both girls nodded. I even decided that Jenny could walk with them, reminding her to do what her sister told her to do. I thought I should reward her good behavior.

My girls were back in about fifteen minutes and I set Alice to watch the baby, who was awake and in need of attention, while I started supper. Afterwards, we sat on the steps and waited for them while I snapped green beans. And down the lane they came just before four o'clock, looking a bit tired.

The cart was loaded with boards and they both set about unloading them, William carrying the bigger ones, but not before Papa came over to hug both his girls and took the baby, just for a moment to kiss her small face. He was like that, affectionate with his family. I got a quick kiss, too.

Billy was especially quiet that afternoon. He went off to get the cows as usual, and William told me our son had given him a shock by disappearing while his father was in conversation with one of the workmen at the hall. "I suppose he got bored. I'd offered to walk him over to see the trains in the yard after we did our work. He didn't wait. I think he wanted to tell Alice about all the trains he saw. And I looked around and didn't see him. I didn't know where to go first. When I called his name, he didn't answer me. I ran down the sidewalk and toward the trains. I could hear whistles and that scared me, a small boy down there who might not be noticed. I never knew so many thoughts could run in my brain at one time. And then I saw him, standing there and watching. I knew he was storing up information, but all I could think about was that he was doing a dangerous thing, being so close to those trains and I ran down the platform and didn't exactly grab him but took his arm and turned him around to look at me. Billy looked scared, then, until he saw it was me, but the smile left his face pretty quick when he saw how I looked."

"We had a long talk, Billy and I, about never walking away like that, no matter how much he wanted to see something. I tried to tell him about the danger for a young boy like him to be there near the trains.' What if you had been in the way, on the track when one started up?' I know he wanted to tell me how he wouldn't be that stupid to go on tracks, but thought better of it when he saw my look. I don't think I've ever been so upset with one of our children." William paused then, and I took his hand.

"You did the right thing to lecture him, William," I told him. "You don't want him to forget. There are dangers out there." I was scared myself, just thinking about what could have happened.

"I think he is just so used to being able to do things on the farm and we do let him wander because he knows the land. He thought he could do that in the city," William said.

"It was the longest five minutes of my life when I couldn't find him right away," added my husband.

I didn't talk to Billy about it that night. I thought he'd heard enough for one day and to have his Pa angry at him was a new experience he would not forget. I knew they would make other trips together to the city when necessary. So, I was glad he would know and understand the rules now. Billy put himself to bed a bit early that night. I saw Alice looking at him and wondering why. I decided there would be no benefit to telling his sister about it. There had been some cake left after all, despite her teasing. William looked at the stairs as Billy went up. "Good night, son, Thank you for your help today."

"Good night, Pa," Billy said quietly.

It didn't last, his stillness. The next day he was up for chores and breakfast and all was as it had been. But I hoped a lesson had been learned and our boy had perhaps grown up a little after that trip.

He did tell me more about his day, that afternoon, as he sat with me on the steps while I shelled peas. First, he told me more about Mechanics Hall. "I never saw such a big hall, Ma," he told me. "It even had upstairs spaces where people could look down. There were some men cleaning up, but it was like an empty church, all quiet, except for us."

Then he screwed up his face, but not as I expected, to confess about his visit to the railroad yard. Billy wanted to tell me about something else on his mind. "Pa told me about the Shriners. They have their place at Mechanics Hall. The men do good," he told me. "They wear red hats with tassels. I saw pictures. Sometimes lots of them march in big parades. I asked Pa if I could be one and he said, 'Catholics can't be Shriners because their religion is different from ours. Our church forbids it.'"

I could tell Billy was curious about this. "I didn't know there were different religions," he went on, "I never thought about it. And then Pa said I could be a Knight of Columbus and they help people too, except they're Catholic. And, I'm a Catholic." Then, he added, "Pa says they dress up, too, in capes and hats with feathers." I didn't quite know what to say to all this, so we just sat quietly for a few minutes. Then, Billy said, "I went by myself to see the trains and Pa was really mad at me."

"Your father was right, though, wasn't he Billy," I answered firmly. "When you disappeared, he was very worried. You are not entirely old enough to take care of yourself yet, especially not in the city."

"I guess so," said Billy, "and I'm really sorry." He did look so.

"You won't do anything like that again, will you, son?" I looked right at him.

Billy looked up at me with his eyes, green like mine, as if he wondered why in the world I would ask that and shook his head, "no," I was sure, though, it would not be the last time he put himself in some danger. But we'd be teaching and watching over him. Billy took my pan of peas and held the door open for me as we went into the kitchen for supper. I have a thoughtful, sometimes mischievous, always curious son and I am happy with that. I playfully pulled on his black curls with my hand as we went into the kitchen. My son grinned at me.

"Pa took me on trips to Boston in a horse and buggy. One time we went all the way to Mechanics Hall where his boss, Mr. Pierce, had business connections to pick up useful lumber and haul it home. Ma made us a lunch for the trip."

~Bill Bennett, Age 90

CHAPTER 37

School

The morning of the first day of school, I laid out the girls' freshly ironed school dresses on their bed with matching bows for their hair. They'd had baths the night before and had their hair washed. I'd spent the last weeks letting down and adding trim to Alice's old dresses. I had also made Alice a new plaid dress for the first day of school with a white collar, waist, and matching belt. I'd saved some of Alice's old dresses for Jenny from when she was five. Jenny's short, gingham smock hung down from her shoulders. She looked darling in it. The girls' low, lace shoes would do. Billy, who didn't care what he wore, had needed new knickers and shirts. His shoes were fine. I checked my scholars that morning for clean undergarments and stockings. The children were excited, but Jenny was beyond that. The night before, I had refused to let her sleep in her clothes, saying they would be wrinkled. As they each, in turn, sat on a kitchen chair, I put bows in my girls' combed hair and wet Billy's hair to get it to lie down. It didn't stay that way.

We all walked down the lane, Mary in her father's arms, to see them off. I was so proud of my brood. We heard the school barge coming and the voices of children. The windows were open on this warm September day of 1923. The monitor stepped down and took Jenny on first, helping her up the big step. Billy and Alice followed. I'd instructed Alice to sit beside her little sister for the first day. Billy joined a tumble of small boys on another bench. I noticed that the bigger boys greeted him by name. A few moments later, we waved them off.

William surprised me by coming in for an extra cup of tea. Maybe he thought I'd be lonely or wanted to take my mind off Jenny. It was nice, though, sitting for a short time together without interruption until Mary woke up. Dinner was quiet. The afternoon went by quickly and we went down to meet them again. This time, I held the baby and William got his younger middle daughter off the big step. The other two followed, calling out to friends, before they jumped down. They all looked a little tired, especially Jenny, but they were all smiles. I had bread and jam for them. We sat around the table.

Even the baby had missed them. She was all smiles and giggles. It had been too quiet for our Mary. The older children had homework. I checked their lunch bags to clean them for the next day. Something fell out of Jenny's. I bent to pick it up. Alice called out. "Jenny brought her crayons home, and she's not supposed to." She rushed over to get them. Jenny seemed unperturbed. "Mama," said Alice, "The teacher does not ever let pupils take crayons home. It's a rule."

She let the awfulness of it sink in. "Jenny will be in trouble to-morrow." I knew she was worried about her little sister, but I had quickly gotten tired of the drama.

"Jenny, did you not listen when the teacher told you not to take them home?" I asked.

Jenny replied with her head down, "Maybe I wasn't listening, Mama? I'm sorry." When she looked up, she didn't look the least repentant to me.

"Well, you'll have to take them back." That got a solemn nod from my middle daughter.

"Maybe the teacher won't notice you took them home. You can sneak them back in your desk tomorrow," offered her brother. I did not thank him for that. Jenny smiled. Alice was still looking concerned. I didn't want Jenny all upset but still thought she should have something happen because she had broken a rule. Then, I had a good idea.

"Alice, you take Jenny to her class tomorrow and explain what happened. Jenny can say she's sorry and won't do it again and it will all be over."

Alice looked at me uneasily. "The teacher might blame me," she offered

"Nonsense," I replied. "She'll know it's not your fault." I looked meaningfully at Jenny, who still did not seem to be involved. It was like a play she was watching. Her eyes had been going all over. William was sitting in his chair. I knew if I looked at him, I'd smile or even laugh and I did not want the children to see that. "Well, that's all sorted out, isn't it?" I announced. Alice's look said it all. I think Billy wanted to say his idea was better, but didn't. I put the crayons up high on a shelf out of temptation.

Billy and Alice settled down with homework. Alice always knew when it was no good talking anymore. Jenny ran out to the barn. William went out to do chores. Later, before supper, Billy left to bring in the cows. They did the milking, and I put supper on the table. William and I always welcomed talk at supper. We liked to hear about their days and believed children should be heard. I thought we were through with school talk until Pa asked Billy about his day and he offered this.

"I like recess. We have this thing we play. The little kids get up on the shoulders of the big kids and we wrestle each other." He must have seen the look on my face, because he changed course. "Only sometimes, Ma, we might knock the other kid off. But, it's okay. We don't get hurt." And he put himself back to eating his supper. I sent William a look, and he sent me one back that signaled, "Later." So, I settled down.

Alice then looked at her brother as if to say, "What did you bring that up for?" It seemed our eldest daughter was putting up with a lot from her younger brother and sister this day.

Downstairs that night before we went up to bed, we sat in the parlor together, William and me, and talked about Billy's story. I was worried that he'd get hurt. "Well, Ellen, this didn't just happen on the first day of school. You noticed the big boys greeting him by name this morning. And he's never came home hurt, not even a scratch."

I had to admit that was true. "But it's such a risk. What if he fell the wrong way and broke a bone? Isn't anyone watching them at recess?"

"Can you truly tell me what your brothers were up to in the school-yard when you were growing up?" I had to admit I had no idea. "Ellen," he said, "Teachers seldom venture onto the boys' side of the yard unless there's a fight. Billy has not told us he's been fighting, which would concern me. This is the way boys play. If Billy minded, he wouldn't do it. I know our son."

All this talk of rough play and getting hurt did not help me to get to sleep that night. I could picture him falling hard to the ground. I decided to check him each day for cuts, bumps and bruises.

He was small for his age, but strong and wiry. Billy was built compact like his father. He had only sisters at home and so no opportunity to play rough. We wouldn't allow it. "Boys do not hurt girls," we told him.

The next day after school, Alice reported, as soon as she got off the bus, that she had done what I said and gone to Jenny's class with her to return the crayons. "Her teacher is so nice. She's young and new and pretty and she bent down to talk to Jenny and Jenny really listened!" I laughed to myself because that wasn't one of Jenny's habits. "Mama, teacher says Jenny is really smart and a helper. Miss. Cain said she believes she didn't understand and won't do it again."

I cannot describe the look on Jenny's face without laughing. She looked like the cat who got the cream. She had not gotten into trouble and her teacher liked her. Alice seems relieved that her sister was not starting a life of crime. Billy seemed entirely uninterested, now that the excitement was over. Papa seemed to be controlling himself by looking away. "What a family I have," I thought to myself.

At that the baby put out her arms to Billy, who carried her into the kitchen. The tea was on and bread and butter and jam out, and the pitcher of milk from the icebox. I looked forward to every afternoon when time stopped just for a little bit before I had to start supper. It was like a gift. My mother told me one time to love the little things in your life because everything could change so fast. The baby's squeals interrupted that thought, and I smiled at Billy as he played gently with his baby sister. I hoped we would always be together like this.

I did not forget to check Billy for bruises when I had him remove his shirt so I could hang it up for another day and later, again, when he was in his nightclothes. His father noticed and sighed at my mothering, but I could not help it. I think Alice must have spoken to her brother because he did not bring up the playground again. We got through supper, this time, with little news of school until Alice said her class was going to do a play and she would be in it. And we could come and see her. Alice was pleased with herself and when Alice was pleased, her face turned into one big smile and we all seemed to get her blessing, even Billy, who was seldom interested in his sisters' doings. Jenny saw herself now as the star of her class. I had high hopes for her teacher, who seemed to understand our daughter. Keeping Jenny very busy would keep her out of trouble, I knew, and had planned to tell her teacher, but she seemed to have figured it after just one day.

I shared all this with William in bed that night but he slept through it. So, I said my prayers and joined him.

"I liked school back then. We had a thing we did at recess. The little kids would ride on the shoulders of the big kids and wrestle each other. Who could knock the other guy off?"

~Bill Bennett, Age 90

CHAPTER 38

Fall

One early Monday morning in November, I picked up the phone on our three rings. The operator put Amelia through. "We'll be coming out to see you next Saturday," she said happily. "We haven't seen you in a long time, Ellen." The family had moved to Waltham from Lincoln.

"I am so happy you're coming. We've missed you," I said into the phone, and handed it over to William who had just walked in. "It's your mother. They're coming," I told him.

"Who will drive you out?" I heard him ask. "Oh, Stephen, that's good. Come early and stay as long as you can. The children will be so pleased and you've not seen Mary since her Baptism."

He called to the children who were just coming in. "Your grand-parents are coming for a visit and your Uncle Stephen, too." Alice wanted to know if Florence was coming. She was the youngest aunt, only fifteen. "Yes," nodded Papa. That pleased our Alice. Jenny looked gleeful. They always spoiled the children with treats. William himself looked pleased. Billy was focused on the car.

"The Bennetts are coming," I told my sisters the next day. Bridget said she'd walk over while they were here. Mary Anne and Fred, though, would be busy that day on the dairy farm and couldn't leave.

I thought I'd make shepherd's pie. They'd liked it in the past and bake apple pie for dessert. I'd see the cottage was very clean. I did wish we had a camera to take pictures of us all. I love company. William had been concerned when his family moved to Waltham, that his parents, especially, would miss living in the country. He wanted to know how they were doing. Some of his brothers and sisters were still at home, going to their jobs.

That November day dawned sunny and cold. I lit the fire in the stove and put the kettle on way before I expected them to arrive. Billy was excited about the car. He would be asking his uncle a lot of questions, I was sure. Jenny had dressed her dolls in their best clothes and knew it was not unheard of that her grandparents would come bearing gifts. Alice thought she should show off her books. She had a small library now on the shelf her father had made her. The baby thought nothing, but was taken by the noisy, festive mood and never settled down for her nap.

By the time they arrived, by late morning, the cottage smelled of meat and gravy. The apple pies I'd made the day before. Finally, the car moved up the lane. The children hardly let it come to a stop before running over. Our company moved out of the car and into welcoming hands. Stephen stood there, tall and handsome, still boyish when he smiled. The folks were the same, Amelia, lovely with her smooth skin and gray-brown hair worn up. Henry William was jolly, calling out our names. He held Jenny high in the air. Alice immediately took young Florence over and they went, arm in arm, upstairs to the bedroom she shared with Jenny. Florence was a high school girl, and she wore a dress with a fashionable dropped waist and lots of trim. Her smooth brown hair was bobbed. Our Alice would be looking up to her. Florence was lively and pretty. I imagined her mother was keeping an eye on this youngest daughter. I suddenly had a picture of my girls at that age and quickly made it go away.

In no time at all, Amelia had taken over the baby in the kitchen. I began to put dinner together. Billy was outside with Uncle Stephen, looking over his big, new, black Model T Ford sedan, full of questions. I could hear their voices. Jenny had put herself and her dolls in Papa's big chair and was waiting expectantly for someone to notice. She'd also seen a large carpet bag come in. She stared at where it rested over by the door. Mary was good-natured, despite no nap. I did think she might sleep through dinner, though. William and his father had walked off toward the barn, looking very much alike.

First thing, Amelia wanted to know about was the children's schooling. "Are they doing well?" I told her they were good at school, even Jenny, the youngest. We all wanted them to go on to high school. Then she wanted to know how I was doing, as she cuddled Mary and rocked her to sleep. We both knew she meant about George.

"I still miss him," I told her, "But now we love this little one just as much, but in another way." She nodded. "I see George sometimes," I told her quietly, "He is happy again and running around the farm-yard." Amelia did not look surprised. She patted my hand. No one of their family ever talked about the young girl they had lost. She had been named Mary, too. William said his mother had been pleased when he phoned to tell her we had named the baby after his long-ago sister. All I know about their Mary was that she had been sick only for a short time. Amelia had given birth to several more children afterwards. She still never talked about her Mary.

I called Alice to come down and help. Florence came, too. I gave them aprons and got them busy. We sat down to dinner right at noon, as I'd planned it. Mary had been carried off to bed. We were all squeezed around the table. I'd covered it with my best tablecloth. Jenny led the blessing. Amelia praised my cooking. The kitchen stayed warm for a long time after we ate and we sat comfortably around the table, trading stories. Bridget came by for dessert. The Bennetts now lived not far from the Waltham Watch Company, that immense building on Moody Street. William had told me about it. I've never been to Waltham. Henry William told us he'd found work on a farm in the west of Waltham. It was not all city. Amelia kept house on Brown Street.

His parents wanted to know when he might come home for dinner. William said he'd try to arrange it. I knew it would be a job to get every-one into the buggy and have someone come to milk the cows before he got home in the evening. I noted that William accepted, "coming home," even now because it was his parents' house. It would always be so. When our children came to see us when we were old, I suppose they would call it the same, "going home." I tried to see myself old.

We talked for the rest of the afternoon. I sent the children off to play. William's father laughed aloud at tales of our children, especially Jenny's escapades. After a while, Mary woke up and was passed around the table, finally landing in her grandfather's lap. We heard that the other Alice had a new beau. Stephen told us little about himself. I think he was walking out with more than one girl. He was that handsome. My husband's brothers and sisters would soon marry and have their own families. The boys were all working. It was hard for me to imagine my children all grown up.

Amelia directed Jenny to go get the big bag resting by the door. Inside were doll clothes, embroidered aprons, and bean bags made out of leftover cloth. They immediately started tossing them around. Also, for Alice, a pretty blouse, and a little carved car for Billy. I saw his grandfather's hand in that. There was a rag dolly for Mary, lolly-pops for all, and also a big tin of Grandmother's cookies. And then Henry William reached into his pocket and pulled out a postcard of the Waltham Watch Company. From the picture, it looked like it went on for blocks. I could see Billy ruminating on the biggest ship, and now the biggest building in the world. We were all impressed. Billy instantly wanted to go to Waltham. Alice, I could see, would find a way to be included in that expedition.

Too soon, it was time for them to go. Stephen was rushing them a little. I would not be surprised if he had plans for later on that evening. They got all bundled up. The day was turning colder. Florence was slow coming downstairs. I thought I could have her to stay some time. Alice would love that. Billy was out there watching Stephen get ready to start the car up. We would be hearing about this marvel for a while. Once they were all settled in, Stephen took the crank handle in his hand and cranked it hard. Then, he jumped in and did things with pedals and lever and a stick. Billy was right there watching it all. I think Stephen liked having us witness to what an expert he was. We waved our goodbyes. Billy ran alongside the car while it rolled down the lane. William looked a little sad when we turned to go back in the house. I took his arm, and we walked in.

"We had a telephone with a party line. If the operator rang the phone, we counted three rings for us to answer the phone and hear the operator. It had speakers and a little holder which a lot of people would ease up and listen to. That's how word spread."

"Pa's family lived in Waltham, fifteen miles from Dover. The grandparents had no car except when Uncle Steve, who had one, would drive them out sometimes."

~Bill Bennett, Age 90

CHAPTER 39

Christmas (1924)

WINTER

The snows had come early this year. Already, the farm was covered with drifts from the night's storm. The animals still needed to be tended. Billy was big enough, now, to be a help to his father. School was closed again. I had the children all day long. Mary sometimes didn't take naps. There was just too much going on. Billy started tossing a ball one day and broke a plate. He took himself upstairs after saying he was sorry. Pa had a talk with him. Alice was busy drawing pictures and writing stories about them. Jenny was all over the place. I put her to work dusting the furniture, but that didn't last long. She placed a sheet over the big wooden chair and had Mary crawling in and out. I let that go. It kept the baby amused. I told my husband to take them all out to muck out the barn with him. If I can't be alone, neither can he.

Another snowstorm was coming. William could tell. I told the children that Santa Claus was watching. Alice gave me a sideways look at that. Jenny seemed the most affected. She sat still for at least ten minutes before rushing off to another one of her projects. This time it involved her and Mary banging on pans with wooden spoons. I stood the racket for a while and then put the baby in for a nap and handed Jenny her

Peter Rabbit and told her to read to me, now that she was in grade one. She did quite well, knowing many of the words when I quizzed her.

It has always seemed funny to me that the cows like to go out in the snow. Sometimes they lay in it, a comical sight, big beasts that they are. Billy led them into the warm barn at night. There was frost on the inside of the windows in the parlor and in the bedrooms. The children scratched and drew with their fingernails in the ice. This is not what I came from in Ireland. When I got into a mood, I'd blame William for the snow and the cold. He'd just look at me. Thank God, on one house-bound day, Papa decided to take them sledding. He'd found an old sled in the barn and fixed it up. I put them in as many clothes as I could find, fastened mittens, hats and gloves and pushed them out the door. I thought how grand it would be to have a picture of them in the snow.

They lasted a long time out there, sledding on the hill. It was almost dusk when they came in. Time to bring the cows in and milk them. William had been having fun, too. Alice and Billy were arguing about whether it was better to go down on the sled sitting up or on your belly. I quieted them and put Alice to work peeling carrots. Their wool coats smelled as they dried on a chair near the stove. I could imagine the odor at school with dozens of coats all drying at once. Jenny came down the stairs in her best dress, saying she was a princess. She had made herself a paper crown. I admired her and then sent her skittering back up the stairs to change. Jenny was never still. She did not ever fall softly into sleep at night. She just suddenly turned off, like when you pull a switch. Billy was like that, too. Alice was the one with the books until I turned off her light. We still rocked the baby most of the time. My mother would have said that she would never learn to put herself to sleep. But I thought Mary was my last baby, and I wanted the feel of an infant going to sleep on my shoulder a bit longer.

I began my Christmas plans early. My sister Kate sent books, including one of fairy tales for Jenny. She'd also found an illustrated one about ships for Billy and Pollyanna, for our Alice. I'd read through it as soon as it came. I knitted hats for everyone, even the baby. Our old landlady in the center of Dover had given me a red wool coat, which I had made over into a coat for Alice. I like red. I'd give it to her Christmas morning before church.

Money was the same this year, but we could provide some gifts for our children. We got them all bird whistles. You fill it with water and it sounds like a canary. Billy got tinker toys. He likes to put things together. We got Jenny a little girl's stick horse. And I sewed a doll together for her. Alice was that in between age. She was turning eleven in the spring. She still had her dolls, but really didn't play with them anymore. So we got her a little figure porcelain girl doll in an Indian costume of fringed dress with dark braids and headband to keep it on the shelf with her books. All of this was from the Sears Catalog. For the baby, we got a small stuffed bear. When the parcels came, I hid them under our bed. I would wrap each one with tissue paper later for under the tree.

One night at the end of supper, instead of getting right up to clean the kitchen, I decided to tell them a story. Seeing how Alice, especially, was interested in my life in Dorchester, I decided to recount my first Christmas there. "Since Christmas is on our minds," I announced, "I think I will tell you about my first Christmas here in America."

"It was to be our first Christmas not at home in Ireland. We had already put together a package to send home with small gifts for our parents and brothers and sisters. I'd written a very long Christmas letter and put in a little extra money, too. Ma had sent each of us a parcel. I could picture her carrying them to the post office in Ballynacargy and the post master asking her about her daughters in Boston."

"How far away is Ireland?" asked Alice.

"Remember," I told her. "I came over on that big ship and it took ten days."

Billy nodded. He remembered the big ship. Jenny was still wondering how Mama could have a mother and father and brothers and sisters so far away. She'd never seen them, only the aunts who came over.

"We had the day off from service and would be going to dinner at the Rafterys where we had stayed when we arrived, just over a year before. They were nice to us and the closest we got to family in Boston.

I did hope for mince pies and Christmas cake. I knew they were having a big turkey."

Billy liked the part about the food. Jenny needed to understand where I lived. "Remember Mrs. Bernstein where we went to visit? I worked for the Bernstein family, doing cooking and cleaning and helping to take care of the children."

"That sounds like what you do now," offered Alice. She is so smart, our Alice.

They seemed ready for me to go on. "We had both been given some hours off, too, on Christmas Eve. So we went over to the Rafterys where, despite being busy with Christmas preparations, had us to an early supper of fish chowder and brown bread. They had put a holly wreath up and had evergreens around the house, lighted candles in every window, and water buckets too."

"Just like us," called out Billy.

I paused to remember, "The turkey had been plucked and cleaned and sat in a large pot with a cover on the back porch. The kitchen was well cleaned, and the windows washed and shining with starched curtains. Carpets had been beaten and floors polished. The Rafterys would be going to midnight Mass. We would come to them the next day, after morning Mass."

I had only just got started, "Christmas day opened cold and sunny, no snow coming down at all."

"I'd had this awful picture of waking to a snowstorm and not being able to get to church or to dinner after. What a Christmas day that would have been." They all looked adequately horrified. "I left hot porridge for the Bernsteins on the back of the stove and filled the kettle. I'd permission to leave early for Mass and to spend the whole day away. I was not expected back until the evening. It was generous of Mrs. Bernstein, I thought. They did not celebrate Christmas or Easter, being of the Jewish faith, I knew, and had their own holidays." Billy wanted to know about Jewish people. He had recently learned there were different religions. "Later, Billy," I told him. Jenny looked shocked that anyone not keep Christmas. Alice wanted to know what I wore. "Well, Alice, I had only two sets of clothes, one for working: a plain skirt and blouse and two aprons. For going out: a coat, a woolen skirt, pretty white blouse and felt hat. I wore shiny boots. I felt dressed up." That seemed to satisfy her.

"At Raftery's, we were welcomed into their warm house, now filled up with family and friends and with the smell of roasted turkey and stuffing. On one table was what appeared to be a Christmas cake and a plate of mince pies. I felt at home. We all sang carols after dinner, then helped Mrs. Raftery clear the table and wash the dishes. The men seemed to drift to the divan and parlor chairs where they snored, having eaten heavily and had some drink. All the women and girls chatted, and the few children played on the rug with their new toys. After that, some of us took a walk along cold Dorchester streets, instead of the lanes of Rathcaled and along the canal as we would have done at home. Most people were still indoors where you could hear merriment. We saw men outdoors smoking their pipes and children sliding down a hill on their sleds. That did look like fun."

"I love sledding," remarked Jenny.

"I didn't get on a sled until I was already a young woman." Jenny was amazed at that. "No snow in Ireland," I told her.

"Yes," said Alice, imitating me. "Everything is all green."

I continued my story. "After our walk, we went back to the house for the rest of the day's entertainment and it was not even getting dark yet, dinner having been served at noon. The men were waking up, and the tea was on, and yet another cloth on the table and more plates and Mrs. Raftery's best tea cups. The Christmas cake was put on the table and a pudding, and the mince pies. We sat down, a crowd again, and cheerfully ate our way through the desserts with a little more drink here and there. There was story-telling and more songs, and finally I looked outside and saw it was drawing dark on this winter afternoon, and soon we would have to leave. Christmas day was fast becoming Christmas night, and we were due back to our jobs. It had been a wonderful Christmas and yet there was not one of us who did not think of the people home in Ireland that day and what they would be doing and how we missed them." The children all looked a little sad at that telling.

I was almost at the end of my story, "There were hugs at the Raftery's and thank-you's and a fast wrapping of sweets for us to take back with us. We ran outside into the cold. Everyone agreed that snow was on the way. And so we walked to the streetcar. My sister got off two stops before I did, and I walked home alone and let myself in the kitchen door. On the table was a small package with my name on it. 'From Anna Bernstein. Thank you for all your good work,' it said on the small card attached to it and inside, a little sewing kit with a lovely silver thimble. Well, I supposed it to be a Christmas gift, although she did not celebrate. It did brighten my return and made me very pleased to be working for such a kind and generous woman. I would thank her the next day."

"Mrs. Bernstein," said Alice. "She is nice." I agreed.

"She gave us presents, too," added Jenny. "And it wasn't Christmas."

I got on with the story, "I would have given anything on that Christmas night to be at home in my parents' small house, sitting at the table and having a last cup of tea, and chatting with my mother. But I had succeeded here and sent money home and learned so much and had so many plans, too, I did think, even then, that Mary Anne would be the first to marry. I was taking my time."

"Until you met me," That and a wink from William. I ignored him.

"And then I went to sleep."

"And Santa Claus came," added Jenny.

"No," I told her, "Santa comes for boys and girls. I was grown by then." Jenny, I could tell, had never thought of that.

Billy chimed in, "Ma and Pa never get anything from Santa Claus."

We all got up from the table and cleaned up. I was feeling very tired. I'd enjoyed telling my story, but it had worn me out.

Christmas was a week away. They were all excited. Jenny's feet no longer touched the floor. Alice was trying hard to believe in this Santa who came around secretly, was never seen, and left presents. Billy had no problems with any of it.

One afternoon, William took the children up the hill and into our woods to pick garland to hang inside our cottage. While they were gone, I located the candles and the tree decorations. The crib had gone up the week before. Jenny had rearranged the figures of the Blessed Family many times since. Sometimes the shepherds and the three kings left entirely and went off somewhere else. She never got tired of it. I would put them back in order after she went to bed. We hung the garland over the doorways and along the walls. It looked lovely.

Two days before Christmas, they went to the woods again, this time to pick out the tree. I could hear them coming back. Pa was singing with them. They knocked the snow off the tree and pulled it into the house and then into the parlor where the stand waited. It was still afternoon, so we had time to put the ornaments on; inexpensive ones and others made by the children. The candles went on last, each in its little holder. I was feeling tired again and went into the kitchen to sit down. William joined me, looking concerned. "I'm all right," I told him. "I just do not seem to have much energy."

"You're probably worn out from the baby," he offered. "You'll soon be weaning her?"

"In the new year," I told him. What I did not tell him was that I had discovered a small lump in my breast. I did hope it was nothing and did not want to be bothered with the doctor yet. I thought it might have something to do with the nursing. Mostly, I tried to forget about it. Alice had lugged the baby down from her nap. I could hear Mary crowing in the parlor. The door would remain closed to the children until Christmas Eve, when we would light the candles on the tree and in the windows to welcome the Holy Family.

It was Christmas Eve. We all looked forward to the next day. Each Christmas morning was the same. I would make breakfast. Pa would have something to do in the barn. A door would bang and he would return. We would open the parlor door and Santa Claus would have come and left presents. It was my favorite day of the year. I vowed to put my problem entirely out of my mind until after the holiday. At that point, Jenny flew in to ask how many hours until Santa came? She offered to go to bed early if it would make him come sooner. I tried not to laugh.

"That doesn't work," her brother told her. "You just won't be able to sleep. He never comes until after breakfast."

"Breakfast?" said Jenny. "Why do we have to have breakfast on Christmas?"

"We go to church, too," said Alice. "But not until after we've opened our presents."

"Church?" Jenny was beside herself. She'd forgotten.

"Remember the stable at church? Tomorrow the Baby Jesus will be in it. It's His birthday." This from Papa. Jenny sighed.

After supper, we lit all the candles in the windows, each one with a bucket or bowl of water on the floor near it. Then the candles on the tree. Beautiful. The children were enchanted. We had to keep the baby from crawling right over. Her mouth was a perfect circle. We sat for a while and then I sent them up to bed and deposited a sleeping Mary into her little crib. It did not take long to get quiet. William carefully put the candles out on the tree. He'd already snuffed the candles upstairs. We sat quietly together for a while and contemplated other Christmases. Then I brought down the tissue-wrapped packages and put them under the tree.

Jenny actually slept like a log. It was Billy I could hear get up several times to go to the window. I wondered how he could stand the cold on his feet. I supposed he was looking for Santa. I even heard Alice get up once. I knew all their footsteps. I also knew they had seen or felt the lumpy stockings at the foot of their beds. It was very early, not even light out, when they opened their stockings to apples and oranges and nuts and candies inside. Santa had been good.

Next, we came downstairs. Billy went out with his father to feed and milk the cows. I made eggs for breakfast and nice thick toasts with butter and some preserves from last summer. I had my hot cup of tea. Pa ate his breakfast and then, as usual, had something to do in the barn. I kept the children with me in the kitchen. Then we heard the door bang, and he came in to announce that he thought Santa had come. I ran and opened the door to the parlor and the candles on the tree were lit. Underneath were the few gifts we had for them. Jenny froze, but just for a minute. I'd printed their names on each white tissue-wrapped gift. We kept it calm by handing each child a package, waiting while they opened it and then passing the other one out. It didn't take long at all. The bird whistles worked. Birds warbling everywhere. Lovely. I just perched comfortably in a chair with my cup of tea and enjoyed their pleasure. William did the same.

Alice tried to interest Mary in her little stuffed bear, but she was happy crawling amongst the tissue paper left on the floor. Alice solemnly told me how she would have to keep her porcelain Indian princess doll up high and away from her little sister, who was now tearing around the room on her stick horse. Billy had dumped all the pieces from his tinker toys onto a little section of floor and was putting them together. The books would wait for a quieter time. I blessed our Kate for sending them.

"Church," I called into this activity. "I'll give you just enough time to play a little more and then you can get into the clothes I got ready for you. I'll bathe and dress the baby first." A while later, I called Alice to me upstairs and showed her the red coat. She was so pleased, and it fit perfectly. She twirled around and around. I fixed both girls' hair and pushed a comb through Billy's and then took the baby from Papa so he could go out and get the buggy. We all piled in and off we went. It was a pretty day and no snow coming. As we got nearer to church, we encountered more families, and the children shouted out, "Merry Christmas!"

The music was wonderful. We all sang loudly. At the end of Mass, we marched up the aisle to the crib so they could see the infant Jesus in His bed. William drove home fast, so I could prepare for our company. Bridget and her family would walk over and we had invited Mr. Norton, the old farm tenant, to come to us from town. Soon, he arrived. He brought some wine which was nice. Bridget came with the Christmas cake. I'd made mince pies.

Dessert was finished. We all felt stuffed. Soon, it would be time to tell stories. The cleaning all done, we joined the men and children in the parlor. Mr. Norton came in from smoking his pipe outside on the steps. We all found places to sit. It felt very cozy. It was easy to think about past Christmases. So, Bridget and I would share our memories of Christmas in old Ireland.

"Pa let the cows out even when there was snow on the ground because they needed exercise and they didn't mind it, trudging through the snow. Some of them even lay down in the snow. They stayed in the warm barn at night."

"I remember Christmas. I went with Pa to pick out the Christmas tree. It was on the property. And we would pick garland, too, green, to drape around the house. The tree had real candles, the size of birthday candles. And they didn't go on fire. On Christmas Eve, we would also have candles in all the windows and water buckets everywhere. We would go to bed early and in the morning, the parlor door would be closed. Ma would take us into the kitchen for breakfast. Pa would have something to do in the barn. Then, we would hear a door bang and he would return. The parlor door would open and Santa Claus had come. The gifts, they would be under the tree."

~Bill Bennett, age 90

CHAPTER 40

A Christmas Story (1924)

SHADOWS

Bridget and I sat on the divan together in the parlor while the children sat on the floor near the Christmas tree. The candles were not lit yet, but would be as soon as it got dark. "Your Aunt Bridget was only a little girl when Aunt Mary Anne and I left Ireland. So, we'll tell the story together. Sometimes Bridget will fill in for me. Her memory is fresher."

"I'm much younger," said Bridget with a big grin.

The children laughed.

"At home in Rathcaled, on Christmas Eve, candles were lit in all the windows of our small house. This was after weeks of cleaning and clearing out."

"Oh, don't I remember that," said Bridget. "Ma had no mercy on us at all. Tell them about the whitewashing, Ellen."

"The inside walls and outside were carefully whitewashed. And the curtains taken down and washed, floors swept and scrubbed, and the hearth cleaned thoroughly."

"Remember the holly wreath on the door, Ellen? That was our father's job. He wanted it just so and evergreens hung all over." Bridget was reaching now into her memory. "I'd forgotten how much he had to do with the decorating," she said. "And we would be so excited and there was company in and out all day on Christmas Eve."

I continued. "At noon, the forge closed. Our father was a blacksmith, an important job in our small townland." I thought how they would never meet their grandfather and made that thought go away.

"Were the presents hidden in the forge when you were at home, Ellen?" asked my sister.

"Oh, yes, but I only knew that because I was one of the oldest."

Bridget looked over at me. "I found out," she told me. She reminded me of Jenny, who was looking over at the mention of presents. "I looked all over until I found them."

"Santa Claus left them there," I told them quickly. Alice looked skeptical. I went on. "There would be a turkey plucked and cleaned and resting in a pan of water for the next day."

"Ellen, do you remember the Christmas cake with the liquor poured into it?"

"Of course," I told her. "And the mince pies, too, pretty and brown, resting on a plate."

"Bridget, did you still go to midnight Mass?"

"Oh, yes," she told me. "And we were very excited to stay up so late."

I told them about the candles in every window to guide the holy family on their journey which we lit when we returned from church. And the little table set for three with mince pies to feed them.

Alice had never heard of it, this food left for Mary and Joseph and Jesus. Bridget told her that it was as I said and probably still done in Ireland.

"There was a pageant at the school every year. Do you remember that, Bridget?" She did. "We would all go to see the little ones act out the nativity and sing songs, all dressed up as Mary and Joseph and the shepherds and even the three kings, although they did not really arrive until later on the Epiphany." I looked over at Jenny. "Is that why you keep moving the three kings away?"

"Yes, Mama," my daughter said. "That's why." I thought her brother and sister would fall over laughing, but they mostly contained themselves.

"The performers would giggle, but the sweetness of the story always came through and the children's innocence." I thought the adults in the room would understand that.

Bridget continued, "We would be lively going home with the sweets we'd been given and the giddiness of looking forward to two whole weeks of no school."

I added that I thought the schoolmaster and schoolmistress shared some of that joy at a release of two weeks from their young scholars.

"Then, we would all go to midnight Mass," added Bridget. "On Christmas, walking there down the lane to Saint Matthew's."

"And into the crib would go the baby Jesus, just after midnight when He was said to be born."

"You would be asleep in the pew by then," I told Bridget.

"Later, when you moved to America, I would stay awake," she countered. The children were watching us, their heads going back and forth.

"But when you were little, you would be carried home by one of our brothers. I remember that." I recalled something else. "Bridget, everyone was crying the day we left for America, but not you. You said we'd be back in two weeks."

"And, I waited for you," Bridget was not her smiling self. "But you didn't come back at all."

We both looked at each other.

"But then you came over yourself," I offered.

"But not for a long time," said Bridget.

I thought we should continue with the Christmas story. It made me too sad to remember when we left them all behind, especially Bridget. Alice was listening, though. I don't think she'd ever thought about how hard that had been.

Everyone had been quiet while Bridget and I told our story. At the conclusion, Alice thought we should go to midnight Mass next year. I said her father and I would think about it. Billy wanted to leave food for the holy family. I thought we could certainly do that. Jenny had got up to move the three kings somewhere I could not see. I thought I might not find them for weeks. We were all tired but did not want Christmas to end. So we sat longer. Finally, the baby got me up because I needed to change and feed her and put her to bed. I could tell the other three children hoped I would not notice they were still up. So, I didn't. Bridget and Martin and small Margaret prepared to leave. They only lived down the road. I held Bridget's hand just for a moment. I'd never realized how abandoned she'd felt when we left Ireland. Mr. Norton told us what a fine time he had before he, too, left for home.

In bed later that night, I said a little prayer for George. I always did at Christmas. I examined my breast again. Surely, there was nothing wrong, I told myself, but I would tell William during the next few weeks and I would see the doctor. We'd had little conversation, Mary Anne and I, these past busy few weeks. I thought I might talk to her about this first. She was always so practical and would tell me what she thought I should do. I did not fall asleep for a while. When I did, it was strange dreams I was having. There were shadows in my dreams. I woke up the next morning not as rested as I usually was.

CHAPTER 41

Winter (1925)

It was over a month before I talked to Mary Anne about my problem. I was busy weaning the baby over to milk in the same little cup I'd used for her sisters and brothers. They all went back to school. But, then, Jenny got sick. She came home one day and put herself to bed. I put her into her nightclothes. She was shivering. In the morning, she didn't feel any better. It seemed like a bad cold. I sent the others off to school. I sat up with her several nights. She had a cough and ran a fever. I stayed with Jenny. Alice went into Billy's room. William called the doctor to come out.

The doctor came. He took Jenny's temperature and said it was not very high. I'd known that. He listened to her chest. "No problems with her lungs." He looked at her throat. "Looks fine." I felt relieved. He instructed her to cough. "Not a dry or hacking cough," he said. "Do you have her sleep sitting up"?

"I sit up with her at night and have her up on a pillow."

"Well, Mrs. Bennett, you do right to keep her away from the other children. She has a flu. It's not a bad case and Jenny seems very healthy."

"I can give you something that will make her feel better and rest more." He took out a glass jar and in it was something called Vicks Vapo Rub. "It is a salve. She's congested and this will help her breathe

244

more easily. Apply it on her chest and under that little nose of hers," He looked over at Jenny and smiled. She managed one back.

A few days later, Jenny was calling downstairs, first for food, and then for company. We had both been sleeping nights, and that made a big difference. I had begun using the ointment right away. It improved things immediately. It smelled good, too, of Eucalyptus and menthol and maybe a bit of nutmeg and thyme. It made her less congested and she could breathe through her nose. I decided Alice could be trusted to read to her, and that would give me some time for chores. At the end of another week, we went back to our own rooms. I found out that Alice had been reading to Billy from Pollyanna each night. He had no complaints. I was glad to get back to normal, but still the worry about my breast persisted. The lump had gotten larger. It was past time to talk to Mary Anne.

It was late January. I could not put it off any longer. I looked for a way to talk to my sister, Mary Anne alone. Always, when she came, it was a big crowd, and we enjoyed ourselves but found no time alone. Finally, I called her and asked that she get Frederick to drive her out one nice day when the children were in school so we could talk. She knew from my tone that I had something to tell her, and she made it that week. As soon as Frederick dropped her off that morning, I sat her down in the kitchen and made tea. She made a fuss at Mary being so big, and then I got the baby occupied with some toys and faced my sister across the table. Bridget would be over soon, and I wanted to talk to Mary Anne first.

"I have a lump on my breast," I told her, seeing no reason not to get right to the point. The look on her face was strange. I couldn't fathom it. "I thought it was due to the nursing, but I'm done with that and it's gotten bigger. I don't know what to do." I stopped then, to give her a chance to say something.

I was concerned because her silence went on by several minutes. Then, she spoke and I will never forget her words. "I have a lump in my breast, too, Ellen." And then she said something even more unexpected. "I'm frightened, Ellen." I grasped her hands in mine across the table.

"We've always solved problems together, Mary Anne, and we will do so now." I told her. My voice was shaky. My throat hurt with holding it in. And then we both broke down crying, and that was how Bridget found us. She was shocked. We told her. She immediately informed us that we should both get to the doctor. She looked right at me first. "Ellen, you will have William take you tomorrow to town to see Doctor Arnold. Why in the world did you not make an appointment when he came for Jenny?" I had no answer. And then she turned to Mary Anne. "And you do the same, tomorrow." This was our little sister talking.

At that point, all Mary Anne and I could think of was telling our husbands. And there would be no putting that off. They needed to know, and it would have to be tonight. There was to be no more hiding this news. Then Bridget looked at both of us. "Everything will be all right," she told us.

Well, all of us knew better, but we accepted that Bridget spoke that way to make us feel better. She didn't know what else to say. None of us dared to talk about tumors or cancer or, God help us, sickness and death. We were all too young yet to think of it. We felt like the world would tumble down right then.

The rest of the day, until it was time for Mary Anne to go, was difficult. Bridget gave me instructions for the next day, "You should head off in the morning after the children leave for school. Bring Mary right to me. I will be here if you are long and Martin can take care of the cows. To Mary Anne, she said, "Louise can watch the other children if you are not back. I suppose you can go to the hospital? And I expect to hear from both of you right away." She was ordering us around, but I saw the strain in her face. She did not want to say what we all thought. People like us did not survive cancer. We did not have operations. We did not have that kind of money.

That night was awful. I so wanted to have another regular evening before I told William what was wrong. I thought of Mary Anne going through the same. I did not like my week upset with a trip to the doctor in town. But I could not put it off any longer, now that Bridget knew.

She would not let me, which was, in a sense, a relief, but still I wanted to go back to that place where I could put it out of my mind.

William's eyebrows went up when I said, "William, I have a woman's problem." He looked at me as though to say, "What can I do about that?" I quickly told him about the lump in my breast. He got up and stood in front of me where I was sitting in my parlor chair.

"Why didn't you tell me before, Ellen?" and he reached out for me, pulling me up and against him. "I would have taken you straight away to the doctor. You should not have worried about this alone. I knew something was not right."

I refused to cry. I wanted to do this the right way and not lose control before I'd even been to the doctor. I had only bits and pieces of information on this problem. I knew lumps on the breast were a bad thing. I knew what cancer was. "It doesn't hurt," I told my husband. "But it doesn't belong there. I prayed for it to go away."

"Well, it hasn't," responded William firmly, "And we will go to the doctor tomorrow."

"Bridget will watch Mary and be here for the others," I told him. He looked surprised.

"When did you arrange that?" His voice got louder.

"When Mary Anne came. I wanted to talk to her before I did to you. She's always so practical. I've been daft over this."

"And what did she say, Ellen?" he looked a bit upset that I'd gone to her first, but that went away when I told him that my sister had the same. He shook his head in disbelief. "That can't be." I saw his world fall down as ours had earlier. I took a big breath. I was not one for drama. We talked.

It was a while before we went up to bed, for all it was getting late. We agreed that the children were not to be told anything. We would keep it to ourselves, leaving for town the next morning, right after they left for school and Bridget came over.

"Maybe it isn't so much," I said, looking for a way out of it. "The doctor will do his examination and tell me to watch it and come back if it doesn't go away" I was grasping for a better answer than I thought I would really get in the morning. William didn't disagree with me.

When I got my nightgown on upstairs, I left the top buttons undone. I had been taught to be very private in my ways, but I thought William should see. He looked and tenderly touched me there, making me cry softly because I would not wake the children. I saw tears in William's eyes, which he tried to hide. We slept nestled together that night. I had no dreams at all.

CHAPTER 42

Winter and Spring (1925)

The morning did not change anything. We both got up quickly and did our morning chores. The children knew nothing of it at all. I got ready. I wore my shawl wrapped around my coat. I was shivering, not just with the cold, but with dread.

Bridget came over to get Mary. I had bundled her up in sweaters and a small blanket. She cried when I left. William put me up on the seat beside him and off we went. It wasn't very far. I felt bad that one of the few times we went out alone together had to be on such an occasion. We did not talk and only nodded when we saw people we knew in town. We sat in front of the doctor's big house. I did not want to get out, but William stretched out his hands to me and lifted me down.

The doctor's wife told us to wait. She was very nice. We did not have an appointment, but she was sure he would see us. We didn't wait long. I went in alone. Mrs. Arnold directed me to a chair in the examining room, then left me. I had just enough time to read the doctor's framed medical certificate mounted on the wall, and in he came.

"And how are all the little Bennetts?" he asked me.

"They are fine," I told him. "Jenny is fully recovered. I am here about myself."

"Tell me about it," he said quietly.

I took a breath. "I have a lump on my left breast." I told him.

He nodded. "When did you notice it?"

"In September."

His face got somber. "I am going to examine you. I will have my wife come in and help you undress." He left to go get her. I was feeling cold.

Mrs. Arnold came right in. "You need to open your blouse and your brassiere." she told me, "And then we'll get you comfortable and the doctor will come back in."

So we did that. He had me lie on the examining table. It had a little step on it to help me up. I had never had that kind of examination before. I was nervous. He was gentle when he probed it. He let me sit up and cover myself. Mrs. Arnold stood nearby.

Then he said, "I am going to be honest. I think this could be well-advanced." I swallowed hard. "I am going to do a biopsy before I attempt a diagnosis. That's when I draw liquid from the lump with a needle to determine what we have here. Then, I'll know more." He got a big needle ready and told me it wouldn't hurt much and it didn't. I tried to see his expression when he looked at the liquid, but he was looking away from me.

He came back over and said, "Mrs. Bennett, I am going to have to send this sample to a laboratory where they will examine it under a microscope. I cannot conclude anything until then. If the liquid had been clear and I hoped it would be, I would have called it a cyst and sent you home, but this makes it more serious and you've had it a while." He did not scold me for not coming in sooner. That was not his way.

"While you get dressed, I'll go out and get your husband."

A few minutes later, he came in with my William, who had gone pale. He grabbed my hand and sat down next to me. "I've just told your husband what I told you. I've also informed him that it could be up to two months before we know anything, and this will be very hard on both of you. It is serious, but I do not want you to spend all your time worrying. I will call you when I have the results."

"My sister has the same," I blurted out. "And she also goes to the doctor today."

I think he did not know what to do with that information, and so he just patted my hand. Mrs. Arnold saw us out. We climbed into the buggy and drove toward the farm. When we were almost home, William stopped and sat. "You know how much I love you, Ellen." I shook my head. "Well, we will get through this together. It's not the first time we've had to deal with hard things," I could only nod. We drove home the rest of the way in silence. I wondered how soon I would hear from Mary Anne and know her news. I took big breaths.

Bridget greeted us in front of the cottage with the baby in her arms. William took Mary and went inside. I don't think he could bear to hear me talk about it.

"I won't know for two months," I told her. Her eyes widened.

"No, you don't mean it," she said loudly. She covered her mouth, then, and let me continue. I explained about the biopsy.

"Does that mean it might not be a tumor?" she asked. I could tell she did not want to use the word, cancer.

"Maybe," I said. "Maybe there's some hope." I doubted it, though. The doctor had been very direct.

She knew there was nothing more to talk about and went home. I went into our cottage, where I saw William taking out pots and pans. "I will cook dinner," I told him in even tones. "I am not an invalid and will continue to do my chores."

"That's my wife," he laughed, "giving me orders." We ate our noon dinner. In the afternoon, the children scrambled into the kitchen, having walked up the lane, and everything gave over to our normal ways. I sensed Mary Anne had probably heard something similar and would call me the next morning. It was enough to have a regular night. The telling was past now and the doctor. It would be just a matter of waiting, and I could do that. God would give me strength.

Of course, Mary Anne's news was the same. She did call me the next morning. Her doctor, though, had reprimanded her for waiting so long. She'd told him off. She'd gone to see him at the hospital. I knew they could be overbearing there. We talked about it, but not for long. There was not much to say. We had to get on with our lives. Maybe we

252 – ELLEN DEMERS

would get a reprieve, maybe not. It was all up to God now. I turned my attentions back on my family. I told Bridget I did not want sober faces around me.

In February, we had a little birthday party for our Jenny. I'd made her a new doll. We ate cake and sang Happy Birthday at supper. She'd not grown much at all for being now six years of age. Jenny is both smart and mischievous. I think, often, those two things go together.

In March, my young lady turned twelve years old. We had a family party with cake and presents. We gave Alice the books her Aunt Kate had sent. I'd not let Kate know anything of our troubles, nor had Mary Anne or Bridget. We were waiting. I did try not to think of it all the time. William certainly did not talk of it.

We had an early spring. It got warm in April and the trees turned green and all about us was beauty. The wild forsythias were in bloom. A litter of kittens mewed in the barn. Jenny had not lost her love for animals. She was out there a lot. I loved the spring warmth before the heat of summer. We were waiting every day in anticipation of the call from Doctor Arnold.

I would not live this day again. Doctor Arnold called for William and me to come to his office. Bridget took Mary as before and we went off in the buggy. He'd dressed up a bit, like it was an important occasion. I put my church clothes on as I always did if we went into town. I was shaking despite the mild weather. When we got there, William lifted me down. Mrs. Arnold sent us right in. There was no one else in the waiting room. We sat stiffly together until the doctor came in. He had some papers in his hand. He gave us a small smile and asked after the family, then he told us.

I had cancer. The results showed it. There was no treatment. Even if we had the money, the doctor told us, the operation was brutal and did not necessarily prolong life. I did not like the sound of that because it meant I was going to die of this. I did not want to ask him how long I had, and he did not tell me.

"Mr. and Mrs. Bennett, I want to be clear and give you all the information you need. I want to get that part over with. This is not easy to take in, I know. I've had other patients. All I can tell you is that only God knows how long you have. What I possess is the medical end of things. Your cancer will spread. It will get more uncomfortable, but when you begin to feel pain, you must tell me. No waiting. I will give you medicine to ease it. I have nothing else to tell you. I had hoped it would not come out like this. I am so sorry. I'm going to leave you alone for a few minutes. Come out when you are ready." He looked very sad. I wondered if that was his habit, to leave people alone after giving bad news.

William and I sat there for a few minutes. I fought to keep my composure, as did he. Although I had expected this news, I'd also kept a thought in the back of my mind that God might give me a miracle. It had not happened that way. I suddenly felt old and weary before my time. This was not the life I'd envisioned for us with me dying early. All these thoughts came to me, one after another, in terms I had not allowed myself to face up to until now. I did not speak them aloud. William needed time to take in this news in his own way. His hand had gone over to hold mine.

After a few more minutes, William looked over at me, and then he stood up. "Come, Ellen, it's time to go home." That's all he said. And I got up. William shook hands with the doctor who told me he wanted to see me in two weeks and reminded me I was to report pain when I felt it. We left in a dazed state, I think, like when something is too much to handle. I wondered if I'd ever sleep again with all this on us.

We climbed into the buggy for the trip home. I thought of Bridget saying that everything would be all right. I thought of how I did not want to tell her the truth. William let me go quiet on the ride home. We sat very close together. It was a beautiful, breezy spring day. When we set out, I'd thought maybe on such a day, I would get good news. But instead, we got bad news. Bridget was waiting.

William took the baby from Bridget. Mary was walking now and demanded to be put down. Papa held her hand as she toddled along beside him. She had begun to talk and learned to say, "Ma" and "Pa." I cried inside at the thought I would not see her grow up. But, then, I would not see any of my children grow up because of this damn disease. Bridget knew the news just by looking at me. I did not have to say anything at all. I could not blame her for looking so miserable. She just went back inside. We would talk another time.

The call came from Mary Anne two days later in the middle of the morning. "I'd rather have put this in a letter, Ellen," she told me. That's when I knew what she had to tell me. Unlike me, she had been informed of how many more months she probably had. My mind dizzied at "months." I'd not yet thought in those terms. Mary Anne was quite forward. "I have maybe until October," she said. "He does not recommend surgery, even if we could afford it." It was like she was telling me when and how she would be leaving on a journey. I suppose it was like that, but it was too soon for me to grasp it as she did. I knew she was just holding herself together by leaning on the facts of the disease; still, it bothered me to hear her talk like that. But I could sense the shock and the tears behind her telling, and I was gentle back.

"We have families to care for," I told her. That's all I had to say.

"We'll be talking," she told me softly, and said goodbye.

I went right over to Bridget's cottage. She knew about Mary Anne when she saw me, and this time she broke down. We went inside together and shut the door. No one else was home.

"You're both leaving me again," she cried, her face all wet with tears. "I can't stand it." She fell into a chair, her hands over her face. "And you're not coming back and I'll never see you any more. I'll be alone without my sisters."

"Hush," I told her. "What about God? We'll see you again some day in heaven after you've lived a long life and died a very old woman."

She was not having it. Bridget was like a child in her weeping and inconsolable. I stayed quiet and rubbed her back.

After a while she began to settle down. She dried her eyes and looked at me very clearly. "I have to ask you," she said softly. She took a long breath. "How long do you and Mary Anne have?" There, it was out.

I told her. "Months, Bridget." That's all I had to say. She fell into tears again. After she calmed, I went home. William had put Mary in for a nap and I had a little time, so I composed a letter to our Kate in New York. I thought she could write to the parents in Ireland to prepare them. I would write myself later. I felt strangely calm, as though I was drawing on some kind of strength I hadn't known I had. I had questions for God. Why would God let this happen? But I knew He was helping me. I thought of the Blessed Virgin, too, and sent a prayer up to her while I was at it.

I'll tell you this. First you live with hope, then despair, then you have a new hope there's something on the other side. All my religious teaching tells me that is so. It makes sense there is a Heaven to go home to. The impossible is happening, and the world goes on despite it. The cows get milked. The baby fusses. The children make noise. William spends time looking off into the distance, as though there is something to see there. Then he looks over at me. He does not know I notice this. I look up the hill at George many times during the day. Physically, I don't feel any pain yet, just tired and uncomfortable. I am truly terrified at what is growing in me. I have tears sometimes, but there is nothing to be done, so I just go on. I don't need the crowding in of other people's feelings right now. I told Kate what she needed to know in my letter. She will have written to the parents by now, so one day soon, I will sit down and write to them myself. I hold myself outside of all this, sometimes, and tell it to me, like the storyteller I am. I don't want pity or special attention. I just want to live out the rest of this life doing what I can do. I don't know how to prepare the children. I've put it out of my mind for now. It hurts too much.

CHAPTER 43

Spring and Summer (1925)

LOVE, THOUGHTS, AND FEELINGS

I was tired and it did not go away. I did not always sleep well, and my energy was low after a short bit of it early in the morning. Bridget got into the habit of taking Mary for a while each day. It was the month of May and the children still in school, so she would come back with the baby at noon and help me get the meal. William would come in from the field for lunch and Mary go in for a nap. Then my sister would go home. I would rest then and have my thoughts. Bridget made me laugh, recounting Mary's antics, but I had jealous thoughts, too. It would not do to let them take over. In the future, Alice, Billy, Jenny, and Mary would be under the care of their father. I did not know how that would go. I thought of the Bennetts living in Waltham. I knew I would never leave the farm, but the family might. I was already envious of who might help in raising my darlings. Who would take care of them when I was gone?

On 29 May, William and I were married thirteen years. We had moved into our little house in Lincoln that happy evening of our wedding day in 1912 and set up housekeeping. This night, I'd made a nice supper of roast chicken. Afterwards, William and I walked out into the warm night and talked together. It was better to go back in time than discuss the present, so we did. "Remember our wedding night, William, when you reminded me that the priest said he expected great things of us and he meant children and we had them, didn't we?" He laughed quietly.

I'd left Alice in the kitchen to do the dishes with Billy. I could hear Jenny laughing at them and hoped the kitchen would be in one piece when we went back in, but I was not ready to return yet.

William looked at me. "I will never forget how you said you were now ready to marry me, Ellen, after having met the family in Lincoln and then told me I had to ask you again properly, which I did, and sealed with a kiss, all of this on the way to the train station." William's eyes were bright.

I remembered, too. "It was so hard leaving you that Easter evening for the ride back to Dorchester. I felt so alone on the trolley. When I returned, Mrs. Bernstein guessed at our betrothal but only teased a little and let me keep it to myself. I ran upstairs to see Benjamin. He was my first baby."

"Did you think of me in bed that night, Ellen?" said my husband, with his big grin.

"That is not a proper question, husband," I said, hiding my smile.

I got serious. "I know I'm leaving you, William. But not yet." He took my hand. "But times like this make it better. I choose to live until I'm gone. We have much to be grateful for, but still I am angry. I've been having a long argument with God these days and nights and I'm not through yet."

William had not a word to say about that. I think it felt safer to him to stay out of this argument I was having with the Lord. I'm sure he had his own conversations, with himself or with God, I did not know. It had gotten quiet in the cottage. It looked all cozy inside, where we could see the children moving about. I could hear their voices and knew I should go in and organize them for bed, but it seemed like a long time since we'd been alone like this, so we stayed a bit longer, being quiet together.

Then a small person ran out the door and down the path to us. "Alice says I have to go to bed first, and I think I'm too big now to go up before her. She's being bossy." Papa scooped her up and said she should listen to her big sister, but he wasn't insistent about it. That was not his way, and Jenny knew it. I would have to be the one to direct her up to bed. But I wasn't so inclined yet, and we stayed outside a bit longer with Jenny, until it became cool and then we went in.

Alice and Billy were engaged in a game of checkers. I told them I was not aware they were allowed to stay up that much longer, and didn't they have school the next day? They put the checkers away and began their way upstairs. Jenny had already been in her nightgown despite her not wanting to go up first, so she scooted up, too. Soon, it was quiet. They had done a good job cleaning up the kitchen and I put a fresh cloth on the table and prepared to sit in the parlor with my book. It is true that when you know your time is limited, you cherish it more.

I was not feeling any pain yet. William asked me all the time. It was my feelings that were hard to manage. It had been a bad afternoon when I opened the letter from my mother. She told me they prayed for a miracle. Ma wished she could to hold us close. The priest had told her it was God's will, but she was not having it. They were praying. I feared a Mass would be said for me and Mary Anne in Saint Matthew's Parish in Emper, before the year was out. I planned to write the family in Ireland soon, letters full of news about the children. That would be best.

I was slowly teaching Alice how to do the housework. "You're a big girl now. You can help me. Some day, you'll be a wife," I told her. She could cook, now, simple meals. I supervised her. She was glad of the attention, but I did not let these lessons go on too long because I wanted her to do her schoolwork. Billy still did farm chores. Jenny, I grabbed her sometimes and handed her a cloth to dry the dishes or recently, I'd had her make her bed with Alice. She's not inclined to stay still long enough to get much done. I understand that. She's only seven. I make time with Mary in my lap when she'll settle. I sing to her, which often brings the others around because they like music. I hope that will be a memory of me they'll keep. I do that now, as I go through the day, I think of good memories I can leave them. I tell them stories because I want them to remember my voice.

In June, we had a first birthday party for our Mary Martha. I had my sisters. It was the first time I'd seen Mary Anne since that awful time in the spring when we'd both gotten the same bad news. She looked like I felt, drawn and tired. We spoke a little but did not dwell on it at all. William had been acting funny for weeks now. I put it down to his worry about me, but the day of the party, he seemed to keep looking down the lane as though someone might be coming. I thought it strange. In the afternoon, Martin went out for something he said he had to do. A while longer he came back in the cart and sitting next to him was someone familiar. It was Kate! All the way from New York City.

She jumped down and ran over to us. Martin stood behind her with two big bags. There were tears. There was laughter. For a while we forgot about our illness and fell into what sisters do. I observed our Kate had matured. She was a housekeeper now for that family in New York and used to running things. She had one week, she told us to stay, and intended to keep us all in order. The children, all of them, stood and stared. She'd managed to come to some of the Baptisms, but not recently. She was the aunt who sent books and other gifts. They were amazed by this crush of sisters, all talking at once and laughing with joy.

It didn't last, their silence. Jenny was the first to burst out. "Who are you?" she demanded, hands on her hips. Kate laughed and summoned her over.

"I'm you long-lost aunt," she said. "Come over here, all of you, and tell me all your names. I know this one is Jenny." Margaret moved away from her mother and said her hello and then the rest of them followed her. I had more tears, but for the first time in a while, I was happy. I looked over at William, who had that big smile on his face he gets when he surprises me. It was a long and happy day. It was not until evening when the men left us to ourselves and the children were in bed that we sat down to talk. We said it all and left nothing out. The Flood girls would stay this night together. Frederick had taken their children home and Mary Anne would stay the night with us. Between Bridget's cottage and mine, we had room for both her and Kate.

We had a little something poured into our tea from a bottle Kate had brought with her. We became a bit giddy. Our mother would have hushed us, but instead we carried on. We began to sing together and then Bridget got up and danced, around and around, her face all pink, arms in the air and her feet moving to the beat we made with our hands on the table. Then, our Kate, her dignity forgotten, joined her with more waving of arms and feet moving fast. Mary Anne and I watched this, singing and tapping our feet. This is all for us, I thought, an offering, a thing of beauty, not yet a goodbye or good journey but something like it. And we forgot all about cancer for a while. Then, it got quiet as Kate and Bridget joined us back at the table. We looked first to the door where William and Martin had appeared just a little time before, clapping for us. And then we looked to the stairs where Alice and Billy and Jenny were sitting with their mouths all wide open, and they looked so comical, we laughed again. I did send them back up, though despite their Aunt Kate thinking they should stay. And thus ended the evening.

The next day we all went to church, Bridget, too, who did not always make it, I'd noticed. Our two buggies went down the road together. Frederick would come to get Mary Anne at noon. After Mass, we introduced Kate to our friends. Dinner was a shepherd's pie Bridget brought over with carrots and potatoes. Kate told us about her job and how she enjoyed being in New York. We had once plotted to have her find work near us, and Bridget, too. Bridget had returned, but not Kate.

I was tired after Mary Anne left but did not want to sleep and miss anything, but they told me to go sit down and I could hear them in the kitchen cleaning and doing the dishes. I fell asleep to their voices. It was nice. When I woke up, Bridget had gone home and Kate sat in a chair in the parlor reading a book. She looked a lot like Ma. She noticed I was awake and went to the kitchen to make tea. She brought it in on a tray with some cookies in a tin. She told me William had taken the children on a walk, the baby too. So we had some time to ourselves.

We agreed it was up to William what happened with our children. I doubted he'd stay on the farm. I wanted him to keep all the children with him. We'd not discussed it at all. I knew his family would help. It wasn't so hard talking about this once Kate got me started. She just let me talk.

"I need to work," said Kate. "But I'll send things to the children, keep in contact and visit. I have none of my own."

Now, Kate was younger than me, but I felt it not my business to talk to her about why she did not marry. She liked her life. She'd made her own road, just as I had made mine.

"Bridget is very upset," Kate said. "You are so ill."

"It's not my decision to have this sickness. I'm not choosing this journey. I'm going to die. I'm suffering more than she is." I was sharp with my words. And then I paused and listened to what I had just said. I did not like what I heard. I did not often lose patience with my Bridget. I loved her.

Kate did not seem at all shocked at my temper.

"We can, neither of us know your illness or your feelings," she said quietly. "But only imagine them."

I nodded at that, my temper gone. If she'd corrected me, though, I'd been ready to explode. I explained to Kate how I was angry with God, too. Kate accepted that as well, for all we were good Catholics. I knew she'd understand. She changed the subject.

"Alice seems quite grown-up," Kate observed. "She's your reliable one."

"I've heard that before," I told her. "She'll be the first of all the children to understand that I'm so ill. I want to handle her gently, even as I begin to depend on her. I think she'll remember me best."

"Billy is very quick and intelligent," said Kate. "He watches everyone and everything very carefully to see what he can learn." I agreed.

"Jenny is wonderful. She's funny and energetic and brings a special kind of joy," said Kate, smiling. "I like her forwardness."

"Right again," I responded.

"Mary is an angel." Kate's eyes got soft.

I smiled at that and then, more sadly observed, "I doubt she will remember me."

"Infants remember things," Kate told me. "I have memories of our house curtains and Ma lifting me up to see out the window, and I was no age at all."

We sat quietly for a few minutes, sipping our tea. It was comfortable. I didn't feel like crying anymore. She'd brought me some peace, to be allowed to talk the way we had.

And with that, they all burst in from their walk with Pa, stomping around the parlor, bringing the fresh air in with them. Billy handed me a bunch of wildflowers. I sent Alice for a glass to put them in. When she came back, she sat down near her aunt and began to talk about books. Jenny ran around chasing little Mary. It brought back an image of them chasing George around when he was little. I gave William a happy look. He looked content.

The June weather was glorious, not hot yet. Our roses were in bloom. We took short walks every day. The baby started going to Kate when she held out her arms. I let myself think of what a good mother she'd make. I was not yet able to think of anyone in terms of mothering my Mary, though. It was too soon to think of that. Jenny rattled on with stories for her aunt and even brought her out to the barn to share the kittens. Bridget was over every day. We called for Mary Anne to come again, but she was too tired. I left her and Kate to have their private conversation on our phone. It was hard not to see her again. It took a little away from the joy.

And then it was Saturday, again and time for Kate to leave. I had to bear it. There was no other way. This time, William would be taking her to the train. Kate had put on her deep blue skirt and matching jacket and her city hat with the feather on it. She looked very nice. We'd said our goodbyes the night before; Kate, Bridget and myself. We'd stayed up very late talking.

The children were yammering to go with Aunt Kate to the station. I said, "yes," to Alice and Billy, but thought it might be a chore to keep an eye on Jenny, too, until I looked at her small face and signaled she could go too. She ran before I changed my mind. Then Margaret sped over from her house, and in she went. Kate was swallowed by nieces. Billy was riding up front with his Pa. I'd heard something about ice cream, so did not think I would see them for a while.

I stood with Bridget, waving until we couldn't hear or see them anymore. Mary cried, and I took her inside the cottage where it was as though a light had gone out. Bridget gave me a hug, took the baby, and went back home with her. I was alone again.

CHAPTER 44

Summer Days

ALICE AND BILLY

In July, we had a birthday party for Billy. He turned ten, finally achieving his sister's double-digits. He was happy with his cupcakes and freshly churned ice cream. We gave him an odd gift for a young boy. William found him a ledger like his because our son is fascinated with numbers. We thought he would like to have his own. He was delighted and diligently copied the farm accounts into it from his father's book.

Alice seemed to be sticking closer to home. I released her, sometimes, from her chores, because I wanted her to be a young girl for a bit longer. She was insistent, though, that she did not want to go anywhere for the day or have her friend over. I wasn't sure what she was thinking. She didn't even want to leave me to go berry-picking.

I caught Alice looking at me one morning. I'd just turned around from my cooking and she was there. "Mama, you're sick," she said. That's all. I'd not wanted this day to come, but, still, I had prepared for it.

"I want to know what's wrong with you, Ma," Alice looked very serious, as though in asking, she both wanted and didn't want this knowledge.

I explained to her how I had a disease and it made me very tired, but it didn't hurt yet.

Alice focused on my "yet," She is very smart.

"Tell me what's happening to you, Mama."

I sat her down at the table. "What do you want to know, Alice," I asked, trying to hide my feelings. "These are things I talk about with your father," I told her, keeping my voice firm. She was not having it. Alice had on her face the identical expression to mine when I am being stubborn. She would know more, and she would know it now.

"I have cancer," I told her. There was no other way. Then she looked like a little girl again. She started to cry. I held her hand and hoped no one would come in, so my oldest daughter and I could do this alone. I held myself together. "This is not your problem," I told her. "We will handle this, your father and me." I could tell she was not yet ready to talk about death and dying, and I did not push it.

"I'll help you all I can, Mama," she sniffed as she said it.

"I do need you," I said. "I get tired and can't always finish what I begin. That's why I've been teaching you the housework, not just for that reason, though. I also like your company." I smiled at her. I think Alice and I considered that enough for one day, and I sent her upstairs to get the baby and to give myself a moment to get my feelings under control. She came back with a smiling Mary.

"I'm going to stay in all day and help," she said, "and maybe you'll get better." We left it at that. I thought maybe I should have William talk to her. And then I wondered about Billy observing us all the time. Maybe him too? It was a lot for one day.

In August, the pain started. I kept my promise and told William. The doctor came the next day. William and I met with him in our bedroom upstairs with the door shut. Bridget had taken the children to her cottage. Alice's eyes had gotten big, though, when the buggy had pulled up with the doctor in it. She had looked at me once and then hurried with the others, holding Mary close. Billy gave me a backward glance. It was not time for his chores yet, but he saw no need, I could tell, that they should have to go to his aunt's house. He kept quiet about it, though. Jenny just trotted along, game for any change at all.

The doctor had me pull my blouse open and looked at the lump, now large, and then at the growth under my arm. He said it was growing, too. We were both quiet, William and me, while he did this. He let me tidy myself while he went into his bag and pulled out a brown bottle of some liquid.

"This is laudanum. This medicine will make you feel better," he said comfortably. "It's what you need right now. It will take the pain away." He paused. "I should tell you something about it. This is a potent painkiller. You will take it with a teaspoon. It's very bitter, but I don't think you will mind that because it will help you so much. You will even feel an alleviation of your distress over this hard time you are going through, and you will rest, too. It will calm you."

He paused then. "Mr. Bennett, you will administer this to your wife. I will show you the exact dosage. It's very important to get it just right." He then showed William how to measure it out. I got my first dosage. Then he continued. "I know that you are careful with your children, but it is extremely important that they not get into it. It would be poison for them." We both thought of Jenny.

"I can lock it up," said William. "I have a metal box." I thought he must mean the same one where he locked up the shells to his shotgun.

Doctor Arnold then prepared to leave, but not before turning to face us and saying, with some feeling what a nice family we were and how he thought, looking right at me, that I would leave a legacy to my children of love, joy and respect. That said, he quickly went downstairs to let himself out, but I could hear his voice and wondered at it because I thought no one was home. Alice's voice reached us upstairs. She was saying "good day." to the doctor. We heard him reply and off he went.

I would not leave her alone down there. William helped me up and down we went. Alice was making tea. I did not correct her for leaving her aunt's house. I think we both knew then that things had changed. She would have a part of this not shared with her sisters or brother. Part of me did not desire this while the other part wondered at the daughter we had raised. We briefly told her that the doctor had brought medicine to help me when I hurt. She nodded.

"I am already feeling better," I told her truthfully. And I did. It was good to know that I had something to relieve me. It would help me to keep my resolve to live my life as long as I could under my own terms. I did not feel so frightened as before when the pain started. I could have some control over it. When Bridget brought them back, we were sitting drinking our tea, and she had bread, which she quickly sliced and put on a plate next to a jar of jam. It felt almost normal. The good feeling the doctor had promised began to go over me. Alice looked very determined.

Before Bridget left, she took me aside and told me that Alice had insisted on going back home.

"She had your look," she told me. "And I did not attempt to stop her." I managed a small laugh at that.

"Alice is my dependable one," I told her. "Everyone has told me so." I thanked Bridget for taking the children and explained about the medicine.

"Thank God," she commented. "There is no need for you to suffer with this." That said, she went on home. Bridget didn't cry anymore, at least not where I could see her. The cottage was filled with the sound of my family and I was content. Alice received my instructions for supper, and I arranged myself at the table to watch with the baby in my lap. Billy went off to help with the cows, and Jenny stopped her play long enough to give me a funny look. I was certainly not ready to answer any questions she might have, so was glad when she went outside.

CHAPTER 45

Come Fall

As August turned into September, Bridget helped me with getting their school clothes ready. Alice had grown again, and Billy, too. I was so grateful when Kate sent a frock for Alice, stockings for both girls and short pants and a cap for Billy. She and I had a steady stream of letters back and forth. It took my mind off things to imagine her life in New York City. The family she worked for lived near Central Park. I'd always wanted to see the wonders of Central Park. It had its own pond and boats. As for the house, it was a mansion. Kate described a system of lights on a board that told her in what rooms servants might be wanted. She wore her keys on a ring attached to a belt around her waist. On her time off she enjoyed going to an art museum, the "Met," she called it, and out to tea. The family respected her. She was always giving orders to what she called the "staff." What a life! I remembered that Alice wanted to travel to New York to see her aunt. I sometimes thought of my children's futures. They will know a world that I will not.

We had some hilarity one afternoon. Jenny got hold of a kitten and stuffed it into doll clothes. Then she pushed kitty in her little doll buggy all around the barnyard. The kitten's face coming out of the bonnet looked so cunning. Alice and I watched her out the kitchen window, laughing. We could see Jenny's mouth moving. She was singing or talking to the kitten. I left her alone, thinking she'd get tired of it soon. I sat down for a while. A bit later, I checked, but she was no longer outside. I could hear sounds from the parlor. I took a peek. Propped up on the divan was the still-dressed kitten. Alice saw it, too. We started laughing, so loud that William came running in to see what it was about. We pointed through the open door of the parlor. His expression made us laugh even louder. Jenny just looked over at us as though we were crazy, carefully picked up her baby, unwrapped her and headed out to the barn, completely unperturbed. Billy had come running, too. He looked over at Alice. "I haven't heard you laugh like that in a long time, Mama." I agreed. It was like old days. It felt good.

Mary Anne and I had a weekly phone call. On a farm, there are no days off, but Saturday was a little different, and that's when we would talk. We mostly did not discuss how we were feeling. It would be all about the old days in Ireland, life on our small lane where we knew all our neighbors. We recalled details like the wind blowing all the time and the soft rain and the smell of the forge. Imagine that, being old enough to have old days. We went back to our girlhoods and school, our first jobs working at shops in the village. We touched on our families, all so changed now; the brothers and sister grown and our parents aging. Then we remembered our early family times here, having babies. Of course, Mary had only just turned a year old in June, so that wasn't so long ago. I always felt better after having talked to my sister. But still, my mind would go back to what was wrong and how things would be ending. One of these days, I knew, we would not be up to talking at all. I did try to put it out of my mind, but could not ignore it. Would I even know my family at that point? I wondered if I would go in my sleep. That was a phrase I remember my mother using, but it was always about some old person and I was still young.

William was in the habit these days of taking us for rides in the buggy. He knew I enjoyed it, and it took no energy to be driven around the countryside. It was about all I could do because the disease was spreading. The doctor said so. William was very careful about giving me my dosage before I started to hurt. He was in charge of that. One day, though, he forgot until we got into the buggy. "Billy," he said, "There is a bottle on the table and a spoon, bring it out here." Billy jumped down and ran into the cottage.

"It's my medicine," I told him, because I could tell he wanted to know. After supper, in the parlor where I went now every night, leaving the clean-up to others, he came in and stood in front of me. I saw a little of his father in him that night. He wanted the truth.

"Alice told me you are ailing," he said directly.

"I am ailing," I told him.

"Is that why you take the medicine?"

"Yes," I told him, "It makes me feel better."

My son nodded. "Then, every time, when we go out, I will bring you your medicine." He straightened his small shoulders. I saw something in his eyes that told me he sensed more than I'd told him. And yet I would not have him know it all. I did not want his memories of me to rest on this illness, but on other things. I wanted him to remember me, but not so much about what was ahead of us. Even Alice could not entirely see that.

"Your father is taking care of me," I told him with a smile.

I wanted to see Mary Anne again, so William arranged it. One fine day, we left in the morning to drive to Westwood. She knew we were coming. As the buggy went up the long road to the farm, young Eddie ran down to meet us. My niece Louise was waiting at the door. "Ma is in the kitchen," she told us.

Mary Anne was sitting in a chair in the kitchen, wrapped in a shawl. She looked thin as I knew I did, too, but the smile was the same. "So, you've brought your brood to visit." And then, more quietly, "I've missed you, Ellen." The men took themselves off, taking Billy with them. Louise and Alice went upstairs. Mary was asleep in my lap. It was time to talk or not talk, whatever we pleased. So, we were quiet for a while.

"Ellen, if I get up, I might fall over." I nodded because I had the same weakness. "I don't know what I would do without the medicine." I shook my head again. I wondered at what happened to the two strong young women we had been just a short time ago.

"Damn this cancer," I said, trying hard not to wake Mary.

"Damn is right," she answered.

"Frederick will remain on the farm with the children," she informed me.

I did not know yet what William would do. We were not people with lots of money and many choices. It would have to be a practical solution. I made up my mind to talk to my husband about it while I still could, but I suspected he'd not decided yet. He was still a young man, after all. It was hard for him to think of going on without a wife. He faced a world without me.

"We've done just what we resolved to do when we left Ireland," said my sister with the same tone she always took. "We got jobs and husbands and had families."

I had to agree. It was just ending way too soon, but I didn't need to say that.

Louise and Alice served us a nice dinner after we had all said grace. I was still unhappy with God, but it was all right to thank Him for our meal and I did have to set a good example for the children. The priest had been to see me and said it was no longer necessary for me to come to Mass. He would bring me Holy Communion. William would not leave me, though, to go to church, so none of us had gone the last months. I saw that we said prayers together, instead. If God did not understand, then He was not the God I had been raised to believe in. I had no regrets at all about it.

We only stayed a short time longer because I was getting weary. We prepared to go home. Billy went to his father, who pulled the bottle out of his big coat pocket. Billy carefully handed it to me and then gave me the spoon and I measured out my dose and took it. My sister and I embraced. There were no tears. That time was over now. I walked slowly back to the buggy and William lifted me in. The last I saw of my sister was of her standing on her porch, supported by Frederick and waving to us. It was time to go home.

"We would go for rides in the buggy. I would bring my mother her medicine in a bottle when she was ailing. I didn't know she had cancer."

~Bill Bennett, age 90

CHAPTER 46

Ellen In October

UNTIL WE MEET AGAIN

It is October and I can no longer manage to climb the stairs, even with William's help. He carries me up each night. The bathroom is up there, too. For during the day, a neighbor had brought over a wooden commode for my use. William manages everything. I spend most days in the parlor wrapped in blankets and shawls. I cannot seem to get warm. Bridget comes every day. The children have formed the habit of coming in to play in that room. Jenny does not like this new mama, I can tell. She wants the old one back. She asked me one day when I was going to be well again. I didn't know how to answer. So, I just said I didn't know. She shrugged and ran outside. Thank God, she does not usually keep one thought in her head for long. Mary, of course, understands none of it. Alice moves around doing the housework I used to do. She still goes to school most days. I insist on that. Billy gives me looks. He is, I can tell, trying to put it all together in his mind, what's happening to me.

One sunny Saturday, William decided I should go for a ride. He said the leaves were at their peak colors and he would have me see their beauty. So, off we went with me nestled inside the buggy with all my shawls and blankets. William had carried me out. Billy had followed carefully with the bottle of medicine and spoon. The baby was excited and Alice held her up to see out the window. Jenny was quiet for once, and Alice, too. It was a long ride. We went down Farm Road to the center in Medfield and saw the church. There was a bridge I loved and the railway station and at the end of it, we drove by the Norfolk Hunt Club, where the horses were outside on this beautiful autumn day, their coats gleaming brown in the sunshine. At home in Ireland, there would be sheep everywhere, and roses still blooming and the hedges coming out to meet the lane. I had become a country girl again, out of love for my William. We slowly drove home again.

This time, when I settled back into my chair in the parlor, I went in for a long nap. Actually, I slept the rest of the day, only waking up to the smell of supper. This evening, Alice brought me my meal on a tray. She could tell I wanted to be still. At bedtime, they all came in to kiss me. Again, I stayed where I was and listened to them upstairs going to bed. William came back down after a while. We didn't talk. I was too tired. He only asked me if I'd enjoyed the ride, and I told him that I had. He carried me upstairs. My body feels more like the size of Alice's now. I'd grown down, and she'd grown up.

And now I can't get out of my bed anymore. The doctor came, and I overheard him say that I didn't have much longer. What a thing to hear! Even now, I'm not resigned to it. I continue my argument with God. I bargain for a bit longer, but in my heart, I know it's almost over. The children come in from school and visit me in the bedroom. I don't want to eat anymore. I know that disturbs William who still has thoughts deep down that maybe I would last longer if I only ate. The doctor told him to increase the dosage of my medicine. "To make her more comfortable," he said. It also gives me dreams and I see things. Yesterday, I dreamed of a little old man, my father, telling me to eat. I was in our kitchen again on the morning of our departure from Ireland, during another October long ago. I saw my mother look right at me, her eyes filled with tears. And now, I think my final rest is coming. I both welcome it and rail at it. My family needs me so much and I will be leaving them soon. It is too much to bear, and yet I must. William says the priest is coming tomorrow. Oh, well, he's become used to me.

Alice

Mama wanted ice cream today, and Papa sent Uncle Martin to get it in town at the drugstore. Mama ate a few mouthfuls and then she sat up and talked to us about ice cream and summer, and picking blueberries. Then, she spoke of the days when we were born and how happy she and Papa had been, looking at each of us, as she said it. Her eyes look different now. But today she smiled and talked. It was nice.

"I want you to go to Ireland some day," she said, looking at all of us.

"I know, Mama," I told her. "Everything is so green there."

And then she fell asleep again, and Papa had us all go downstairs. The next day was October fifteenth. When evening came on, Pa called for the doctor to come and the priest. I put the baby to bed but Billy and I and even Jenny stayed up, sitting in the parlor together. Aunt Bridget and Uncle Martin were upstairs with Papa. Cousin Margaret sat with us.

I let the doctor in and he went right up. Next the priest came and also went up. I knew he carried the host and the holy oil. All was quiet and then we heard Aunt Bridget weeping and we all started to cry, too. Papa came down and said, "She's gone." That's all. I led the way upstairs with my brother and sister and cousin. Mama was lying there, and she looked so quiet and her eyes were closed and I knew they wouldn't open again. Billy knew, too. Jenny just looked surprised. Papa motioned to me to take her downstairs. Billy soon came down too.

Billy

Mama died last night. Tonight was the night of the wake. While we were at Aunt Bridget's house, the undertaker came. When we came back, there was Mama in the parlor in the casket with two big candles on either end. And they were lit. I understand she's gone now. Aunt Bridget is keeping the baby at her house, and Jenny. She's too little. People that we know came in and said prayers. Then they sat around and drank tea, mostly. Father led us in the Rosary. They all went home after a while. Pa says the Bennetts and Aunt Kate are coming tomorrow for the funeral. I went to bed, wishing it was a dream, losing Mama, but when I woke up, I knew better.

We got into our church clothes. Pa was wearing a black band on the arm of his coat. I'm still too young, he said, to grieve that way. The Bennetts, he said, will meet us at church. It's a long drive for them from Waltham, and a longer trip for Aunt Kate on the train from New York. As we got into the buggy, I looked behind and saw the undertaking men go into the cottage. I saw them load the coffin onto the wagon. As we set off, I could hear the bells tolling. At church, my grandparents and aunts and uncles were waiting outside. They came over and hugged us and cried, and then we all went inside up the stairs inside the church. Mass was so long. Jenny was wiggling in her seat. A neighbor had taken Mary. When we got home, we found out that Aunt Mary Anne had died, too. Pa said they're together in Heaven now. Jenny says they'll be back in two weeks.

So, the next night, we went to Westwood and Aunt Mary Anne was laid out in her coffin with two big candles, again, one on each end. We went to her funeral the next day. She's buried at the same graveyard in Medfield, next to my mother. We went home then, but it isn't really like home anymore without Ma. Mr. Pierce sent a maid over from the big house to help out. She's Irish like my mother and she asked me if I'd like her to be my new mother. I didn't think much about it. A few days later, Pa told us we are going to go live in Waltham in a big house with our aunt and uncle and cousins. I've never even met these cousins. And then my Grandma and Great-Aunt Tressie got a ride out with Uncle Stephen. They talked quietly with Pa in the parlor, and it was decided that Mary would go to live with Aunt Tressie in Lincoln. I don't even know where that is. Pa says it's not far from Waltham. I can't sleep at night. All the changes are too much. Every morning, I wake up and wish it was all a dream. Jenny still says they'll be back in two weeks.

"My mother died and there were two big candles lit on either end of her coffin in our parlor. We went to her funeral and when we got home, we found out my aunt had died. We went to Westwood. She was laid out just like my mother, with the candles at each end. They are buried together at Vineland Cemetery in Medfield. Mr. Pierce sent over a maid to help out. She asked me if I would like her to be my new mother. I didn't understand her at the time. Later, when we were in Waltham, I would wake up in the morning, hoping that it had all been a dream."

~Bill Bennett, age 90

The story isn't over yet. The family went to Waltham. Billy was just ten years old. It was a new, confusing world of grown-ups. He became a city kid, but he never forgot Dover and missed his mother for the rest of his long life. I feel privileged to tell her story. She was the Irish grandmother my family never knew. I got to know her, though, by telling her story. William was my grandfather and Billy was my father. He told me all about Dover. Ultimately, he meets his Phyllis and marries her. He goes to war. He comes home. They have a big family. But the next book is about Billy's adventures as a boy in Waltham, growing up without a mother. Some of the characters remain the same and new ones emerge in his young life. It is his voice. I think he and his sister Alice had their mother's ability to tell a story, their father's charm, and both their parents' humor.

I found the elusive Ellen Flood, through the help of my cousin, Charlie Naff, and his wife, Anne. Charlie's grandmother was Mary Anne. I visited the Flood family's birthplace in Ireland and found an Irish cousin, Tom Nally and his wife, Sheila. Tom's grandmother, Teresa, was sister to John Flood. So, the Floods are rediscovered and will never go away again. Ellen and her sisters must be happy.

~Ellen Bennett Demers

Ellen Flood

What of an Irish grandmother
You've never seen,
Or hugged
Or spoken to
Who exists in the memory of your father
On the farm
With his family
Until he is ten
Ireland is all green, she said
And then the wake,
At home with big candles at either end of the coffin
And a small boy orphaned
The elusive Ellen Flood
I, who never touched you
Found your home in Rathcaled, County Westmeath, Ireland
And now you are a young girl again
And my grandmother, too
And I think I've touched you
Love,
Ellen

ACKNOWLEDGEMENTS

Nathan Demers, my Editor

Stephen Demers, my husband who read and advised me on my chapters

My friends in the Writing Group at Osher Lifelong Learning Institute; University of Massachusetts-Boston for their help, patience and appreciation for my story of Ellen's journey.

The Archives at Waltham, Massachusetts

My father's Memoir

Printed in the USA
CPSIA information can be obtained
at www.ICGtesting.com
LVHW021226191023
761201LV00006B/57